Praise for ...

'Pure rocker perfection in every single way ... marriage of romance and comedy, a possibly even better book than its stellar prequel, and I would recommend it to anyone who likes their love stories with a side of giggles'   Natasha is a Book Junkie

'Kylie Scott is quickly becoming one of my favorite authors at combining funny with sexy, and I can't wait to read more from her. *Play* is a definite must-read book!'   Smut Book Club

'*Lick* is a breath of fresh air with a unique story line, think *The Hangover* meets contemporary romance'
                                          The Rock Stars of Romance

'Mal is taking us all by storm . . . go buy this book. Seriously. You won't regret it'   Fiction Vixen

'Engaging, humorous, and at times a heart-breaking picture of first love . . . a swoon-worthy romance'   Smexy Books

'*Play* does not disappoint! It's sexy, naughty and hilarious with a sidenote of serious that makes it all so real. I'm an affirmed Stage Dive groupie and I'm ready to follow those men on tour wherever they go! Rock on!'   Up All Night Book Blog

'I'm now officially addicted to Stage Dive. I highly recommend it to readers out there who enjoy rock-star romance books and the new adult/contemporary romance genre'   Book Lovin' Mamas

'With each book in this series, I become more attached to the characters and more enamoured with author Kylie Scott'
                                          Book Reviews

Dirty

Kylie Scott is a long-time fan of erotic love stories and B-grade horror films. Based in Queensland, Australia with her two children and one delightful husband, she reads, writes and never dithers around on the internet.

www.kylie-scott.com

@KylieScottbooks

By Kylie Scott

The Stage Dive Series

Lick

Play

Lead

Deep

The Dive Bar Series

Dirty

Dirty

Kylie Scott

PAN BOOKS

First published 2016 by St Martin's Press, New York

First published in the UK 2016 by Pan Books
an imprint of Pan Macmillan
20 New Wharf Road, London N1 9RR
Associated companies throughout the world
www.panmacmillan.com

ISBN 978-1-5098-0629-4

1 3 5 7 9 8 6 4 2

A CIP catalogue record for this book is available from the British Library.

Printed and bound by CPI Group (UK) Ltd, Croydon, CR0 4YY

*For Astrid, who passed away during the
writing of this book. She was terrible and
she was great. She was the best dog
a girl could ask for.*

CHAPTER ONE

Fuck.

I stared at my cell phone, mouth slack in horror. Man, they were really going for it. Tongues wrangling, teeth clashing. There was no hesitation, no holding back, as they ground their bodies together. The angle and lighting were crap, but still plenty sufficient to catch all the porny action, god help me.

This couldn't be happening. What the hell was I going to do?

From out in the hallway came voices, laughter, all of the usual sounds of happiness. About what you'd expect on your big day. The smut on the small screen, not so much. I didn't want to see it, yet I couldn't look away. Whoever had sent this to me had blocked their number. They could have only had one aim in mind, however.

Shit.

God, the sure way they touched, so obviously familiar with each other's bodies, killed me. My stomach churned, bile burning the back of my throat. Enough. I swallowed hard and threw the cell onto the brand-new super-size bed. Video still rolling, it lay discarded among the scattered red rose petals like some sick joke. Should have chucked it at the wall. Stomped it, or something.

Chris had said they were going to hang out, take it easy. Just him and his best man, Paul, knocking back a few drinks and talking about the old times. Sure as hell, there'd been no mention of them tongue wrestling because I would have remembered that no matter how busy with wedding details I'd been.

My eyes itched, a muscle quivering in my cheek. Had this been going on behind my back all along, in which case, what kind of idiot was I? I wrapped my arms around myself, holding on tight, doing my best to keep my shit together.

It wasn't working. Not even a little.

The bitch of it was, now that I thought about it, there'd been signs. Chris's libido had never been what you'd call raging. Among all the dinner dates and outings that made up our whirlwind romance, there'd been lots of hand holding and kissing, sure. But little to no actual intercourse. There'd always been excuses. His family was religious, we should follow tradition and wait for the wedding night, it would be so special when we finally did it, yada yada. It'd all made sense at the time. His simply not being into pussy had never crossed my mind. The man had been so perfect in every other way.

Only, he wasn't. Because according to that video, Coeur d'Alene's golden boy had most likely been using me as a goddamn beard and had planned to keep doing so for the rest of our natural-born lives.

Deep inside, some part of me broke. My heart, my hopes and dreams, I don't know what. But everything hurt. Never in any of my twenty-five years had I experienced anything akin. The pain was excruciating.

Voices out in the hallway came closer as the moaning and groaning on my cell grew louder. The Chris on the video clearly into all the cock wielding his best man was doing. Bastards. To imagine, I'd finally thought I'd found a home. How stupid was I?

No damn way could I go out there, face all those people and tell them what a fool I'd been. Of how thoroughly I'd been duped. Or at least, not yet. My mind needed a chance to wrap itself around the enormity of what Chris had done, of how thoroughly he'd screwed me over.

Boom, boom, boom! went a fist on the other side of the bedroom door. I jumped, eyes painfully wide open.

"Lydia, it's time," announced Chris's father.

And yeah . . . no way. I was out of there.

Blind panic seized me and I ran. Not easy to do wildly out of shape and in full wedding regalia, but I managed. Hell, I fucking flew. It's amazing what terror can do.

Out the French doors and onto the patio. Across the expanse of manicured green lawn, my stiletto heels sinking into the soft ground with every hurried step. The hum of soft music and conversation filled the air. All of the guests were gathered out front awaiting the service, followed by cocktails and canapés. So through the back garden I plowed, pushing past shrubbery and flattening flower beds. Thorns from a rosebush caught at my stockings, stinging, scratching my legs. Never mind. No time to waste. For hidden behind a tree sat a compost bin, placed perfectly beside the six-foot-something-high fence separating this property from the next.

Yes. Awesome. Escape was mine.

Let Chris explain to them all why his bride had fled. Or better yet, let Paul, the slimy, two-faced, man-stealing bastard.

Thank god I hadn't gone for the floor-length gown his mother had tried to squeeze me into. Calf length would be tricky enough what with all the tulle underskirts. I hitched them up, clambering onto the hip-high bin without too much trouble. It wobbled like a bitch as I climbed to my feet. A scarily high-pitched noise escaped me. I grabbed hold of the rough wooden fence, hanging on so tight my knuckles turned white.

Normally, I wasn't much for prayer. Surely, however, the Big Guy wouldn't let me take a tumble and break my ass. Not today. If he really and truly felt the need to smite me some more, it could wait. Today I'd suffered enough.

Nice deep breaths, standing tall and steady. I could do this. In the yard behind my and Chris's overdone mini-mansion sat a small silent house.

Perfect.

French manicure already scratched to shit, I lifted myself up, wiggling and squirming until my hips sat high enough for me to get a leg over. The pressure that position put on my crotch was not pretty. I swear I could hear my labia screaming, let alone the rest of my girl bits. And what with me hoping to still be a mother one day, I needed to move . . . pronto. Wooden palings dug painfully deep into my belly as I lay down, balancing my torso atop the fence. Beads of sweat dribbled down the sides of my face, probably carving out canyons in the inch-thick makeup (artist recommended by Chris's mom).

"Aunt Lydia?" asked a small high voice. "What are you doing?"

I squeaked in surprise. Luckily, there just wasn't enough air in my lungs for an all-out actual scream. Down below stood a little girl, her big brown eyes inquisitive.

"Mary. Hi." I smiled brightly. "You surprised me."

"Why are you climbing the fence?" She swished the skirt of her white satin flower girl dress this way and that.

"Ah, well . . ."

"Are you playing a game?"

"Um . . ."

"Can I play too?"

"Yes!" I gave her a twitchy grin. "Yes, I'm playing a game of hide-and-seek with your uncle Chris."

Her face lit up.

"But no. No, you can't play. Sorry."

Her face fell. "Why not?"

This was the problem with small children, so many questions.

"Because it's a surprise," I said. "A really big surprise."

"Uncle Chris doesn't know you're playing?"

"No, he doesn't. So you have to promise not to tell anyone that you saw me back here. Okay?"

"But how will he know to come find you?"

"Good point. But your uncle Chris is a smart guy. He'll figure it out in no time." Especially since I'd left my phone behind with that evil porno still playing. Damn hard to feel bad about outing him, given the situation. "So you can't tell anyone you saw me, okay?"

For a long moment Mary pondered her already scuffed satin slippers. Her mother would not be impressed. "I don't like it when my brother tells on my hiding places."

"No. It's annoying, isn't it?" I felt my leg slipping and muttered an F-bomb, which I thought was under my breath.

Pink lips formed a perfect O. "You shouldn't use that word! Momma said it's naughty."

"You're right, you're right," I hastily agreed. "It's a bad word and I apologize."

She let out a little sigh of relief. "That's all right. Momma says you weren't raised right and we have to make all . . . allow . . . allowan . . ." Little brows drew together in frustration.

"Allowances?"

"Yes." She grinned. "Did you really grow up in a barn? I think living in a barn would be fun."

This. This is what comes from letting stuck-up rich bitches influence the young. Chris's sister was a prime candidate for stick-up-the-ass removal. His whole damn family was, for that matter.

"No, honey," I said. "I didn't. But I bet your momma would feel right at home among cows."

"Moo." She laughed merrily.

"Exactly. You better head back now. And remember, don't tell anyone you saw me." I gave her a finger wave, trying to wriggle into a more comfortable position without toppling off the precipice. As if that were possible.

"Promise! Bye!"

"Bye."

The kid took off racing through the garden, soon disappearing from sight. Now to get the hell down off the fence. Whatever way I played it, pain was sure to follow. Fact. I stretched and strained, my thigh and calf muscles screaming in protest. If only I'd gone with Chris to the gym all those times he'd suggested. Too late now. Slowly, knee first, one leg, then the other went up and over. Splinters caught at my dress, threads pulling and silk ripping. I slid down the opposite side of the fence, dangling in midair for one excruciating moment while the rough wood tore my hands to pieces and my muscles stretched beyond endurance. Then gravity kicked in.

I hit the ground hard. It hurt.

So much for being plus-size. My extra padding hadn't cushioned a damn thing. I rolled onto my back and lay in the long grass, wheezing like a pack-a-day smoker. Pain filled my world. Maybe I'd just die here. It was as nice a place as any.

"Lydia, are you out here?" a voice called. Betsy, the receptionist from the real estate agency. "Liddy?"

I hated being called that. Hated it. And she knew it, the bitch.

I held my silence, lying there, sweating and breathing heavily (as quietly as possible). No way could she see me without climbing the fence herself. Small chance of that. Generally, Betsy wasn't any more athletic than me. I was safe for now. Overhead, a wisp of white cloud passed, marring the perfect blue sky for a moment. Such wonderful weather for a June wedding. Seriously, you couldn't have asked for better.

Betsy's voice receded. Time to move.

Ever so slowly I climbed to my feet, every muscle aching. In the distance, my name was being called out over and over again by a multitude of voices. They were starting to sound panicky. Meanwhile, here I stood. No money, no cards, no phone, no nothing. Truth be told, my emergency escape plan was a little flawed. At least I'd made it over the fence.

The neighbor's yard was a jungle, completely overgrown. Lucky, otherwise I might have actually broken something when I fell. A cute gray bungalow sat beneath a circle of big old pine trees. It had a lot of charm. Places like this were why I'd gone into real estate. To have the opportunity to help people find a wonderful home for the rest of their lives. A place where they could raise their children and get to know their neighbors, have block parties and BBQs. As opposed to dragging their offspring around the country in search of the next big opportunity, living in one crummy thin-walled rental after another.

Unfortunately, instead of selling homes, I'd wound up pushing soulless condos and talking people into properties they couldn't begin to afford. I'd been beyond naive. Cutthroat didn't even begin to describe the industry.

But back to my current situation.

Sanders Beach was a pretty quiet area and they'd soon be looking for me. Out on the street, I'd be found in no time. That wouldn't do. I needed to catch my breath and pull my shit together. Wait until the video outed Chris as the cheating lying vile scumbag he was and then . . . well, I'd hopefully have some sort of plan figured out by that time.

So what I liked best about this pretty bungalow in particular was the wide open back window.

I pulled up the ruins of my skirts and kicked off my one remaining heel, before making my way through the tall grass. No immediate signs of life from inside the house. Perhaps they'd gone out and forgotten to lock it. The window opened onto a small bath-room, everything inside dated and dusty. Still nothing stirred.

To trespass or be discovered? Not a hard call to make. Call me Goldilocks. I was going in. If I got eaten by a bear, then so be it. At least I'd make a decent-size meal.

The window wasn't high. This time I climbed up without any trouble. I grabbed hold of the edge of the bathtub for balance while the other hand reached for the floor. Everything was going great, right up until it came time to squeeze my hips through. Wooden casing bit deep into my sides, pulling me up short. I was stuck.

"Shit," I said, keeping my voice down just in case.

I wriggled and twisted, grunting in exertion, feet flailing in the open air. Thank god no one was around to see. So help me baby Jesus, I could do this, I could. After all, what was losing a bit more skirt or skin at this stage? Nothing, that's what. I gripped the edge of the bathtub and gave a final almighty heave-ho. Material tore and my girth gave way. I plummeted toward the floor. My face broke the fall and my body followed, crashing down. Given the amount of noise involved, it was kind of surprising the neighbors didn't come running along with the police.

"Oh god," I whimpered, struggling to breathe.

Pain and humiliation levels had officially bypassed bad and gone straight to horrific. What a clusterfuck of a situation.

Carefully, I took a slow deep breath in through the nose and out through the mouth. Okay, it worked. No ribs broken, I think. Nose still intact. I ran my tongue around the inside of my mouth, check-ing for loose teeth. All good. Just the same, it felt like I'd been in a bar fight with an angry mob. My right cheek throbbed like a bitch and for a long while I just lay there, stunned. Neither daring to move, nor quite able. The old bungalow remained quiet. I was alone, thank god. Alone was best, I got that now.

Just in case someone came looking, I dragged my sorry self into the bathtub and pulled the shower curtain closed. Then carefully, I arranged the remains of my silk and tulle skirts around me.

It was time to face the facts. To face them and let them fill me. My man was in fact not my man, nor was he my best friend. There would be no happy home. And my dream wedding? Screwed sideways and then some.

Never mind, I'd found somewhere safe to hide and wait out the day. Let Chris deal with the mess he'd made. I needed to put myself back together.

Hot tears started flowing down my face. They didn't stop for a long, long time.

CHAPTER TWO

Heavy footsteps roused me from my stupor. I don't know how long exactly I'd been sitting in the bathtub, staring off at nothing, pondering the catastrophe my life had become. Couldn't have been too long since sunlight still lit the room.

The footsteps came closer and closer. And then they entered the room. Oh, shit. I froze, not even daring to breathe. There was a loud yawn, followed by the cracking of joints. Then a large hand reached in beside the closed shower curtain and turned on the tap. A torrent of ice cold water poured down. It was like a billion itty-bitty knives stabbing at my skin. All of the scratches and raw patches from earlier stung like shit. I gritted my teeth, shoulders hiked up to around my ears as if that would provide any protection.

Yep, I sat there, all huddled up, listening to the man take a leak.

Awesome. Just plain awesome.

Wasn't like I could jump out and interrupt the man midflow. And say what? I knew this was not a good situation to get caught in.

1. I'd basically broken into this guy's house.
2. And had then gone on making myself right at home, having a messy emotional breakdown in his bathtub.

Normal, rational people didn't do this sort of thing. I didn't even have a criminal record, had never particularly done anything outlandish or interesting until now. This was all Chris's fault, the bastard. I'd just have to make the best of it and hope this guy had a sense of humor.

Just as the water began to warm, he flushed the john and freezing cold water drenched me anew. I'd been about to open my mouth and announce my presence, but that put an end to that. Needles of icy cold water pelted down on my skin. I fucking froze. Teeth gritted, I suppressed a squeal of pain and rage.

Then the shower curtain flew back.

"Shit!" The man was very tall, very naked, and very surprised. He stumbled back a step, a hand clutching at the bench behind him, eyes furious and wide. "What the hell?"

Good question.

I opened my mouth, closed it. Language skills had apparently abandoned me. In total silence, the man and I stared at each other.

Even with no clothing to take cues from, the dude was clearly the epitome of cool. He looked about my age, or maybe a little older. He had longish red-blond hair, dark blue eyes set in an angular face, a lean but muscular torso covered in tattoos, and a rather large cock. Not that I meant to check him out, it's just kind of hard to ignore a penis and scrotum when they're dangling right in front of your face. I tilted my head, trying to get some perspective. Every viewpoint, however, was equally shocking. There was dick as far as the eye could see.

And I should stop ogling him. Right.

"Hi." With a calm I didn't even vaguely feel, I reached up and turned off the tap. Much better. His monster penis had momentarily derailed me, but I was back on track now. Time to talk myself out of this mess. "Hey."

"What the fuck are you doing in my house?" he asked flatly.

"Right. Well . . ." I neatly tucked my dripping-wet shoulder-length blond hair back behind my ears. As if that would help. My winged eyeliner and false lashes were probably halfway down my cheeks. "I, um, I . . ."

"You what?"

"I'm Lydia," I said, the first thing to come to mind.

No reply. His handsome face, however, took on a distinctly pissy expression. Even his strawberry-blond hair seemed a fiery hue. Fine, so we weren't swapping names and getting cozy. Fair enough. You wouldn't believe how hard it was, keeping my eyes on his face. The struggle was real. It might have been due to my not seeing one in so long, but his dick seemed almost hypnotic. The thing had magical powers, I swear. It was so big and mobile, subtly swaying every time he moved. My gaze kept darting down despite my best efforts.

Finally he put me out of my misery, grabbing a towel off a nearby rack and wrapping it around his waist. It made for quite the hot-looking miniskirt. Not just any man could have pulled off such a look.

But back to my explanations.

"Ah, firstly, I'd just like to say sorry about this." I waved a hand at him and his bathroom and, well everything, really. "For any inconvenience I might have caused here in your bathroom."

The guy stood tall, looming over me with his hands on hips. Tattoos covered his arms to his wrists. Still, he had a whole lot of sinew on show. Definitely not the kind of man you'd want to mess with. Dude could probably snap me in half in a second. I bet he was a tattoo model, or a biker, or a pirate, or something. Something a lot hot and more than a little scary.

Shit. I really should have chosen another house.

"I don't normally break into people's places and hide out in their tub," I babbled, on the verge of incoherency. "So I'm really sorry. Seriously. So very sorry. But you've got a lovely home."

"That so?"

"Not that, I mean, that's not why I'm here. I just . . ." Fucking hell, my mind was a disaster. I took a deep breath, letting it out nice and slow, before trying again. "I love the old Arts and Crafts bungalows, don't you? They have such soul."

His brows drew tight. "Are you high? What the fuck are you on?"

"Nothing!"

"You haven't been popping any pills or snorting something?"

"No, I swear."

"Nothing to drink?"

"I haven't had anything," I said, but the suspicion and anger still lined his face. Paired with the stubble on his chin and the shadows beneath his eyes, my unwilling host was one tired, cranky man. Couldn't really blame him.

"So you're completely sober," he said.

"Completely."

A pause.

"You're thinking I'm bat-shit crazy now, aren't you?" I asked, despite the answer sitting plain as day on his pretty face.

"Pretty much, yeah."

Oh, god. "I'm not. I'm sane."

"You sure about that?" He looked down the long line of his nose at me, distinctly unimpressed. "Seen a lot of weird shit in my years. Stuff like you wouldn't believe. But I got to tell you, right now, this . . . you, are taking the cake."

"Great." And I was so definitely probably going to jail. Someone ought to give me a cookie. My ability to take a bad situation and make it worse today was amazing.

"You touch any of my stuff?" he asked. "Take anything?"

"Yes, your sofa is cunningly hidden down the front of my dress. You won't believe where I fit the TV."

Again, his eyes narrowed dangerously. "Between you and me, probably not the time to be funny, babe."

Crap. "Sorry. I'm sorry. I didn't mean that. You have every right to be mad."

"Damn right, I do."

I nodded, contrite. "I haven't touched any of your things."

The dude just stood there, staring. Lots going on behind his eyes. None of which I could read.

A stray tear trickled down my face. It must have saved itself up just for the occasion. Gah. How pathetic. I sniffled, brushing it off hurriedly with the back of my hand.

"Fuck's sake," he muttered.

"I really am sorry about this. The truth is, I just needed somewhere to hide for a little while. I didn't mean to freak you out."

He sighed. It wasn't a happy sound. "Lydia?"

"Yes?" Despite my best efforts, my voice trembled slightly.

"Look at me."

I did so. He still looked cranky and crazy cool while I remained a hot mess.

"I'm Vaughan," he said.

"Hi."

He tipped his chin and silence fell between us once more.

With the tip of his tongue rubbing at his upper lip, he looked at the wide-open window, and then back at me. Yep, that's how I'd gotten in. Houdini had nothing on my mad skills.

"What are you doing in my house, Lydia? The truth."

"It's kind of a long story, actually." Along with being excruciatingly embarrassing. But then, what wasn't about this day?

Vaughan crossed his arms over his wide chest and waited me out while I fussed with my ruined skirts and tried to come up with a way to spin the story to not make me look a complete fool. Christ, the holes in my stockings were huge. On one side, my entire foot stuck out. So screwed.

Vaughan crouched by the side of the tub, resting his arms on the side. Up close the shadows under his eyes seemed even bigger and darker against his pale skin. And there were bags big enough to use as carry-ons. Despite the strong lines of his lean face, the man looked done-in. Ready to sleep for a hundred years.

I knew that feeling.

"Looks like a wedding dress," he said quietly.

"Yes, it is. I was going to get married today." I took a deep breath, wiping my face with my hands. Just as expected, my palms came away smeared with black eye makeup. "Ah, boy. I must look a wreck."

Without comment, Vaughan reached out and grabbed a towel, handing it to me. It was sort of threadbare, old. Dated like the rest of the house. I hadn't seen more than one room, but real estate agents got a feel for these sort of things. Minimal upkeep for the past five or so years would have been my guess. Perhaps it'd even been left empty. Bushes out front hid the house from view, so I'd never gotten a good look at it before.

"Thank you." I patted myself dry with the towel as best I could. What remained of my beautiful dress was a sopping-wet ruin. "I'm sorry I broke into your house, Vaughan. I swear I don't normally do this sort of thing."

"No," he said, his voice deep. "Figured as much. Where'd you come from?"

"The big house at the back."

His brow wrinkled. "You climbed over the fence?"

"Yes."

Tired, red-tinged eyes appraised me anew. "That's a tall fence. Must have been one hell of an emergency."

"It was a disaster."

For a long moment he studied me, deep in thought. Then he sighed yet again, climbing to his feet.

"Are you going to call the cops on me?" I asked, my throat tight with tension. "I know you have every right to, I'm not disputing that. I'd just, I'd like to know. Mental preparation and all that."

"No. I'm not."

"Thank you. I appreciate that." My whole body sagged in relief.

Then he clapped his hands together, startling the crap out of me. "Okay, Lydia. Here's what we're going to do."

"Yes?"

"I arrived late this morning, have only had a few hours' sleep. If I don't get some coffee soon, things are going to get ugly. And you probably need to get dried off." With no fuss, he held out his hand. "Let's get shit sorted out. Then we can sit down and you can tell me the long story of how the hell you ended up in my house. Agreed?"

"Agreed," I said, voice lightening.

He pulled me up. Then, with strong hands on my waist, lifted me out of the tub. Immediately water started dripping off of my saturated dress, pooling on the scuffed wooden flooring at my feet. Chris would have been distinctly unimpressed. Chris didn't like messes. But as Vaughan didn't seem to care, neither did I.

"You're really not going to call the police?" I asked.

"No. Hold still," he said, carefully plucking a fake eyelash from my cheek.

"Thank you."

"Your dress is kind of fucked." He looked me over from top to toe.

"I know," I said sadly.

"I'll leave you to get changed."

"Wait. Please. I can't get out of it on my own."

More frowning.

"It's vintage," I explained with a grim face. "There's no zip, just a line of little buttons up the back."

" 'Course there is." Without another word, he turned me around and got started in on said buttons. As he worked, he hummed beneath his breath, the song vaguely familiar.

"Aren't you still mad?" I asked, perplexed.

"Nuh."

"But I broke into your house."

"Window was open."

"I still trespassed."

Busy fingers kept working on undoing the dress. "You sat in the tub and cried because some dickhead fucked you over."

That shut me up.

"Or that's what I'm assuming, given the dress and all. I take it he's the one that gave you that shiner on your cheek?"

"No. No one hit me. And yes, you assumed right about the being fucked over." I tried to look back at him, but I couldn't see a thing beyond my wild-ass hair. Impressive how it'd survived the shower. The stylist clearly knew her shit.

"You sure no one hit you?" He did not sound convinced.

"Yes. I lost my grip and hit the floor when I was climbing in the window. My home invasion skills need work."

"I'd suggest you try a different career." He finished with the buttons and took a step back, scratching his head. "You okay with the dress now?"

"Yes, thank you," I told his reflection in the mirror. "For everything, I mean."

"Sure." He almost smiled and gave a small shake of the head as if he couldn't quite believe what was going on. Or maybe it was disbelief that he wasn't kicking me straight back out the window through whence I'd come.

Lord knows, it'd shocked the shit out of me.

He turned toward the door. "See you out there."

CHAPTER THREE

Beneath the sodden wedding dress, things weren't so bad. My petti-coats and corset were actually pretty dry. Or would be soon enough in the warm weather. I fixed up my panda eyes and wrapped my hair up in a towel, turban style. Nothing more could be done.

Time to venture out in search of the kitchen. It was easy enough to find with the tantalizing scent of coffee leading me on. The bungalow had roughly an L shape. Obviously at some stage it'd been remodeled and given a more modern layout.

It was nice, charming.

French doors opened out from the kitchen onto a back deck where several pots containing long-deceased plants sat. All of the light inside was hazy, care of the unwashed windows. Tiny flecks of dust floated about in the golden afternoon air.

Vaughan waited at the table, a cup of coffee in his hands and another opposite. He wore jeans and a wrinkled gray tee with some band on the front. Even slouched in a chair, he looked good. Different from Chris yet still immensely appealing. Vaughan was so slacker cool with his long, lean body and his hair falling in his eyes. Man, I hated people who could appear so effortlessly attractive. Me relaxed resembled an oily hair and sweatpants party for one.

"Hi." I raised a hand in greeting.

He'd been busy staring off into space, lost in thought. Now, however, he blinked repeatedly, slowly looking me over. Even though I'd seen him naked, being in front of him in my flouncy lingerie had me hesitating. So stupid. Much too late in the day for me to be getting embarrassed. On the plus side, the corset turned my extra flesh into a fabulous hourglass. Something Vaughan definitely seemed to notice. I wasn't seeking any sexy times. Though, some honest male appreciation for my womanly assets felt nice. Onward and upward and all that.

"I tried to clean up the bathroom a little," I said, pulling out a seat. "Hung my dress up to dry."

"Okay."

"Thanks for the coffee."

"No worries," he said in a gruff voice. "Hope you take it black. I haven't been here for a while so there's no sugar or creamer."

"Black's fine." I took a cautious sip of the brew. Ah, coffee. My one true friend (beside vodka). There must have been some beans hiding in the freezer, because it wasn't half bad. I'd have suffered through a cup of crappy instant; it was nice not to have to, however. Small pleasures mattered. "That tastes amazing."

A grunt.

With caffeine pumping through me, I started to feel more myself. Less Miss Havisham sitting in her tattered dress and more modern capable woman. I shook off the shit, sat up a little straighter.

"Vaughan, I really am sorry about all of this, dumping my problems on you."

"I know." He didn't meet my eyes due to still noticing my assets. Maybe he'd zoned out, what with being so tired, and that just happened to be in the vicinity where he'd been looking when it happened.

"It bears repeating. You've been great about it, really."

Another grunt.

Had to admit, curiosity filled me about this man. Wonder what he was like when he wasn't sleep deprived and dealing with a trespassing runaway bride. Was he the sort of person who smiled a little or a lot? I couldn't tell. For someone who made her living reading people and talking them into buying big houses, today I officially knew shit.

"You didn't even get to have your shower," I said.

A one-shoulder shrug. "Later."

"I promise after I finish this coffee, I'll get out of your way."

"No rush." Still no eye contact.

I shifted in my seat.

He really was appealing in his way. His lips were neither thick nor thin. Just nice. It would be good to see them curved in a smile. To know I hadn't entirely trashed his day with my drama.

"This really is a lovely house," I said. "You don't spend much time here?"

"No."

"Shame."

Maybe he'd been all talked out and didn't want a conversation. Fine by me. But I don't think that's what was going on. He'd zoned out, all right. I highly doubt it was due to tiredness, however.

I cocked my head, studying him. "Vaughan?"

"Yeah?"

"Nice weather we're having, isn't it?"

"Great."

"It is. It's so great," I enthused. "Love the weather."

Handsome face blank of expression, his fingers remained curled unmoving around his half-full cup of coffee. If it wasn't for his monosyllable responses and the whole chest moving with each breath thing, I'd have wondered if the man had croaked. And it wasn't my makeup-smeared face or crazily knotted hair he was gawking at. In fact, I don't believe he ever got that far.

Seemed my would-have-been-neighbor was a tit man.

I have to admit my Elomi bridal lingerie was exquisite. I'd been so certain it would wow Chris, spur him into some post-matrimonial lustfulness. What a joke. A strap-on might have been a better idea.

"I just wanted to say thanks again for being so understanding about all this," I said.

"Sure," he told my boobs.

"You've been great."

"Mm."

"Other people wouldn't have been so understanding."

"Assholes," he said, lips pressed tight in disapproval. I'm sure my breasts appreciated his support immensely.

I drank my coffee, waiting for him to get bored of them. And then I waited some more. Wasn't happening. The clock on the wall ticked loudly, the only sound in the room. While I couldn't claim innocence regarding his groin, at least I hadn't gawked at him to this degree. I'd been discreet(ish).

"Vaughan?"

Nostrils flared on a deep breath. "Huh?"

"You're staring."

"What?"

"My breasts." I waved a hand around the pertinent parts of my anatomy. Though I'm reasonably certain he already knew where they were. "These things, Vaughan. The baby feeders and pillows of sin. You're staring at them."

His startled gaze jumped to my face.

"I wouldn't mention it, but it's been a while now and I'm beginning to get a little uncomfortable."

"Shit," he muttered, as realization hit. He turned his face away.

"Don't get me wrong. Since you're probably the only one who'll ever see me in this, it's kind of nice to see some appreciation. But yeah, getting awkward."

"Sorry, Lydia."

"It's okay." I tried to hold back a smile. Tried.

Brows drawn down, he concentrated good and hard on drinking his coffee. "Didn't realize I was doing that."

"It's fine. You like boobs. I get it," I said, inspecting the girls. "They are kind of out there in this corset."

"Yeah."

"And to be fair, I did see you in all your glory not so long ago."

He snorted out a laugh. No idea how he made it sound attractive, but he did. Then his lips curved into a small droll smile. And that smile? It was lovely.

Wonder how things were going over the fence for Chris & Co.? Not that I cared. A fiery gateway to hell could open up beneath their garden party and I wouldn't have helped a single one of them. Guess I'd entered the bitter and twisted stage of mourning my relationship. Sure as hell I was done with denial.

"You were going to tell me about your wedding disaster," Vaughan prompted.

"Right." I folded my arms over my chest. A purely defensive, batten-down-the-hatches kind of move. All it did, though, was plump up my boobs. Immediately, Vaughan's gaze was there, making me shift in the chair uncomfortably. "You wouldn't happen to have a shirt I could borrow, would—"

"No."

"No?"

He cleared his throat. "Sorry."

"You only have one shirt?"

"Yeah, ah . . . see, the airline lost my luggage."

"I thought you said you'd been driving all night."

"Right, right. Flew then drove. Decided to hit the road in Portland, catch all that scenery."

"At night?"

"Yeah." He turned away, scratching at the golden-red stubble on his chin. "All the stars and shit. It was real pretty."

Huh. Okay. Probably no point asking about towels. The only ones I'd seen were now hanging up wet in the bathroom. To steal the sheet off his bed and make a toga out of it might be going too far. No problem, I could brazen it out. Obviously my host had no issues with letting it all hang out physically. Though he'd been hewn from stone, while I was more marshmallow. Chris had liked to call me his "dumpling." He'd made it sound sweet, but it'd niggled none the less.

How much exactly had I ignored or excused? Good question. I bit at my thumbnail, folding in on myself. No. Enough. I would not allow him and his set to continue undermining my self-confidence. The video had woken me up. No more excuses.

"I believe my fiancé is gay and has been using me as a beard," I announced, chin held high. "That's basically the whole story."

Vaughan's eyes widened. "Shit."

"Yes."

"What happened?"

"I was getting ready for the ceremony and someone sent me a video of him getting it on with another guy."

"That's why you ran?"

"That's why I ran." I slumped back in the seat. "Why? What would you have done?"

"Gotten the hell out of there."

I gave him a nod, relaxing further. "Good."

"Dick isn't my thing. Would have had to have been drunk as fuck to have gotten engaged to a guy in the first place." From beneath his brows came a sly look. "But yeah, I'd have definitely bolted."

"Ha-ha."

The smile came slowly, but again it was definitely there. Strange—he smiled and the weight on my shoulders lightened. All of the dust and darkness in the house faded from view. Maybe it was just me not feeling so alone, I don't know. But it helped.

"No way I could've pulled off the underwear and dress as well as you," he said contemplatively, thumb rubbing over the rim of his coffee cup.

"No?"

"I lack some of your finer assets."

"Aw, that's sweet," I drawled, laughing softly. "I'm sure you look lovely in drag, Vaughan. But I appreciate you saying that."

"No problem." He took a sip of coffee, watching me all the while with those intense blue eyes. Not once did they stray down to the assets in question. Probably too busy admiring my fine collection of scratches, bruises, and general hot bridal messiness.

I shifted in my seat, fussed for a minute. Though really, what was the point? I looked like hell. Might as well just roll with it. I huffed out a breath and did my best to let all of the dross go. Everything would be okay. Life would go on. Me and my insane situation had even managed to raise this man's spirits a little.

Yes, I'd made a mistake. Shit had definitely happened. But things weren't so bad. Apart from my fine collection of scratches, bruises, and aching muscles, I still had my health.

"You've got a killer smile," he said, still staring.

Heck, he was serious. Probably just being kind. "Thank you."

A nod.

He rubbed at the stubble on his chin, little lines appearing between his brows. "You weren't tempted to have a show-him-up, out him in front of all the guests?"

"Honestly?" I took my time and pondered the question, turning it over inside my head. "I wasn't afraid, exactly, I just . . . they weren't my people. All of those guests were business acquaintances, contacts, friends of his family. Most of them I'd never even met. Guess I haven't been in town long enough to make my own friends. I've been either busy working or I've been with Chris. My parents couldn't make it and I've pretty much lost touch with the girls I went to school with.

"I don't really care what those idiots over there think of me. As for what they think of him, he made this mess. He can clean it up himself. I just wanted to remove myself from the entire situation, pronto." I stared over his shoulder, lost in thought. "I guess I was embarrassed. How could I not be? He played me for a fool."

He made a small noise.

"Anyway."

"And that's how you wound up in my bathtub?"

"Yes." I gave him a strained smile. "I realized a bit late that I had no money or cards. Hiding out for a while until things settled down seemed like a smart idea. Have my meltdown in private."

"Mm."

"Speaking of which, guess I better head back around, check out the damage." I took a fortifying gulp of coffee. "Get out of your hair and go fetch my purse."

"No rush."

"Think I've probably taken up enough of your time with my drama," I said with a small laugh. It fell flat. I should give it a few days to sink in before attempting to make jokes. Right now things still felt raw, on edge. Like I might burst into tears again at any moment. Either that or go into some sort of psycho rage. Too many emotions were bubbling away beneath the surface. It didn't feel like there was enough of me to contain it all. One small crack and everything would start pouring out all over again.

No. Nope. I straightened my spine. I could handle this. I could and I would.

"Seriously." He waved a hand, motioning for me to stay seated. Then he stretched, raising his arms up above his head then gripping his elbows and cracking his neck. "You don't really want to go back around there yet. Fuck knows, I wouldn't want to."

"Are you sure?"

He nodded. "Yeah. You being here also gives me a damn good excuse to put off dealing with my own shit."

"You've got drama too?"

A shrug. "Doesn't everyone?"

"A side effect of breathing, I guess."

He smiled.

CHAPTER FOUR

"Nothing about your sex life didn't make you think he might be gay?" Vaughan asked.

"Um . . ."

"If you don't mind me asking."

"Well, yes. I mean no, I don't mind you asking. But *yes*, our lack of intimacy should have made me think twice." Oh, god. It really, really should have. What with the lack of screwing, I'd screwed up magnificently. Shame filled me. "I still can't believe I fell for his crap."

"Guess he was convincing."

"He sure was."

"Least you didn't go through with the wedding."

I huffed out a breath. "Hell no. As soon as I saw . . ."

A nod.

"I'm not sure it's actually sunk in yet, that I'm not getting married today. I'm not spending the rest of my life building a home with him."

"It's big."

"Yeah." I folded my hands in my lap. "I got carried away and took a leap of faith. It just didn't pay off."

He said nothing. Not like there was anything to say.

"Trust is a bitch. Anyway." I shook it off. Time to move on, et cetera. If I kept telling myself as much, eventually it had to sink in. "To answer your question. Honestly, Vaughan, we didn't have much of a sex life to speak of."

"What?" Elbows on the table, he leaned in, getting closer. "When was the last time you two fucked?"

I blinked. Not "had sex." Not even "made love." Fucked. Like language even mattered, and yet . . . maybe I was a prude. I'd never thought of myself as one, though as today was showing, I knew shit.

"Lydia?"

"Sorry. Just mentally beating myself up again."

"Stop it. That's not going to help."

"No, it's not. But kind of hard to avoid today."

"Mm."

Tattoos covered his arms to the wrists. Black and gray, mostly, with traces of color erupting here and there. An electric guitar with an ornate skull above it. A diving bluebird surrounded by licks of flame. Beautiful ink work. Whoever he went to was an artist.

Opposite me, he pushed back his pale-red hair, waiting on me to answer his question.

"Well, we were waiting to have sex. His family are religious and quite traditional." My fingers meshed and twisted in my lap. "Big on appearances and stuff. Yeah . . ."

Little lines appeared between his brows.

"But he told me he loved me all the time. And he'd call several times a day just to check on me, to see if I needed anything," I said with just a hint of desperation. "He respected me. Without a doubt, he's the most adult, well-adjusted person I've ever been in a relationship with. We wanted the same things, a stable economic future and a family, two kids. We were both ready to settle down. Marrying him made perfect sense."

"Sounds great," he deadpanned.

"I thought it was."

He sat forward, leaning his elbows on the table. "Let me check I've got this right. You guys were together for months, getting married."

"Yes."

"And absolutely nothing between the sheets?"

I pursed my lips, readjusting my turban-towel hairdo. You know, buying some time. If only I'd kept my mouth shut and just let the guy gawk at my breasts. Much better than having this humiliating conversation, especially with him. The man was obviously some sort of ridiculously cool Idaho sex god. Who the hell even knew such a thing existed?

"Lydia?"

I growled or moaned. It was definitely one or the other, I'm just not sure which. Emotionally, things were in upheaval. "There was some couch action. We messed around, we just didn't go quite that far. Well, we sort of did it."

His brows went up. "Sort of?"

"Yes."

"Babe, if you're not sure what you did with this prick was sex or not, then it's not. Let's get that straight right now."

My grin was a forced, ugly thing. "Right."

"Guy was dating you and he didn't want any?"

"Mm-hmm."

"Does he have a dick?"

"Yes, Vaughan, he has a dick."

"You sure about that?"

I looked to heaven. No help was forthcoming. "It's kind of you to think that."

He laughed, gaze sliding down to my breasts for a millisecond. "No. Just being reasonable."

"Some people believe in celibacy before marriage."

"You don't."

He had a point. No way was I acknowledging it, however.

"Do you?" he persisted.

"I believed in him." My pride was a sad small thing. I could feel it sinking slowly to the floor to play dead. "You know, I thought talking about this would help, but it's not. Can we stop now?"

"No. I want to understand this."

"God, get in line." This time, it was a definite moan of despair. Pitiful. "I'm not even sure I can explain it anymore. And you don't want to understand it, you want to mock it."

"That's not true. C'mon, I'm trying here."

Brows high, I gave him a look most dubious.

"I am. But you had to suspect."

"Or maybe he was a damn good actor and I was one of those sad lonely women who get taken in." The ugly truth. My stomach twisted and turned, making me want to heave.

"But—"

"Stop. Please." God help me, I could take no more. I softly banged my forehead against the tabletop and stayed there, face-down. "Can I convince you to press charges? I think maybe I should go to jail after all. A nice, quiet jail cell might be just the thing."

"You're not going to fucking jail."

It'd been worth a try.

"Hey, I'm sorry you got screwed over, but shit will sort itself out."

The weight atop my head shifted and then my towel turban disappeared. Straggly damp blond strands feel around my face. I sat up, pushing back the whole mess.

"Sorry," he said, throwing the towel in the general direction of the kitchen counter. "I was trying to give you a comforting pat on the head."

"Thanks."

A pause.

"No straight guy could stay away from that rack," he said quietly. "Just saying."

"Not everyone's a tit man."

"Well, they should be," he scoffed. "Breast is best."

I snorted, laughing a little despite myself.

The room quieted again, both of us lost in our own thoughts for a moment.

"I'm on your side, Lydia."

"Thank you," I said. "And I know what sex is, Vaughan. Okay? There were hands, but neither of us came. Things got interrupted. He interrupted them, there was an important business call or something. Therefore, 'sort of' on the sex."

Dead silence from the other side of the table.

"What?"

He held up a finger. "I'm still not mocking you."

"Okay."

"But anyone who'd stop feeling up or finger banging a woman in favor of taking a fucking phone call is an inconsiderate asshole you shouldn't be opening your legs for."

"I'm seeing that now."

"I'm serious, Lydia."

I studied the tabletop, needing a moment to pull myself together. "How long have we known each other? What, half an hour, an hour?"

"Ah." Turning in his seat, he checked out an old wooden clock on the kitchen wall. "Yeah. About that."

"Are you aware that most people wait a little longer before

discussing the rules of etiquette in regards to finger banging? Who they should and shouldn't open their legs for? Things like that."

"That so?"

"It is."

"Well, fuck." He sat back, outright grinning at me, and it was stunning. Ridiculously so. The wide pull of his lips over white teeth, the amusement lighting his eyes. His thumb beat against the tabletop, moving the tendons in his arm, shifting all of the complex ink work on his skin.

Couldn't help but wonder what his own drama was over.

"Most people don't turn up in my tub in a wedding dress. But tell me, babe, how's that worked out for you? Following all of the rules, being polite and toeing the line? Doing what most people do?"

"My name's not babe."

His shine dulled down to a patient smile. "How's it worked out for you, Lydia?"

"Isn't that obvious?"

"Why did you have no one to run to today? Why's no one got your back?"

"A last-minute emergency came up with my parents' business. They were really apologetic, but . . . sometimes things happen, right? It's nothing personal, they're just the kind of people that live to work. That's their life. I can pretty much count on one hand the number of birthdays, Thanksgivings, and Christmas's we celebrated on the actual day." I got busy finger combing my hair as best I could. It kept the fidgets from taking over. "Just as well they didn't come to the wedding."

Nothing was said. Though there seemed to be a sadness in his eyes, an understanding. Chris had blue eyes, but different from Vaughan's. Darker. Flecks of hazel muddied their depths. Chris's eyes had never struck me as being particularly expressive. Not like Vaughan's. I guess it was all the secrets he was keeping, all the lies. Eyes as windows to the soul, or not. You can't see into someone if they won't let you.

"Honestly? The way I've lived my life has worked out shit for me, Vaughan."

He just stared.

"Apart from letting Chris make me look like a total idiot. I was working with my fiancé, so I'm assuming I'm now out of a job. I gave up my apartment to move into the big house, so I have no idea where I'm sleeping tonight." I crossed my arms over my breasts, covering up as much as I could. Nothing about laying myself open felt good. Of course, maybe it wasn't supposed to. Especially not to a veritable stranger.

Whatever. The situation was what it was, and no matter how much anger I worked up at Chris, I'd played my part in getting here. I'd made bad choices. No point pretending otherwise. "It's not just Chris's fault, though. I think you could safely say I'm exceptionally shitty at relationships. We were constantly moving around when I was a kid. After a while I just didn't bother making friends anymore, you know? It's easier."

He just watched me.

"I even pretty much kept to myself in college. Just concentrated on study and my waitressing job. Because work is everything, right? The guy I dated was pretty low key too. Neither of us were party animals." I breathed out through my nose, shoulders slumping. "That romance kind of fizzled out after graduation."

"Yeah?"

"He had this great opportunity overseas and I just wanted to find somewhere nice and settle. I tried a few different places. Coeur d'Alene was the first one that felt right. I'd make some friends outside of work, get to know my neighbors." I stared off at nothing, avoiding whatever expression he had on his face. "That's what's normal, right?"

"One version of it, sure."

"Hmm." God, listening to myself try and explain my life made me want to forcibly throw myself off the nearest cliff. Or have a really full-on spa day. Either would probably do. "Given my history, its amazing I thought I had a clue what I was doing with Chris at all. I was the perfect target for his fuckery."

I forced a smile. "Idiot is definitely the word."

"Don't say that," he admonished. "You're were a little naive maybe, inexperienced. But you're not an idiot."

"Thanks. Anyhoo, enough of my pity party. So," I said, squaring my shoulders and looking him straight in the eye. "I'm guessing you don't follow the rules or worry about being polite and toeing the line. How's that working out for you?"

The corner of his lips twitched. "Honestly?"

"Honestly."

"Shit," he admitted, lacing his fingers behind his neck.

"Yeah? How deep?"

"Broke, out of work, probably about to lose this place."

"Wow." I slumped in my chair. "Aren't we a pair?"

"Aren't we?" His self-deprecating smile grew. "No money. No hope. No nothing."

"Basically."

His head fell back and he gazed up at the ceiling. The strong lines in his neck were way pronounced in this pose. I couldn't quite see the tattoo peeking out beneath the collar of his tee. Words, but I'm not sure what. He raised his head enough to look at me from beneath his brows. "They have booze back over the fence at your fancy party?"

"Heaps. Really good stuff too. Lots of craft beer."

"Nice. We should go steal some."

I nodded instantly. Crazy ideas deserved support. "We should. It's half my wedding, it wouldn't really be stealing. You're going to have to help me get back over the fence again, though. I think I pulled every muscle from the waist down getting over it the first time."

"I can help you get back over the fence."

"Done, then," I said. "Tomorrow, we figure our lives out. Tonight we'll toast to our crappy situations and drown our sorrows."

We smiled at each other in kinship.

"How serious are you about this?" I asked, more curious than afraid. Mostly.

A shrug. "You got to go back there sometime. Might as well make it worth the trip."

"I guess so." My forehead furrowed. "Alcohol would be good."

"I definitely need a drink to deal with being back here." He slowly shook his head, lips curved downward. "Shit is fucked, babe. Like you wouldn't believe."

I didn't mean to laugh. Not at his misfortunes, nor mine. Lord knows, nothing about it felt funny. Vaughan frowned at me. Only, then he started laughing too. First a little, then a lot. Soon the noise filled the room, startling the old house from its silence. He laughed until his wide shoulders shook and all that bright hair fell in his face, obscuring the cut of his cheeks. I in turn cackled my ass off until tears streamed down my face.

None of it should have been funny, but it was hilarious. And we, our lives, were the joke.

I guess sometimes there's no right response but to laugh. So we did. Strangely enough, it really did help.

Sitting in a stranger's kitchen, confessing all, was the last damn place I expected to find myself on this day of all days. Yet here we were. I'd spilled a stack of doubts and deep, dark secrets while the man opposite remained a mystery.

Just then he combed back his wild hair with long fingers,

looking my way. A smile still lingered about his lips. A warm one. Perhaps even a suggestive one?

I don't know.

It was certainly starting to heat me up inside. He didn't break eye contact, just kept giving me his friendly, easy, sexy-as-sin smile. So gorgeous. Though this guy would be dazzling peeling potatoes or putting out the garbage. Look up "hot" in the dictionary and there'll be Vaughan, making eyes at you from on the page.

Chris had always held my hand or put his arm around my waist when we were out. I'd taken these moves as him being proud to be seen with me, of him liking my body even if he wished I'd work on it a little. Instead he'd been clinging like a limpet to ward off rumors regarding his sexuality. I wasn't his life partner, just his patsy.

Vaughan admired my breasts, but how he felt about the rest of me I had no idea.

Uptight capitalists such as myself may not be his thing. His clothes were comfortable, old blue jeans and a faded tee. I couldn't see any jewelry on him, just all the ink. His body wasn't bulky, but athletic. Fit and strong if the way he'd lifted me out of the bathtub without pulling his back was any indication. Around my age, maybe a little older.

And as for the house, someone had loved this place once. Taken care of it. There was dust but not dirt, if that makes sense. Photos and personal mementos were missing, the house stripped bare apart from the furniture. A collection of cool vintage from the fifties and cheap pine shit. Crackling white paint on the ceiling, but the cream on the walls seemed almost new. Unmarked. It was as if the place was waiting, but for what?

Curiosity over him owned me. I wanted to wander around inside his mind, fondle his hot body. Things along those lines.

Also, he was still looking at me that way.

"Least you finally made a friend," he said.

"Ha." I squirmed in my seat. "I guess I have. How about that."

Intended or not the man had my body in the palm of his hand. In and out my lungs pumped, gaining speed with every breath. Even my blood was rushing faster. As for my sex . . . god help him. Everything between my legs had started tingling in awareness of him and all the good things he could no doubt deliver. My vagina was waking up and roaring, ready for action. The man should have been afraid, not still giving me sexy looks. He didn't understand the ravenous sex-starved animal he was dealing with. No control. Zip. Zero.

Casual no-strings sex between new friends. It was needed. Now. No big deal. I was here. He was here. Let's do this.

Just before I could jump him, he looked at me anew. "Wait. You said this guy's name was Chris?"

"What?" I blinked repeatedly.

"Your groom's name. It was Chris, right?"

"Um, yes." Cold water. Icy cold freezing water poured all over my lust. "Chris Delaney."

"Delaney?" He slapped his thigh, shaking his head. "Oh, yeah. He likes dick. Thought everyone knew that."

"What?" I hissed.

The man just shrugged, blasé as fuck. "Dude used to date the captain of the football team back in high school. Can't remember the guy's name. They were on the sly, but everyone knew."

"Everyone knew." My jaw hit the floor, literally. Well okay, not literally. Close to it, however. "Everyone."

"Probably. I'd say so, family like that in a place like this."

My mouth worked, but nothing came out. So much nothing it nearly choked me. I wanted to bang my head against a wall. Rant and rage. Climb back over the fence and set the house on fire. I wanted to lose my shit, big-time.

"O-kay," he said. "You should probably take a breath."

I shook my head, quietly hyperventilating. My whole life might not have flashed before my eyes, but the last four months came through loud and clear. Stupid, stupid girl. Vindictive, scheming asshole.

"C'mon, Lydia."

Everyone knew. My fingers gripped the edges of the seat, nails digging deep into the wood. It was like I'd been on a roller coaster this whole time and here came the ultimate, dizzying, final fall. White spots danced before my eyes.

"Babe? Hey. Breathe."

"I hate this town," I babbled first, then took the breath because no one was telling me what to do. Sensible advice or not, I was done with being handled. Managed. Maneuvered. My lungs worked hard, pulling in air as fast as they could. "That duplicitous manipulative little piece of shit."

"Yeah, that's him."

"I want to hurt him. Bad."

"Understandable." Vaughan's tongue worked behind his cheek as if he was deep in thought. "Looks like he's sure as hell given you reason. Tell me, are his parents still trying to be the Kennedys of Coeur d'Alene?"

"You just described them perfectly."

"How long you been in town?"

"Four months. It was a whirlwind romance." I blinked back hot tears. No more. Not a single fucking one. "I thought I finally had it all figured out, but I was clueless. No one told me."

"No, well . . . you're new, they wouldn't. At heart, this place is still a small town."

"Right."

"So," he said with a sigh. "There you go."

"There I go." Everyone knew. My humiliation was complete. I

stared off into space, visions of Chris's bloody severed penis dancing through my head. Violent tendencies weren't my natural setting. Chris, however, had all but walked me to the edge of reason and pushed me over. Garden shears would be wonderful. Also an ax. I bet axes were awesome for working out aggression. Probably fantastic for building upper body strength too. Hooray for multitasking. You'd have to imagine it'd make a godawful mess of his junk but never mind. Chris's dick was dead.

"Babe?"

"That's not my name," I said, mouth on automatic pilot.

"Whatever. You're looking a bit homicidal over there. Everything okay?"

"Yeah. Figuring out the best method for separating him from his manhood."

Vaughan winced.

"Can you blame me?"

"No, no." He set his clasped hands on the table. "Dude worked you over big-time. But before you start washing the streets with his blood, think about it from his perspective."

"You're defending him? Seriously?" I gaped.

"Fuck no, of course not. But you jilting him, how do you think that'll go down with the pack of uptight assholes he calls family and friends, huh?"

I stopped. "They never thought I was good enough for him. Me rejecting him so publicly . . . he'll be completely humiliated."

"Yeah." His vicious grin was glorious. It set the sun to shame.

"They'll be talking about this for years."

"Longer. Places like this never forget this sort of shit."

"I also left the cell phone. Unless he somehow got to it first, they're going to see him and Paul in action." My smile was equally all sharp teeth. "Everyone will know why I did it."

Vaughan clicked his fingers. "Paul. That was the guy's name."

"What guy?"

"You know. The football captain in high school. Fancy them sticking together all these years."

"Yeah. Wow," I said drily, rising to pace the room. There was too much anger in me to sit still. Too much manic energy. "It's beautiful. True romance."

"Sorry." He not so successfully hid a smile behind his hand.

"I wonder who sent the home porn?"

"Number was blocked?"

"Yes."

"If Chris is anything like the prick he was back in school, it's not like he'd have a shortage of enemies." His eyes narrowed on me in scrutiny. "You seem nice. Why'd you want to marry him anyway? Money?"

"No." I bristled, shoulders squaring. "I told you, he was really good to me."

"Right. He called you and shit."

"He wooed me. Almost every night he'd take me out to restaurants and shows in Spokane, all sorts of things. We had a lot of fun."

"Public things where you'd be seen."

"Yes." My lips flattened in anger. "Public things where we'd be seen so people wouldn't think he was gay. Nothing about us was real. I get it, okay? And what the hell is wrong with being gay, anyway?"

He reared back like I was dangerous. Smart man.

"Well?" I demanded.

"I got no problem with it. Not my thing, but whatever."

Then someone tapped on the kitchen door, opened it (without invitation), and stepped inside. Someone dressed in a sharp black tuxedo. Rage got me in a stranglehold and I jumped to my feet.

"I'm going to fucking kill you!"

CHAPTER FIVE

"You," I roared, charging at him.

Chris's handsome face instantly hardened.

A strong arm wrapped around my middle, lifting me off my feet. I was pulled back against a rock-hard body, my feet flailing in midair for the second time that day.

"You lied to me, you bastard. All along, you lied." I struggled, pushing at Vaughan's arms and kicking at his legs. All he did was grunt and tighten his hold around my waist. Damn, he was strong. I was getting nowhere. But did I let that stop me? Hell no. Reason and I had long since parted ways. "You like dick, not pussy. You used me!"

"I have no idea what you're talking about." Chris sneered. "Get yourself under control, Lydia."

"I'm going to kill you."

"Babe, calm down," Vaughan whispered in my ear.

"Let me go."

"Don't think that's a good idea. You wanted to stay out of jail, remember?"

"I want to kill him more," I panted. "Much, much more."

"No, you're a nice girl. You follow the rules."

"Fuck nice. I want to dance on his grave!"

"Are you drunk?" With sharp movements, Chris tore at his bow tie, removing the scrap of silk from around his neck. His gaze raked over me, clearly unimpressed. "You are, aren't you? God knows, you look ridiculous. What the hell happened to you, Lydia? We've been searching everywhere for you. Do you realize how many people are waiting over at the house?"

"They'll be waiting a hell of a long time. I saw you and Paul together."

Fear flashed in his eyes. But he covered it quickly, raising his chin sky high. "So? I told you we'd be having a few drinks last night. That can hardly be the cause for all this."

"You were making out."

All expression left his face. "You don't know what you're talking about."

"Having sex."

"Stop it."

"Screwing."

His hands curled into fists. "Shut your mouth, Lydia!"

"You don't talk to her that way," said Vaughan, voice low and deadly. Still holding me back, however.

Loud banging came from the front door. Next thing we knew, Chris's demonic platinum-blond excuse for a mother came marching inside, glowering all the while. His father came a step behind her, expression equally thunderous. Awesome. Now the party could really begin.

"Fuck's sake." Vaughan hefted me up, holding me closer. "No one in this town respect property rights anymore?"

"You should really lock your doors," I mumbled, giving up the struggle. For the moment, at least.

"Windows too." He grunted, unamused.

"Samantha. Ray." I stood tall. Or as tall as Vaughan's grip would allow. The woman's laser-like eyes cut through me, not even bothering with the guy who owned the place. Next my cell phone was thrust in my face. The all too familiar moaning and groaning of Chris and Paul's porn filled the room.

"This is your phone," she hissed. "What the hell is this?"

"Why, it's your son and his bestie having sex."

Behind me, Chris made a strangled sound. It warmed my cold hard soul.

"Impossible." The woman swept into the house, her husband hot on her heels. It was almost impressive the way she could constantly look down her nose at everything. You'd think it would give her a headache eventually. Paul came skulking behind them, sticking to the wall, ready to bolt at any moment. As well he might, smarmy bastard. Were it not for Vaughan's hold, I'd have been tempted to attack him too.

My blood, it boiled. "No, it's not impossible. You see, Samantha, when two men really love each other and have some lubrica—"

"Lies!" The woman bared her pearlescent teeth. "How dare you."

"Me? It's your son that's been lying, not me. And considering half the damn town apparently knows about him playing for the other team, I highly doubt you were caught completely unaware."

"Those are nothing but malicious rumors!" One bloodred talon pointed straight at my heart. "You did this somehow."

"Me?" I scoffed. "Right. So what . . . I bought a strap-on, dressed up as Paul, and somehow convinced Chris to let me peg him on camera?"

Vaughan huffed out a laugh, his grip on me loosening.

"You're right. I can totally see that happening. It's all my fault." Save me from the woman's stupidity.

"If you'd only made more of an effort to be attractive for him," she said. "Done something with your unsightly fat ass, then this never would have happened!"

I lunged, Vaughan again hefting me back, holding on tight. Red colored my world. I was so damn mad I couldn't even think of a decent comeback. "Oh yeah? Come over here and say that."

Thin lips strained, the she-demon advanced, taking up the invitation. Only, her son had other priorities. Chris snatched the cell from his mother's hand, the outburst of violence as far from his usual cool-and-in-control as possible. Face red and eyes bright, he threw it on the ground and proceeded stomping. Once. Twice. Three times. Screen cracked and innards lying bare, the phone had been smashed to smithereens. The homemade porn moaned and groaned no more.

"Good, it's gone," said Samantha. "It was obviously a fake anyway. I mean, who could have recorded such a thing?"

"Ooh, good question." I didn't even have it in me to be mad about the phone. My ex-fiancé's furious demented expression was reward enough. Ray's mouth gaped. Even Samantha seemed mildly stunned. Only Paul remained unmoved. Unsurprised, even.

"You sent it," I said, realization dawning.

Paul did an awesome deer-in-headlights impersonation. "No, I didn't."

"You did. God." I slowly shook my head, amazed. "You wanted me to know. Why?"

His mouth moved, but he said nothing.

"Were you jealous? Tired of hiding? What?"

"Paul," Chris fumed. "You wouldn't."

The big guy flattened himself against the wall even further. If he could have melded with it, he would have. "I . . ."

"Tell me you didn't."

"Fuck." Vaughan wiped a hand across his face. "This is unbelievable."

"Christopher, you told us you outgrew this nonsense," said Ray, visibly shaking with anger. "That it was just a phase."

"Oh, god." Samantha collapsed onto the nearest worn leather lounge chair. "This is an absolute catastrophe. What will everyone think?"

The half-a-head and superior body mass Paul had on Chris didn't matter. Not even a little. Chris grabbed him by his lapels, shaking him roughly, making his head whip back and forth. "You betrayed me! You fucking betrayed me!"

"I love you," shouted Paul, a tear trailing down his cheek. "How the hell could I just stand by and watch you marry someone else, even if it was bullshit, huh?"

"I knew it." My hands curled into tight fists, lungs laboring. I couldn't get enough air. Anger filled me to overflowing, leaving room for nothing else.

"Yes." Over on the lounge, Samantha's eyes lit with glee. "We'll tell everyone it's her fault. That she did something."

"Excellent," said Ray. "Perfectly believable."

"What?" I asked, voice low and deadly.

"You love me?" Chris stumbled back a step.

Face taut, Paul followed. "Of course I do."

The two men stared at each other, lost to the rest of the unfolding drama. Meanwhile, Ray and his wife talked in hush tones. Vaughan just leaned against the wall, his expression somewhere between shocked to shit and bemused. Fair enough, it wasn't his life going to hell in a handbasket. It was mine, making it time to take action.

"But you know she means nothing to me," said Chris. "Nothing."

"I know." Tentatively, Paul reached out a hand, cupping Chris's face for a moment. How tender. How sweet. And really, I'd about had enough. Some part inside of me had cracked wide open.

Fury pounding through my veins, I advanced on the two secret lovers. The fuckers. Chris turned to face me, oblivious as to my intent. Or perhaps not entirely. He tried to raise a hand, but too late.

With fingers curled tight and muscles tensed, I swung. My fist drove into his perfect straight nose with awesome aim. Pain resonated up my arm as blood gushed from his nostrils. Man, there was a lot of it. Niagara would have been jealous.

Wow.

Chris yelped, doubling over, hands covering his face. From behind me, Vaughan's hand descended upon my shoulder. It seemed everywhere people were yelling. Sure, my knuckles hurt. But it was pure satisfaction curving the smile on my face. I slowly stretched out my fingers, flexing them. Painful, though they all worked. Nothing broken. Far out, I'd actually hit someone and I couldn't think of anyone more deserving than my own fiancé. The room was a whir of action, everyone on their feet. Lots of noise. All I could hear, however, was the pounding of blood behind my ears.

Only one last thing to do before I was truly free.

Such an obnoxiously large diamond ring. Not me at all. I wrestled it off my finger, dropping it at his feet. He looked up, eyes crimson and face a bloody mess. I'd done that. Me. The nothing to which he'd been referring. My most likely demented smile grew even wider.

"Fuck you, Chris. We're done."

I had no idea the police could arrive so fast. It was like the old joke about pornography giving young women unrealistic notions of how long it takes a plumber to arrive. One minute Vaughan sat holding ice to my hand, the next I was facing the long arm of the law.

Boom.

The cop who questioned me turned out to be an old school friend of Vaughan's (who in this town hadn't he gone to school with?). Officer Andy seemed sweet and somewhat amused by the whole situation though he hid it well. What with my entire statement consisting of "Hell yeah, I did it," however, my hopes for remaining at liberty were low.

I hovered in the front doorway, keeping an eye on Chris and Co. Much was ado in the front garden. Samantha had been loudly pushing to charge me with assault while attempting to break the sound barrier via her shrieking.

More than a few neighbors had gathered to watch.

Apparently, according to Samantha, I'd turned into a dangerous criminal out to destroy her family (truthfully, I just wanted to escape them). Also, I apparently made Moby Dick look anorexic and I needed to get a life.

She was probably right about the last one.

Her husband, meanwhile, paced back and forth along the small garden path speaking on his cell. There was a lot of head shaking and mumbling. Off to the side stood Paul and Chris, heads huddled together. The latter's nose was stuffed full of Kleenex to stem the flow of blood. His once pristine white shirt suit was covered in the stuff. All in all, he looked a ruin. It suited him.

"Here," said Vaughan, draping a checked button-up shirt over my shoulders. "Put that on."

"I thought your luggage got delayed."

"Yeah. I lied. Didn't want you covering up."

"Ha." I smiled. Then I stopped. "I am sorry about all this."

He shrugged. "Had nothing else planned for tonight. What're they all up to?"

"Ah, well," I said. "Ron is on the phone to his lawyer trying to best assess how to destroy me while doing damage control to preserve the good Delaney family name. Samantha, meanwhile, is over there busily trying to push your friend, Officer Andy, into hauling me away in cuffs for assaulting her son."

"Shit."

Chris looked up, giving me a truly malevolent look. Hate filled his bloody face. To think I'd been about to marry the asshole. At any rate, no matter the provocation, the chances of him letting me get away with hitting him were nil to none. His pride would demand I be punished.

No, he was just letting me stew with this show of deliberation. Jerk.

To think I'd believed all of his sweetness and light for so long. I really needed to bang my head against a brick wall at the earliest opportunity. Try and knock some sense into myself.

Paul tugged on his arm and they returned to their intense heart-to-heart. They actually made a nice-looking couple, Chris with his dark hair and chiseled face, and Paul with his Nordic good looks. Pity about the general acts of bastardry surrounding the entire affair.

"Why hasn't he, do you think?" asked Vaughan, studying all the people standing in his front yard.

"I honestly have no idea."

"Hmm." He huffed out a breath. "You've got shit taste in men, Lydia."

"Understatement of the year, *babe*."

He gave me a half-smile. "How's your hand doing?"

"Swollen and sore." I turned it this way and that, letting him see. My knuckles were a delightful chunky blue-black. "But I think it's just bruised."

"Matches your cheek."

"Lovely."

He trudged down the front steps, hands in his jeans pockets.

I slipped my arms into Vaughan's shirt, doing my best to cover my womanly assets. Wondered if jail was anything like on TV. Guess I'd soon be finding out. A shame I hadn't kept the ring. Pawning it to pay for my legal defense would have been beautifully ironic.

Whatever happened, I was done being the resident fool for the Delaney family. Dumb was never cute.

"Lydia." Ray stalked toward me, stopping at the bottom of the couple of stairs leading down off the small front patio. "You're fired, in case that wasn't clear."

Asshat. "Am I, Ray?"

He puffed himself up, preening. Lucky one of the buttons on his shirt didn't pop. "You punched a work colleague, Lydia. One who just so happens to be the boss's son. You do the math."

I nodded. "You're right, I did. Speaking of which, what do you think my chances would be of suing Chris for fraud and emotional distress? Guess I should talk to a lawyer too."

"What?"

"Goodness, what a scandal that'll be. The folks in this town are going to be talking about this mess for a good long time, aren't they?"

The lines around his mouth looked cavernous in the early evening light. "Are you trying to blackmail me?"

"You really want to start digging into the ethics of this situation? I don't know if that would be wise for any of us, Ray."

He growled into the phone for another minute. When he faced me again, he was not a happy camper. "Some sort of settlement might be reached if I was assured that video would never again be seen. It would also involve you keeping your mouth shut about anything to do with my family."

"I also want a reference reflecting my prior work history as opposed to today's unfortunate events."

"All right."

I tipped my chin. Accepted. "I'd also prefer it if your son chose not to press assault charges."

"I'll see what I can do." With a frown, Ray looked to his wife, not Chris. Big surprise who held the reins in that marriage. Not. His wife was a Harpy Queen of Darkness if I'd ever seen one. The chances of me not getting a criminal record tonight were slim.

At any rate, the Delaney's had oodles more money than me if it came down to duking it out in court with regards to my emotional distress, et cetera. Best just not to go there. Doubtless, Ray would destroy my reputation any other way he could. The doors of CDA's social elite would be closed to me now. They'd trash talk me all over town and I'd probably never find work.

However this went down, CDA and I were done. A pity, I'd liked it here. The town had a nice vibe and it was neither too big nor too small. What with the lake and the hills, the town was insanely beautiful. For me, it'd been just right.

Oh, well.

There was always my possible looming stint in jail for punching Chris to look forward to. I should try to be positive. Perhaps I'd just get community service or something, a fine. I wonder if I'd be deemed a flight risk and locked up regardless.

God, when I actually started thinking it over, my options were terrifying. The skin on my arms goose pimpled despite the warm evening air. One small tiny miniscule part of me even regretted punching Chris.

No. Never. I'd reclaimed what little remained of my pride by walloping the douche. My hand throbbed in agreement. Sometimes, violence and mayhem just were the answer.

CHAPTER SIX

"Oh good," said Vaughan in a dry voice. "You found tequila."

He and Officer Andy stood by the dining table. Both staring down at me with disapproving eyes. Little did they know how ridiculous and pompous they appeared. People, so blah. Especially men.

"Yeah, turns out we didn't have to go next door after all." I smiled. "There was some hiding at the back of your pantry."

"Was there?"

"Hope you don't mind."

"Not at all."

"You know, I was thinking about all those celebrity mugshots you see in the magazines where they're a hot mess," I said from my seat on the floor in the corner of the kitchen. "And it occurred to me that this is a once-in-a-lifetime opportunity for me to really go all out there and experience the moment to its fullest."

"Really?" he drawled.

"Absolutely. Life is short, Vaughan." I grinned. "And short or not, I intend to get one."

"One what?"

"One life. Just the one. I'm not greedy."

"Right." The dude did not look convinced. Gosh, I liked him. He was so pretty. He and his cock were the highlights of my day. After a few more drinks, I might even tell him in great rambling detail. What fun. Wonder if he'd let me take a picture for my wallet. Of his face, of course.

"I'll replace the booze," I said. "I promise."

"I'm more worried about your liver than the booze." He walked over, liberating the bottle from my hand and taking a sniff of the stuff. "Surprised it's still drinkable. My sister left it here years ago. It was cheap shit then, can't imagine it's improved."

"It's a little rough on the palate."

"And you're drinking straight from the bottle? Classy."

"I didn't want to put you out by dirtying a glass."

"Kind of you." He took a slug and winced, screwing his whole face up. "Christ, Lydia."

I sputtered out a laugh. "It's not that bad."

"It's fucking awful."

"The first few mouthfuls were the hardest, it's true. But after that, the lining of your throat goes numb. Or it's burned away," I hastily amended. "I'm not really sure which."

With a dubious look, Vaughan handed me back the bottle. Then he took up position standing beside me, legs crossed at the ankle, leaning his hip against the kitchen counter. Despite all of the people invading his house in their wedding finery, he'd remained relaxed. Bare feet, skin a couple of shades paler than his arms. Loose threads hanging from the bottoms of his old blue jeans.

For not the first time, I wondered about him and his dramas. If possible, I should help. God knows, he'd more than earned any and all assistance. Few people would have been so understanding.

Officer Andy shifted on his feet, running a hand over his military-short blond hair. Obviously getting impatient. It'd been a long day for everyone.

"When you're ready, ma'am," he said. "I'd like to explain to you the situation as it currently stands."

"Explain away." I sat up straight.

Officer Andy continued, "The good news is, Mr. Chris Delaney has decided not to press assault charges against you."

"What?" My whole body deflated, sagging back against the wooden cabinetry in relief. I'd have done a victory lap of the house had I been able. "He has?"

"Yes."

"Oh, sweet baby Jesus. Thank god for that." Down went the tequila. Down my throat, that is. Holy hell, the stuff was potent. I wheezed as delicately as possible, covering my mouth with a hand, tears flooding my eyes. "Why isn't he?"

"I discussed the situation with them thoroughly," he said, gaze serious. "With circumstances like this, it's not unusual for people in the heat of the moment to get carried away. Once they've had some time to reflect upon everything that's at stake, the full ramifications of the conflict, they often change their minds about taking any action."

"Huh."

"Yes, well, Vaughan also pointed out that pursuing charges against you would likely raise interest with local media," reported Andy, almost as an afterthought.

I looked up at Vaughan.

"Still got a few friends at the local radio station." One of his shoulders rose nonchalantly. "Would only take a call."

"Really?"

He reached down, seizing the bottle. "No big deal."

"No big deal? You kept me out of jail."

"Eh." He took another swig of tequila, cringing only slightly this time. "Couldn't have them carting you off to the big house. We've made plans to hang tonight."

"You're the best," I whispered to Vaughan, my hero.

He winked.

Officer Andy cleared his throat, sounding somewhat aggrieved. Over what, I had no idea. Honestly, I'd kind of forgotten he was still there.

"Seeing as the last thing they want is any more attention given to this situation," he said, "they decided to let it go."

I blew out a breath of relief.

"They will, however, be taking restraining orders out against you," said Andy

"Restraining orders?" Wow. It almost made me sound dangerous, like some thug or something. Like I roamed the streets of Coeur d'Alene just looking for people to punch in the nose.

"Yes." Andy tucked his thumbs into his police officer Batman-thingy utility belt. "Under no conditions should you try to approach any of the family, or step foot on any of the family's properties, including any and all commercial interests. Understood?"

"It'll be entirely my pleasure to never set sight on those idiots again." And then some. "But what about my things? They're all over at the big house."

"Mrs. Delaney has assured me she'll see to the prompt delivery of your personal effects."

"How kind." My brows descended, my trust for Samantha in the negatives. My options, however, were nonexistent. So currently, I had my bridal lingerie and nothing more. Apart from Vaughan's shirt and goodwill, of course.

"I hate to impose further," I said, reaching up for the tequila to take another sip. "But would it be all right if I crashed on your couch tonight once we're done hanging?"

"Spare room's all yours."

"Thank you."

"And I told Ray he could send any paperwork here until you

get something else sorted," said Vaughan, once more taking possession of his own liquor. This time he downed a whole mouthful, no problem. Impressive. Masculine, manly and stuff. He'd probably catch up to me in no time.

"Thank you for talking them down," I said.

Another chin tip.

"If that's all, ma'am, I better get a move on." Over by the table, Officer Andy stood tall, looking totes competent and stuff.

"Are they gone from out front?" Gah, I sounded so timid. "Not that I'm afraid of them. It's just, it's been a long day."

"They're gone." Vaughan handed me back the bottle with a smile. "Took your douche ex-fiancé off to the emergency room to get his nose set."

"I broke it?"

"That's my bet." We exchanged grins.

With a deep breath, I relaxed for what seemed like the first time in days, resting my head back against the cabinet. "I have no home or job. But I have my liberty."

"I'll leave you two to celebrate," said Officer Andy.

"Thanks, Andy." The men started clapping each other good and hard on the shoulder as guys do. "Good to see you again."

"You too." He hesitated. "Damn shame about Nell and Pat."

"Yeah." The smile on Vaughan's face faded.

"You, ah, wouldn't know if she's dating again yet, would you?"

A long pause.

The happy on Vaughan's face had disappeared without a trace. So much for cool, calm, and collected. I wondered who Nell and Pat were. Obviously people important to him.

"See you later, Andy," he said in lieu of answering the question. The message was delivered just fine. "Right. Night."

"Night." I waved. "And thank you."

He didn't respond. The officer got gone while Vaughan watched with eyes distinctly flat and unfriendly. Had it been me, facing his cold front, I'd have run. Instead, I attempted diversion.

"Thanks for not kicking me to the curb." I held out the bottle to him, shaking it gently.

Mouth still grim, he wandered back into the kitchen, sitting on the floor at my side. "You're welcome."

"I'll cook you breakfast."

"There's no food in the house."

"Damn. All right, if Samantha has delivered my purse by morning, I'll buy you breakfast."

"Deal."

We passed the bottle back and forth in silence for a while. My head grew progressively fuzzier, all of the emotion of the day's events softening to a "meh." For now, I was all humiliated, hurt, and raged out. The knuckles on my right hand stung like a bitch and if I started mentally picking apart all of the what-ifs and could-haves again I'd go insane.

The light over the dining table emitted a soft golden glow, leaving the rest of the house in shadow. It seemed even quieter and emptier as the night set in.

"How long has it been since you've been here?" I asked.

"We played at a small festival a few years back. Not since then."

"You're in a band?"

"I was. We broke up a couple of months back." He'd leaned his head against the kitchen cupboards, eyes closed. "We'd been together for ten years, based down in L.A. mostly."

"What instrument do you play?"

"Guitar."

"That's great." I could see it. It made sense. I shook my head in wonder, making the room turn lazy woozy circles, or my brain did. I'm not sure which. "Not about your band breaking up, I mean about you being a musician. Are you going to join another band or—"

He made a noise in his throat. "Been trying to put one together. Bass player from the old one's still on board, but we just haven't had any luck finding the right people."

"That sucks."

"It sure does."

"So that's your drama?"

He opened one eye. "Pretty much. Only came back to town to sell this place to my sister. Need to pay off the mortgage, get a little to live on while we find a new singer and drummer, get things sorted out."

"Your sister, is that Nell who Andy was asking about?"

"Yeah." His gaze darkened. "She split with her husband a little while back. Figure she'll be happy to buy the place, have somewhere of her own to live. She always loved this house."

"It's beautiful."

His face softened, relaxing into a smile. "You do love the old Arts and Crafts bungalows."

"Yes, I do." When he smiled at me like that . . . whoa. Let's just say the house wasn't the only thing that was beautiful. "I'm sorry you've got drama."

"I'm sorry you've got drama too."

"And I'm sorry I dragged my drama into your house."

"I know." He covered my hand with his much larger one. Warm. He was so warm and lovely and stuff. If the shitty day and toxic tequila had left me with an iota more energy I'd run my no-strings-sex-between-new-friends idea past him. As it was, I'd save it up for tomorrow. At least I had my memories of him bare ass naked to keep me happy in the meantime. And trust me, there was real happiness to be had in having seen this man naked. My dreams had better be full of him, or I and my subconscious would be having a serious talk.

"What?" he asked.

"What, what?"

"You're looking at me funny."

"Am I?" My jaw cracked loud and proud on a yawn. What a day. I laid my head against his shoulder, getting comfortable, closing my eyes.

"You planning on crashing right there?" he asked.

"Mm-hmm."

"Okay."

All I could hear was the in and out of his breathing, the occasional sound of the tequila sloshing about in the bottle as he took a drink. All was calm. Peaceful. For now at least.

"You were a beautiful bride, Lydia."

I smiled, too close to sleep to speak.

"Beautiful."

CHAPTER SEVEN

Fucking Samantha. If the woman was on fire, I'd make s'mores.

After so gracefully passing out on the kitchen floor, I'd woken up on a bed in the spare room this morning. Everything hurt. I'd stumbled into the kitchen in search of water and seen the latest disaster through the glass doors. My almost-mother-in-law had been busy. Real busy.

With Vaughan's cool dude aviator sunglasses to guard against the brain-piercing morning glare, I searched the backyard for my belongings. A bra here, a pair of panties there. You never knew what you might find hidden in the long grass.

Why, it was just like a treasure hunt minus the map.

And the fun.

My green silk blouse hung high in a tree and it wasn't alone. God knows how she'd gotten it all up there. Unleashed her flying monkeys, perhaps? Wicked witch was about right.

A box of books and another filled with personal mementos had been dumped straight over the fence as if they were garbage. I didn't have the heart to look inside and see what was broken. Every muscle in my jaw ached. I wanted to scream and rage, to let it all out. Again. Only if I started, I wasn't sure I'd be able to stop.

A pounding head and queasy stomach didn't much help matters.

I'd done a quick search of the kitchen and come up empty on the Advil front. Tequila, like Samantha, was clearly not my friend. And it had to have been her who'd chucked my stuff over the fence. Chris would have simply paid someone to deliver the lot to the front patio. Thrown cash at the problem to turn it into someone else's. Such was his style.

No, only his mother would delight in this type of fuckery.

"Vindictive bitch," I muttered, adding a pair of boyfriend jeans to the growing pile at my feet. Each item retrieved fueled the fury.

There'd better be a special level of hell to reward her for such spite. One without Botox, where no matter what you did, your dark hair roots showed and the only clothing option was unwashed secondhand sweats. That'd teach her.

Insert insane cackling here. Yep, I was losing it. Lucky for me, there were no witnesses to my descent into lunacy.

Oops, I spoke too soon.

I hadn't heard her arrive, but a woman stood watching from the back deck. Her strawberry-blond hair shone in the sunlight and she was covered in tattoos. Behind her, the kitchen door was open, meaning she'd come through the house and therefore had a key. Interesting.

"Hi," I said.

"Hi. I'm Nell, Vaughan's sister." She made her way toward me, holding out a hand for shaking.

I shook it. "Lydia. A new friend of Vaughan's."

"Nice to meet you." A sweeping glance took in my clothing and one of her eyebrows went up. Probably because none of what I wore was mine. Vaughan had left some clothes on the end of my bed, bless him. Soft gray sleeping pants rolled up at the bottom on account of being made for someone much taller and a Rolling Stones T-shirt. Loved the way the tongue and mouth slogan stretched over my assets. Such a tasteful statement. Luckily, a bra had been the first item on this morning's treasure hunt adventure. Out-of-control breasts were not something I needed.

A hard kind of curiosity filled Nell's eyes. "A new friend? Not that it's any of my business . . ."

"Not that it's any of your business," I agreed, crossing my arms over my chest. "But yes. Just a new friend. I'm in between homes so he let me crash here last night. My belongings had a little accident."

It was one way of describing it. Sort of.

"Yeah. I was going to ask about that. Normally yard sales happen out front." With a finger, she hooked a pair of underwear from down beside her feet. Awesome. Black lace boy shorts. At least they were a nice pair. Definitely not embarrassing to have a stranger checking out my undergarment styling at all.

"Thanks." I added them to the pile, my friendly smile frozen to my face. "Issue with the ex."

"Men." Her lips thinned.

"Mm."

"Think they can get away with anything just because they have something to swing between their thighs."

I snorted. "Pretty much."

"Raging assholes, all of them," she growled, cheeks pink with anger. "We'd be better off if they were just jettisoned into space en masse."

Clearly, Nell was still stuck in the bitter stage of a relationship breakdown. I was moving on to moving on. The damage was done. Now I just wanted to get my shit together and get out of this town. Seek a life somewhere else. Pretty or not, this place hadn't been kind to me.

"Men do suck," I said. "But actually, this was his mother's handiwork."

"You're kidding?" She wrinkled her nose, making a scattering of freckles jump and move. She seemed a bit older than me, petite where her brother was tall. Same pale blue eyes, though. She wore plain black slacks and a T-shirt with a picture of a bluebird above the words "The Dive Bar."

"Nope," I said. "Definitely his mother's style of attack."

"Shit. Come on, I'll help you pick it all up."

"You will?"

"Sure." Nell's smile now was genuine, kind.

"Thanks." This woman's moods were more chaotic than mine. I couldn't keep up.

"No problem. Better than just sitting around, waiting for my idiot brother to wake up. We need something to put your stuff in. I think there's some empty boxes in the garage." Without another word, she strode off toward the side of the house while I watched, bemused.

People. You could never tell.

I rolled my shoulders, trying to work the kinks out of my back. If anything, my body hurt worse today than it had yesterday. Muscle strain times one thousand.

Funny, with Nell helping, the weight of my mess seemed to lighten. Maybe things weren't so bad and the bulk of the human race weren't against me.

Today had been my first in months without a good morning text from Chris.

I mean . . . of course there hadn't been one. My cell phone was broken apart. But the lack of it had been less a mild ache and more of a good hard slap upside the back of the head. I'd gotten so used to being part of a couple. To being "we." Time to adjust back to being alone.

Yep, I was swinging single.

Assorted bugs, bees, and butterflies flitted around, doing their thing. It was, all in all, another perfect summer's day. In another life, Chris and I would have been en route to Hawaii for our honey-moon. Man, I'd been so excited about the trip. Sandy white beaches, fruity cocktails, and fun. Lots and lots of it. Instead, my new black tankini waved in the wind, stuck halfway up a pine tree.

You had to give it to her, Samantha had been dedicated. She must have been out here for hours last night, throwing my shit around.

Nell and I had been working maybe half an hour, picking the contents of my makeup bag and jewelry box out of a thorny bush, when Vaughan appeared. He stood on the deck, yawning; a cup of coffee filled one hand and a pastry the other. Worn jeans, no shirt, even more reddish-blond stubble.

Damn, he was hot. The kind of hot that only got better with age and experience. Not that I was even remotely interested in getting involved with him beyond the new-friends-having-sex thing. Neither of us intended to stay in town and I had only just gotten out of a ruin of a relationship. But good lord, such a northern Idaho sex god.

Primitive man might have worshipped the sun, but I'm pretty sure the sun worshipped Vaughan. The way it bathed him in a golden glow, showcasing his ink. Tattoos had never even interested me before. A stable job and a fixed residence? Yes. This whole "reck-less bad boy living the rock-and-roll lifestyle" vibe Vaughan had going? No. Absolutely not. It went against everything my parents had taught me to value, due to them providing a lack of said things during my childhood.

All the things I probably needed to start questioning, given my recent bad choices. Though, I don't know. What was wrong with wanting a home and a little stability? Yes, I'd rushed into it, a big mistake on my part. Next time I'd take it slow, really get to know the person and make sure we were right for each other. Lesson learned.

At any rate, I ignored the stirrings of lust from my loins, for now. Etiquette dictated that jumping a man in front of his sibling was not the right thing to do. Plus, with my hangover looming large, now did not strike me as the best time to raise the no-strings-sex topic. No, I'd keep an eye on the man, see if he gave off any of the right signals. My poor girl parts would just have to wait.

At least he couldn't see me ogling him because of my shades. I probably had drool on my chin, though. Ever so discreetly, I gave it a rub.

"You've got a nerve," said Nell, suddenly tense beside me. If spikes had suddenly appeared running down her spine I would not have been surprised. "Would it have killed you to call me, let me know you were back?"

"Hi, sis." Another yawn from Vaughan. Then he stuffed his mouth full of pastry, talking around it. Or through it (Chris would have been appalled. Fuck you, Chris.). "Thanks for bringing over breakfast."

"Eat with your mouth closed. God, you're gross." Nell crossed her arms, staring him down. "Have you even evolved since you were eight?"

"I'm taller. And I got over the whole girl-germs thing too." He winked.

"Kind of figured that, what with the way you treated the fly on your pants like a revolving door during high school." For the next part, Nell adopted a low manly tone, "Hey, I'm the guitarist in a band. I write songs and I care about feelings and shit. Come on, you know you want a piece of this, baby."

I quietly sniggered (she did his voice so well).

Vaughan cracked up laughing, nearly doubling at the waist. "Not bad. But you have to offer to play them some broody-ass emo tunes out by the lake. Works every time."

Nell flipped him the bird.

"Take it easy," he said. "I was going to call you today. Things got busy yesterday."

"Oh, I know. The whole town's talking about it. It's how I knew to bring breakfast for both of you."

"Awesome," I moaned. Not unexpected, but still. Two hundred–odd guests had been in the front garden, waiting for the nuptials to happen. Made for a lot of mouths to do a lot of talking.

"Sorry," said Nell. "But your botched wedding is hot news everywhere."

I nodded, mouth curved down in a frown.

"We need to talk," said Nell, turning back to her brother.

"Sounds serious."

"It is. I've been trying to get ahold of you for weeks."

"Sorry." Head hanging low, Vaughan winced. "There's been a lot going on. I'm here now, though."

"Which leads me to the next question. Why are you here?" She tilted her head. "You've avoided this place like the plague for years."

"You just said you wanted to talk to me, now you're giving me shit for being here?" He grabbed at the back of his neck, rubbing hard. "Like you said, it's been a while. Maybe I just wanted to catch up with you."

As eyebrows went, Nell's left one was particularly vocal. The way it arced called bullshit on her brother without saying a word. "What's going on, Vaughan? Last I heard you guys were touring with Stage Dive and everything was great."

He gave a smile completely devoid of any joy. "So fucking great the lead vocalist went solo and our drummer joined another band."

Nell's jaw dropped, her face bloodless. "The band broke up?"

"Yeah."

His sister still gaped.

"Got decided late last year. Once we finished the tour with Stage Dive we were splitting. I've had time to get used to it. Let it go. It's fine." He ignored her reaction, turning instead to me. "How are you doing, Lydia?"

"Hey. Hi. Good."

"I take it you already met my sister. Come inside. There's coffee for you too."

"Okay. In a minute." A glint of metal beneath some leaves caught my eye. Carefully, I dusted off the antique silver necklace my grandmother had given me for my twenty-first.

I hung the pendant around my neck, fingers fiddling with the clasp for a moment before it locked into place. Forget Chris and his family. I'd find my feet. They were nothing to me now, less than nothing. They were so subpar-nothing I didn't even know how to describe just how zilch they were. Moving on.

"Babe, why's your stuff all over the yard?" asked Vaughan.

"Pardon?" I blinked, returning to earth.

"Your stuff, it's everywhere." He downed the last of his coffee in one long gulp, his gaze fixed on my face.

Gah. Like he didn't have enough to deal with without more of my drama. "Yeah, sorry," I said. "I'll get it cleaned up."

"Lydia, stop," he ordered in a stern voice. Then his gaze softened. "What happened here?"

"Samantha delivered my belongings." I said, carefully retrieving my best black mascara from the bush of death. The thing basically consisted of a big evil ball of thorns beneath a couple of leaves. It was Satan's shrubbery. Any more scratches from it and I'd look like I'd been in a cat fight. Close enough to the truth.

"You're fucking kidding." He wandered down the steps toward me.

"Wish I was."

"Hey." He gripped the back of my neck with his free hand, rubbing it far more softly than he'd done his own. The calluses on his fingers were rough, making for such a different sensation than

Chris's soft hands. "This petty bullshit is the worst she can do. Ignore it. You're better than this."

"I don't know. Given half a chance, I'd really like to shoot her out of a cannon and forget to put up the safety net."

"That seriously the best you could come up with?"

"No. Give me more time. It's early."

Sweet baby Jesus, his laugh. It was so low-down and dirty. I hadn't even said anything worthy of such a sound. Disturbingly, I couldn't remember what Chris's laugh sounded like. Had I ever even heard it? No memory leaped to mind. What a sad and sorry statement about his life and the part I'd played in it. And while Chris's problems were most definitely his own, I and mine needed a damn good looking over.

I needed change. Now.

I also needed to stop making comparisons to Chris. He was out of my life. Gone. The end.

Vaughan tipped his chin toward the house, still laughing. "Go grab your coffee and cake. Then you can tell me more revenge fantasies. I want blood and gore, Lydia. Covered in honey and eaten alive by bull ants, that sort of thing. Go wild."

I smiled and headed for the house, my mood about ten tons lighter for having seen Vaughan's smile.

"Not cake, palmiers," corrected Nell.

"Whatever they are, they taste like magic," he said.

His sister snorted.

"It is good to see you, sis."

Sure enough, a second coffee and large brown paper bag sat on the kitchen counter. "The Bird Building" was stamped in black ink on the front. It was a place in midtown, not an area I'd had a lot to do with. In the real estate business, Ray and I had mostly focused on residential dwellings, with him covering the big-money mansions. Chris had dealt with the commercial properties.

My coffee was delicious, I didn't bother heating it up. Years in offices had taught me to ignore temperature. The palmiers turned out to be elephant ear cookies covered in cinnamon sugar. Pastry so perfect and light it basically melted on contact with my tongue. Absolute bliss.

I took my breakfast outside and sat on the steps.

"What'd you need to talk to me about?" he asked his sister.

Nell gave me a brief glance. Awkward.

"I'll eat inside, get out of the sun for a while," I said around a mouthful of deliciousness, hardly spitting out any pastry flakes at all. Screw common courtesy. These palmiers were amazing.

"It's okay. Anything you need to say to me, Lydia can hear." He gave me a wry smile. "We've got no secrets, have we?"

"I guess not after yesterday, but—"

"It's fine." Nell brushed off her hands on the sides of her black jeans. "Really."

I tentatively sat back down. Maybe I'd just excuse myself to go use the bathroom ASAP.

"So?" asked Vaughan. "Shoot."

"I need you to either lend me fifty-six thousand dollars or buy Pat out for the same amount."

Eyes wide, he huffed out a breath. "Shit. That all, huh?"

"I'm serious."

"I get that."

"Will you do it?" Carefully, she tucked her hair behind her ears. Her hands, however, didn't stop there, fussing with the front of her white shirt. The woman was nervous. Terribly so. "Please, Vaughan. He wants out and I can't have him involved anymore. The divorce goes through in a few more days and things are so damn tense I can't stand it."

He let his head fall back, staring up at the sky. "Nell . . ."

"Pat hates me. He's completely impossible. Refuses to work in the bar anymore."

"What the hell happened? You two have been tight since you were fourteen. You can't even get on a little now?"

"You've been gone a long time," she said, face drawn. "He's changed, especially since we broke up. He and Eric can't even be in the same room without fighting."

"Shit."

Nell wrung her hands. "Pat's been making all sorts of threats about what he'll do if we can't buy his share of the business."

"Joe can't buy in?"

Nell shook her head. "He doesn't have the cash. Eric's still paying him back for bankrolling his thirty percent when we opened."

"Christ." He wiped a hand over his face. "This is why you shouldn't go into business with friends or family. It just gets fucking complicated."

"You're right. I should have trusted total strangers with my lifelong dream."

Vaughan's shoulders sagged. "Didn't know things were so bad with you."

"You were busy, touring and recording. I didn't want to worry you. I thought I could ride it out."

"Yeah." A long-winded sigh. "I'm sorry, Nell. I don't have the money. I'd do it for you in a heartbeat if I could, but I can't."

"What do you mean?"

"I'm tapped out. Things . . . they weren't as good as I made them out to be." Hands on hips, he faced her. "In fact, they're pretty much fucked. I was hoping you could buy this place off me. I'm sorry."

Hell, poor Vaughan. If I could have been anywhere else, I'd have been there. Instead, I sat silent and still, hopefully forgotten.

"You want to sell the house? How bad is it?" she asked.

"I'll figure something out. It'll be okay." He licked his lips, studying the ground.

"How bad, Vaughan?"

Slowly, he shut his eyes, letting his head fall back. It took him a long time to answer. "I had to borrow to buy you out of this place."

Nell's mouth fell open. "What? You told me you had it!"

"What'd you think I'd say?" Blue eyes snapped open, laser-like in their intensity. "Like you said, it was your dream, opening the bar. Just like it was mine to play music. You backed me however you could. Did you really think I wouldn't do the same for you?"

Nell covered her face with her hands, swearing softly beneath her breath. This went on for quite some time.

"For a while, it was fine," Vaughan continued. "We were getting gigs, being paid. Then we had a lean time and I had to take out a mortgage."

"You mortgaged our childhood home?" Her voice rose to banshee levels. Guess it was true what they said about redheads, at least of the female variety. "Vaughan, how could you!"

"It's almost paid off. Touring with Stage Dive got most of it sorted, but things hit the wall when the band fell apart."

His sister just shook her head. "If Mom weren't dead, she'd kill you."

"I know."

"And if Dad weren't dead . . . I don't even know what he would do. But they'd never find your body. Or what was left of it."

Nothing from Vaughan. His fallen face said it all.

In the distance a lawn mower roared to life, doing its thing. How bizarre to think our dramas didn't even touch upon the bulk of most people's everyday lives. They seemed so big and all-encompassing from within. Any happiness felt fake, phony. Or worse yet, as if it were about to be stolen away. Which was ridiculous, really: Vaughan would work his way out of his money troubles and I would date again. I'd find a job I liked, or least tolerated, and he'd start another band. Life would go on.

Right now, however, it just all seemed phenomenally shit.

"Okay, here's what we do," said Nell, her spine snapping straight. "You come work for us at the Dive Bar."

"But—" An imperious hand halted him.

"No, Vaughan," she said. "You need money, we need a new bartender. Hell, we're probably about to need more waitstaff too. One way or another, you're covered. You can do Pat's shifts behind the bar for now."

"I only planned on being in town for a few days, a week at most."

Lines appeared beside Nell's mouth. "Fine. Whatever. Work while you're here. You start at six. Don't be late."

"Okay. I won't be late."

"And bring Lydia with you."

"Why?"

"I like her. She didn't mortgage my childhood home."

"Right." Vaughan crossed his arms.

"Thanks for the coffee and pastry," I said.

"No problem. See you later."

It took a while for the man to make any move once his sister left. For a long while, he stood staring after her, lost in thought. Useless platitudes filled my head, the usual reassuring crap. For now, I let it all go unsaid. Neither of us was really interested in hearing the obvious.

This summer was genuinely proving to be a motherfucker.

Wonder what nonsense was being said about me around town. Not that it mattered. No way I'd be accompanying Vaughan tonight to find out. First, I needed to find somewhere to stay until things were settled with the Delaneys. And if I hoped to have anything to wear in the near future, finding my clothes in this jungle needed to happen faster.

I brushed off my hands, leaving the empty cup on the step to throw away later. "You okay?"

"Yeah."

"Liar," I whispered.

"Am not," he whispered back.

"Are too."

He gave me a look most dubious.

"That was a heavy conversation. All I'm saying is, it's okay not to be okay after it."

He snorted, pushing his shoulders back. "You want to talk about feelings, Lydia? Is that what you want?"

"Hell no." I laughed. "After yesterday I'm pretty much emotionally wrung out. I vote we be as shallow as humanly possible."

"Thank god for that." A big hand reached out and smoothed down my most likely still psycho bed hair. "You had me worried."

"But on the off chance it's necessary," I said quickly, "I do want you to know I'm here for you, just like you were there for me yesterday."

"That sounds dangerously like feelings talk."

"Not really."

"Yes, really."

"Fine. Take it how you will." I shrugged, getting back into the search and rescue of my belongings. Something glinted among the long grass. An earring. "I want to do a drive-by egging of Samantha and Ron's place, but they've got this big fence and gate."

"Could be a problem." Beside me, Vaughan dropped to his knees, rifling among the vegetation. "How about we toilet paper their front fence?"

"That could work."

"Knew this guy once who dumped his girl by text. They'd been going out for like four or five years. Serious stuff. She got a couple of syringes full of fish oil and injected it into his car through the gap between the doors. Just squeezed it straight past the rubber lining and into the interior." He gazed up at me with a hint of a diabolical smile. "Dude comes back from touring for a couple of months and the inside of his GTO stinks so bad it's not funny. You couldn't even get near the thing, let alone drive it."

I all but clapped my hands. "That's genius."

"Isn't it." A pair of green silk underwear hung from his finger. "These yours?"

"No. They probably belong to someone else whose belongings were dumped in your yard. But I'll take care of them for now."

"That makes sense." Carefully, he inspected them. "French-cut cheekies, huh?"

"You know your lingerie." I frowned.

"Important to appreciate the finer things in life. Especially when they're to do with a fine woman."

"Smooth."

"You know, I had you figured for those boy-short things," he said with a smile. "Happy to be wrong, though. These are hot, babe. Like seriously hot."

"Glad you approve."

"But if you say they're not yours . . ." He started to stick them into his back pocket.

"Give them to me, please."

"Say you'll come to the Dive Bar with me tonight."

"Oh, boy." I hesitated, everything inside of me rejecting the idea. "A public place. I don't think that's a good idea. I think laying low is my best option right now. Find somewhere to live for the next few days then get gone, start over somewhere new."

"You stay here with me until you're ready to leave," he said, like it was obvious.

"Really?"

"Sure."

"I wouldn't be in your way or anything?"

"No." He passed me my underwear. "Course not."

Quickly, I dropped them into the nearest box of stuff. Given the DEFCON 1 embarrassment levels of the past twenty-four hours, a pair of panties shouldn't have bothered me in the slightest. Perhaps it came down to the man doing the teasing.

"I don't know," I said. "When you get right down to it, we barely know each other."

"It's only for a couple of days. A week at most, right?"

"Yes, but—"

"Are you worried about you or me in this scenario?"

"You," I said, happy to be hiding behind the sunglasses. Those beautiful blue eyes saw too much. "You could change your mind and feel stuck with me. I don't want to add to your problems."

"Lydia, I don't want to add to yours either. But I do want you here."

"You do?" My breath didn't mean to catch, I'm sure of it. It was just an accident. The thought of Vaughan actually liking me thrilled and terrified me in equal parts. He was so hot. And I was so me. But I could pretend to be cool for a temporary period. I could do this. "Why, if you don't mind me asking?"

With a scowl, he stretched out in the long grass, relaxing, for all intents and purposes. "Can I trust you with something?"

"Of course."

He licked his lips again, sighed. "Mom and Dad died when I was twenty. I've never been here without them. Not for more than a night or two. It just, it doesn't feel right."

Hell. My heart ached for him.

"Nell packed up the place, got someone to paint the inside so I wouldn't feel weird, so it would feel like my own house, I guess. But it doesn't."

I sat down cross-legged in the grass in front of him. Picked the head off a dandelion and ran it back and forth across the palm of my hand. "Vaughan, it would be great if I could hang here while I get things sorted."

"Good." A slow smile spread across his face. "And I'd really like it if you'd come with me tonight, see Nell's bar. She'd love to have you there, she said so."

I scrunched up my nose.

"C'mon. You have to go out sometime."

"Hmm, bad idea. I think I've already filled my quota for public humiliation this year."

"You'll have a good time." He shook his head. "No way Nell's going to let anyone hassle you in her place, babe."

"That's not my name." The dandelion fell apart on a warm breeze, drifting off to who knew where.

"All right. Come tonight and I'll never call you babe ever again."

"Never ever again?" I sized him up over the top of my sunglasses, judging his sincerity.

"You have my word." With deliberate slowness, he drew a cross over his heart.

The amount I owed the man was big. Huge. But then so was the thought of going out into the public arena and risking death, dismemberment, and some really nasty gossip. Bitches be everywhere. But also, he was right. I did have to go out sometime.

"Okay." I held out my hand.

He shook it. Then kept holding on, gazing deep into my eyes.

"You're going to have fun, Lydia."

CHAPTER EIGHT

I was not having fun. Mostly, I was fighting the urge to puke. Though in all honesty, the state of my stomach had more to do with my hangover than anything else.

The Bird Building wasn't a mall. Basically, it was a ninety-year-old two-story brick monster in midtown, the ground floor a neat line of retail spaces facing the street. First were a couple of empty shops, the windows covered in aging notices of bands playing in town, lost dogs, street fairs, and the like. Next was the Guitar Den, a tattoo parlor called Inkaho, then the Dive Bar taking up the prestigious corner position.

The Beatles played, filling the warm evening air along with the sounds of cutlery and glassware, the hum of chatter. It flowed through the open windows and doorway of the Dive Bar out onto the quiet street. It looked like they had a decent-size crowd for a Sunday. People flocked to town each summer, but most seemed to stay downtown by the lake. I bet the bars and shops there would be full. Midtown, away from the water, tended to be quieter. More for locals.

With a hand hovering at my lower back, Vaughan ushered me along the sidewalk.

"I'm not going to make a run for it," I said, yet again tucking my hair behind my ears, straightening out the imaginary creases in my black linen button-up top.

The side eyes he gave me were full of doubt. "The thought never crossed my mind."

"Liar."

"The fact that I had to manhandle you out of the car—"

"Signifies nothing more than how very cool I think your car is."

"Right." I could tell he was laughing at me on the inside. "Come on, single lady."

Not so subtly, he took hold of my elbow. The muscles in his arms flexed as if he expected some great escape attempt to happen at any moment.

Liking people was a bitch. Same with giving your word.

As we approached the building, I said, "I've been thinking about your money dramas. Wondering if I can help?"

He licked his lips. "You'll pretty much do anything to delay this, won't you?"

"I'm serious, I've been worrying about you all day, what with Nell not being able to buy the house like you'd hoped. I realize we haven't known each other for long, but I'd like to help somehow if I can."

A sigh. "I'm going to have to sell it to someone else. It's going to suck, but that's where my situation's at."

"I'm sorry."

"Thanks." He wiped a hand over his face. "Don't suppose you'd like to rethink your leaving town plan and make an offer?"

"I wish I had that kind of money. And a job." A couple of years in real estate had enabled me to make a start on some savings. Nothing like what the Sanders Beach home would fetch, however. "I could give you some advice on the market, point you in the direction of a good agent and so on."

"Yeah, ah . . . let's talk about this another time. All right?"

"Sure. Whenever you're ready."

"Thanks."

A couple of young women passed us by, one doing a double take when she saw me. Next thing you knew, her mouth was going rapid fire against her friend's ear. The friend turned back to look at me, giggling. Ugh.

"Maybe tonight's a bit soon," I said, edging back a step. "I mean, you need to concentrate on the bar and, really, Nell will be busy cooking, so—"

In one smooth move, he stepped in front of me, turning so we were face-to-face. His hands grabbed hold of my hips, drawing operation "get the hell out of here" to an abrupt halt. "Lydia?"

I blinked. "Vaughan?"

"We're going in there and it's going to be okay."

"I'm not so sure about that."

He swallowed, stopping a moment to think. "What's the worst that can happen?"

"Everyone could point and laugh at me, forcing me to relive the shame and horror of yesterday."

"Yeah, true." Fingers rubbed at the wide hips of my jeans as he held his face down close to mine. Not doing anything, just being there. "How'd you get through yesterday, though?"

"Running away, you, sarcasm, violence, and last but not least, tequila."

"You can have everything today apart from the running away," he said. "How's that sound?"

"You want me to answer that honestly?"

"Nope. You're going to have fun, Lydia."

I highly doubted it, but it would be impolite to say so.

"And if anyone in there gives you shit, I'll punch them for you."

"My hand still hurts from yesterday, so thanks. I appreciate that."

"No problem."

We stood, staring at each other, smiling for one perfect moment. Then I smacked myself in the forehead. "Crap. It's your first night at work and I'm putting all my drama on you again."

He hung his head. "Yeah, you are."

"I'm so sorry."

Such a long and gusty exhalation. The man had big lungs. Also, bad friends, namely me.

"Vaughan?"

"On the plus side, when you get worked up your tits start heaving up and down with each breath. Magnificent. Honestly, I can't get enough of it." Little lines appeared on his forehead as his hands demonstrated the apparently bouncy-boob-like motions in front of his chest. "I'm tempted just to say shit to get you started, I love it so much."

In the face of his broad grin, I had nothing.

Actually, that's a lie. "I felt bad, you asshat."

The good-looking asshole just smiled. Far in the distance the first star started twinkling and doing its thing in the gray and violet sky. Mountains loomed dark and ominous in the distance. Nature, the show-off. But it had nothing on Vaughan standing there, smiling. Lust, like, or whatever this was . . . I had it in the worst way. Maybe if he seemed in a good mood after finishing work, I'd raise my new-friends-having-sex idea with him. We were both only in town for a few days and the clock was ticking. His gaze flickered between my boobs and face, never quite settling on one or the other.

Nipples are little beasts, always reacting to everything, especially when you'd rather they be discreet. There's a reason titillation starts with the word "tit." So of course they got hard now, reveling in his attention. Ever so quickly, I crossed my arms, covering them up.

"I don't even . . ." The words, they disappeared. "You make no sense. I mean, they're covered. My shirt is buttoned up past any and all hint of cleavage."

"Doesn't matter. I can still see the shape of them. It's enough to keep a man like me happy."

"It's like you have some sort of breast obsessive-compulsive disorder. Have you considered seeking counseling for your addiction?"

He sighed, face carefully set. "Nothing wrong with a man admiring a fine female chest. But if you disagree, feel free to hold it against me."

I rolled my eyes.

"Right, so we've discussed both my shit and your shit. Are we done here?" he asked in an abrupt return to serious. "Can we go inside now?"

"Let's."

A nod.

"You're going to be great," I said, all enthused.

"You're the one who's nervous, not me. I'm all good, babe," he teased.

"Very funny. Call me babe one more time and I'm out of here."

Instead, he firmly guided me up the couple of front stairs and through the old glass doors.

Even though he might not have been nervous, I wasn't so sure about his general state of mind. I think going to work for Nell was messing with his Zen cool guy guitarist philosophy big-time. Combine that with memorizing prices, cocktail recipes, the location of everything, keeping up with orders, keeping out of any other bartender's way, restocking, and doing everything else involved in tending a bar and Vaughan had a busy night ahead of him. Hell, I think all of it, being back in town, breathing the northern Idaho air, living in what had once been his childhood home, his parents being gone, it had to be all screwing with his head. Add in the money woes and his band breaking up for extra damage. I couldn't help but feel for him. We'd both had dreams go lopsided.

All day, he'd kept close, helping me find, then clean and pack, my belongings. We didn't talk about anything deep and meaningful. Mostly just movies and music and places he'd been. Stories from life on the road. I'd gotten the distinct sensation that he wanted to keep himself occupied.

Understandable. Drama, gah. We'd both had our fill.

When we walked in I didn't notice any recognizable faces, but I was still a wee bit agitated to be out in public.

"I'm here to be wowed by your bartending skills," I said, slowly moving through the maze of customers and tables.

"Uh-huh. I'll be sure to juggle some bottles and shit, light something on fire while I make your espresso martini." He flicked the word off his tongue like pronouncing it was a trick all its own. "Or are you more of a margarita girl, hmm?"

"Today, I'm more of a water and ice girl. If you feel like getting fancy, Mr. Bartender, I'll take a slice of lemon on the side. A straw, maybe."

"Yeah?" Only a small smile curved his lips. Not nervous, my ass. He might be better than me at hiding things, but those things lingered there just beneath the surface nonetheless. Anyone willing to watch and care could see.

"Still feeling the pain from the tequila last night?" he asked.

"A little."

He looked down at me, gaze softening. "Lydia—"

"There you are!" Nell rushed over, red hair strictly tied back, wearing a professional-looking black apron.

Vaughan frowned and checked his watch. "I'm right on time."

A brow went up. "Did I say you weren't?"

"Nice place." I interrupted the potential argument before the two siblings gained momentum. "All of the dark wood with the raw brickwork and the giant windows. It's got such a great atmosphere." It truly did. Brutal might be the best word to describe the style of the place. Though there were traces of luxury and nods to the buildings 1920s origins too. A section of wall covered in ancient band posters had been preserved. A fancy black wrought-iron circle staircase sat in the corner, leading up to the closed-off second level. The wooden-topped metal-legged table-and-chair sets had an edgy industrial feel. But there were also booths with luxurious shiny black leather. It shouldn't have worked yet it did. The temptation to settle in and order a drink, a plate of something to eat, was huge.

"It's awesome, Nell."

The wrinkle lines around Nell's nose disappeared and her lips spread wide in obvious pleasure. "You like it?"

"I love it." Chris would have sneered at the place for not being fancy enough, but screw him anyway. The bar felt comfortable, relaxing, despite all of the people turning our way, whispering. No. Okay. That was a lie. I wasn't okay with this. Never had there been such a crappy idea. I should have stayed hidden away at the house.

Oh, no. Wait. My mistake. They were checking out Vaughan in his tight jeans. Fair enough. His ass was a work of art. I breathed out a sigh of relief. Excellent. Tonight would be good. I'd just blend in, chill out, and chat with Nell.

"Eric and his brother, Joe, did most of the work. Come and meet him. Joe, this is Lydia," she hollered, snagging the attention of almost everyone in the bar.

Yeah, okay. Now all eyes were definitely turned my way. Bless Nell and her family's extraordinary lung capacity. If only they'd use it for good instead of evil.

"You know, the one I told you about." She grabbed my wrist and towed me through the labyrinth of tables toward the bar.

"I know," the blond bear behind the bar responded, giving me a nod. Then his smiling eyes moved on to Vaughan. "Nice of you to let us know you were back in town, dickface."

"Yeah, yeah. Nell's already given me a hard time." Vaughan reached across the bar, gripping the other guy's thick shoulder. "Good to see you, man."

"You too. How long you back for this time?"

"Not sure. Got a few things to sort out."

Joe grunted understanding.

Joe appeared to be a mountain-man-bartender crossbreed. A Viking throwback, maybe. He was a big guy with big shoulders and a big blond beard. Clearly, there were far more northern Idaho sex gods than I'd given the region credit for. Further classifications were going to be required. If Vaughan topped the super-cool category, then maybe this new guy should win on the lumbersexual front. Given my abrupt return to singledom, I'd have to give this important man-classification system more thought.

Disclaimer: Objectifying people is wrong and stuff.

"Hear you're hired," said Joe to Vaughan.

"Yep."

"Get on the right side of the bar, then."

Vaughan laughed and did as told. Obviously, the bar itself was old and original. Names, dates, and every other marking imaginable had been scratched into the polished wood over god knows how many years of service. This place had real history. It was a decent-size bar, running alongside one of the interior walls. Behind it were shelves full of liquor. Every kind imaginable. Hidden down lights lit up the glass bottles beautifully. Below this sat a long row of beer taps; all the options were mind-boggling.

Clearly, the Dive Bar took its booze seriously.

"Hey, sis," said Vaughan, lowering his voice.

"What?"

"Be nice."

"I'm always nice." Nell patted me on the arm, before turning back to her brother. "Don't worry, your new girlfriend is safe with me. Right, let me quickly run you through the price list."

"I'm not his girlfriend," I said for the sake of anyone listening. "We're just friends."

"Yeah?" Joe scratched at his chin. "I'm single too."

"Really?" I asked, immediately feeling embarrassed by how shocked I was.

The big guy shrugged, giving me a what-can-you-do look. "Working nights, place like this . . ."

Huh. "Are you trying to tell me you don't meet a lot of women tending bar?"

Swear to god, there was a dimple hidden in that there beard. "I meet a lot of women. Not necessarily the kind you want to take home to Mom, you know? Not necessarily the kind looking to meet Mom either."

"Not that there is anything wrong with that."

"Absolutely not, ma'am." Joe started checking me out with renewed interest, dark gaze lingering over my lady bumps. But as brawny and manly as the dude was, his being Vaughan's friend and coworker made him a complication. Whatever happened between now and me putting this town in my rearview mirror, it would not involve complications.

Over my dead curvy unwed body.

"Sorry," I said. "I'm not looking to meet, or not meet, your mother right now. Just got out of a bad relationship."

"Heard about that," he reported matter-of-factly.

"Yeah." Ugh. "Awesome."

"Did you really climb an eight-foot-high fence in heels and a wedding dress?"

"It was closer to six."

The man puffed out his lips. "Still . . . impressive."

"Thanks."

The Beatles changed into the Arctic Monkeys and the scents coming from the kitchen were making my mouth water. Garlic, beef, food in general, all good things. Despite the music, I was reasonably certain everyone in a two-block radius heard my stomach rumble.

"Joe will be with you all night, ask him anything you need," said Nell, wrapping up her brief tutorial.

"Right. Thanks."

The two shared a smile.

"Remember what I told you about Lydia." Vaughan gave his sister a serious look. "Don't get her wet or feed her after midnight. She turns into this weird growly psycho animal. It's not good."

"I'm not a Gremlin," I said.

"Wait." With great drama, Vaughan smacked himself in the forehead. "My bad. It was tequila that did that. You can get her wet and feed her as much as you like, Nell. Just keep her away from tequila."

I subtly scratched my cheek with my middle finger.

The jerk grinned while Joe snickered. Honestly, Nell was right. The sooner all men were sent to colonize the moon, the better for everyone.

"Anyone actually working here tonight?" A short dark-skinned woman dressed in a black Dive Bar T-shirt stood farther down the bar, tapping her talons on the stonework. She and Vaughan nodded to one another with familiarity.

"Any sign of Stella?" Nell asked her.

"No," the woman answered. "My fellow waitress is still M.I.A."

"That girl's about to be out on her ass. I don't care how great Eric thinks she is with the customers. Oh, Rosie, this is Lydia," said Nell. "Lydia, this is Rosie, one of our waitresses. She's been with us from the start. She was also in the same year at school as Vaughan. Say hi."

"Hi."

"Delaney's runaway bride?" Rosie's eyes lit up with interest. "I've been hearing about you all day. Is it true you climbed a ten-foot-high fence topped with barbwire?"

"She said it was closer to six," answered Joe in his gravelly voice. "Didn't hear anything about barbwire."

The shine in the waitress's eyes dimmed a little. "Still. Not bad for a woman in a wedding dress. Mine was so tight I couldn't even get out of the limo without help. Did you know the groom and his best man took off to Hawaii?"

"No way," said Nell.

My stomach sunk. "They went on the honeymoon?"

It made sense. Otherwise, the tickets would have gone to waste. Well, Chris's tickets, at least. They would have had to buy new ones for the best man. Mine were nontransferable and I highly doubted travel insurance covered cancellation of wedding due to a scandalous sex tape. And yet, Chris and Paul were right now enjoying my romantic beach honeymoon. The effort I'd put into finding the right resort for us, the best room to start our wedding life off together perfectly. Wonder what they'd think of the massages and candlelit dinners I'd booked. Suddenly my face felt swollen, my eyes hard and sore. No more crying.

It didn't matter. It didn't.

"I heard they'd gone too," said a woman at a nearby table.

Too many people. There were too many people all up in my

business. It gave me hives. Suddenly, all of the big windows, polished stone, and glossy worn-old-wood loveliness of the bar felt more like a trap. A stage with bright lights. My shoulders inched up, hiding me from view. Such a shit storm of titillation. I'd never given it much thought before, what it'd be like to be one of those people on the pages of magazines. Trailed around by paparazzi, having your life spread across the pages and dissected at every turn. And this was just a scandal in a small(ish) town. My aversion to attention, especially over something as embarrassing as this, made the Delaneys's need to buy my silence all the more ridiculous. Those people didn't know me at all.

I wanted my privacy back. To be just one more face in the crowd, doing my thing, living my life. Coeur d'Alene and I were done. Through. Kaput.

Amid the madness came a voice. "Hey."

Vaughan's eyes caught me, calming me. Gossip was not the end of my world. A few more days and I'd be out of here. The thought of leaving Vaughan bit, though he'd soon be on his way too. Back to the West Coast and the music biz. I'd make other friends. One day, I might even meet a man I could trust, someone I could make plans with.

"You okay?"

"Sure," I lied. "Why wouldn't I be?"

He leaned over the bar, getting closer, making a safe space just for me and him. "Asshole stole your honeymoon."

"Meh. Bet he catches crabs."

"Bet he gets sunburn on his balls."

"Bet he accidentally gets fed to the sharks," I said with great venom. "And there'll be nothing left but this red froth in the churning water, just like in *Jaws*."

"Nice." Vaughan nodded in appreciation. "How do you see that happening?"

I bit my lip, pondering. "Maybe he'll go out on one of those charter fishing boats and fall overboard. I don't have all the details together yet."

One side of his mouth curved upward, eyes set on me. Like, really focused solely on me. I checked my front teeth with my tongue. Nothing there that I could feel. Maybe there was a mark on my face or he'd just realized I was outside my healthy weight range or something.

"What?"

"You look looser now," he said. "You've lost the bullshit plastic smile."

"Have I?"

"Yeah." He linked his fingers, exhaled. "All good, babe?"

"All good." I was so happy he was there with me, I honestly didn't even mind that he'd used the b-word.

"Don't need me to hit anyone?"

"Nuh. I got this."

"Okay." He turned to his sister. "Nell, look after this woman, feed her."

"On it." Once more, his sister grabbed my hand. She towed me toward the kitchen, located beyond a low partition, apart from the gossip pit. Nirvana. Good food. Peace and relative quiet. And all of this with a view of Vaughan, my favorite combo of friend and man-candy, busting his moves at the bar. Awesome. Saved yet again by my tattooed redheaded hero in blue jeans.

Now if I could just figure out a way to return the favor.

CHAPTER NINE

Nell could cook.

She could also bark orders at her assistant (a harried older guy named Boyd), pump me for information about her brother (not that I had any), and still find time to bitch intermittently about Pat. The woman multitasked like a master.

"Is it always this busy?" I asked, hanging to the side, trying to keep out of the way. Every table was taken and there were a couple of people standing around, socializing by the bar.

"Summer's hard to judge. When the bars downtown fill up, we seem to get some of the spillover, along with our usuals." Nell wiped the edges of a dish clear, then deposited it under the heating lamp to be collected. "Long as they keep coming and paying, I'm happy."

Joe and Vaughan were keeping busy. A second waitress, Stella, had finally arrived to work alongside Rosie, considerably lightening the load. Where Rosie seemed friendly, Stella kept her distance. Though with the less-than-warm looks Nell was shooting her way, I would too. She was early twenties at a guess with short jet black hair and a nose ring. Very cool.

The night only seemed to get busier. For every table cleared, another party would enter. I'd offered to go catch a cab home, to let Nell work in peace. She'd ordered me to stay put. So I taste-tested dishes as directed, chatted with her, and slowly sipped iced water in the impressively shiny kitchen.

"He's watching again; quick, look happy," said Nell.

I turned my head, gave Vaughan a finger wave. "Does he usually worry this much?"

"Not in my experience. But then, it's been years since he's been around."

With a lethal-looking knife, she made short work of dicing onions. Not a single tear was shed. Next she moved onto testing a boiling pot of pasta. "Went and visited him on the Coast a few times. Things were always crazy busy. They'd be in the middle of recording or on their way to a gig. It's not like we really got time to talk."

"That's too bad."

"Then once we opened this place, my life revolved around it. I'm here working or I'm at home catching up on sleep."

"I bet." I'd never run my own business, but I could imagine.

"Since our parents passed, Vaughan's been even harder to get ahold of. I don't know, I guess most families grow apart, right?"

"I'm probably the wrong person to ask. Mine was never close to begin with."

"Yeah?"

"I was an accident. Reproduction never featured on my parents list of things to do. They were always working, trying to make things better. Have the money to buy a big shiny house with the latest everything." I shrugged. "It just never quite worked out that way."

Nell frowned. "Dad worked a lot, but Mom was usually home."

"I don't mean to be nosy. But do you mind if I ask how your parents died?"

"Car accident," she said, the volume dropping on her voice.

"Happened at night. It'd just started raining and there was oil on the road. Dad lost control and they hit a tree. Mom died on impact but Dad lasted longer. They'd managed to cut him out of the vehicle and were on their way to the hospital. Luckily he never regained consciousness after the accident. He never knew Mom was gone."

"I'm sorry."

"Yeah." She shook herself. "Anyway, Vaughan and I were tight through high school. Pretty much part of the same crowd. It was weird when he left, I was so used to having him around."

She stopped to pass me a small dish of feta and olives.

"That's how I met my ex, Patrick. He was a friend of Vaughan's. I stole him. Probably why he's so worried about trusting me with you." She winked. "He's worried I've changed teams," she said sarcastically.

"Mm, sorry. I'm going to have to decline." I popped a black olive into my mouth. Delicious. "You've got a hot bod, but you're too complicated. I'm currently avoiding any and all complications of the romantic kind."

"Ha. I guess we'll have to be just friends."

"I'd like that."

She smiled and checked on the progress of some gourmet pizzas, then plated them up with precision. Halloumi, pumpkin, spinach, and pine nuts. It looked divine and smelled even better. "Me too."

"This place is a lot nicer than most dive bars I've been in." To be honest, it was more along the lines of some hipster restaurant/bar with a small stage set up in a corner. "It's much brighter and the floor isn't sticky."

"We inherited that name," explained Nell. "Andre Bird, the guy that owns the building, his dad opened the Dive Bar here back in the seventies. He died behind that bar six years ago. Heart attack. One minute he was pouring beer, the next minute, gone."

"Huh."

"Pat swears he saw the old guy's ghost late one night when he was locking up. But I think he's full of it." A shadow of a smile lingered on her lips. Then she shook it off. "You know Stage Dive did their first public gig on that tiny stage over there."

"No." My eyes bulged.

"Yep. I was here. They were absolutely awful." She laughed. "Took them a few years to get to the point where they were actually worth listening to."

I stared at the stage, mind officially blown. Then I quickly checked out how Vaughan was doing. He was busy restocking the beer fridge. Seemed all good.

"We get diehard fans coming in to get their pictures taken on the stage pretty regularly." She plated up some sort of stuffed chicken breast, spinach and soft cheese oozing out of the middle. "Some are a bit wacked, kissing and stroking it. Eric and Joe had to throw one guy out for trying to hump it. We're pretty sure he was high as a kite. Still, can you imagine the splinters he would have gotten? Ouch."

I snorted. "Ouch, all right. That's amazing that you saw Stage Dive so early."

"Vaughan was in school the same year as a couple of the guys. Had some classes with them. Ask him about it sometime." Nell paused, grimaced. "Maybe don't, since his band's broken up and they're bigger than ever."

"Think I'll keep my mouth shut. Can't be easy, being a musician and coming from the same town as them."

A couple of women in tight-fitting dresses were at the bar, flirting with Vaughan. Not that someone flirting with him was any of my business. Mostly. The amount of alcohol-fueled sex offers bartenders must get . . . though those guys had a lot going for them no matter the situation. Tattoos, muscles, general coolness. Us normal folk never stood a chance.

Why would they settle down when they could live the free and easy lifestyle forever?

"It's great that this place has such a rich history," I said, making myself look away from him. Maybe I should tape my head to the wall. Use a staple gun, perhaps.

Again, Nell made that short sharp almost startling sound of joy and/or amusement. It was hard to say if she was laughing or yipping or what. "Oh, there was history. You should have seen the amount of mirror tiles and velvet wallpaper and shit we had to pull down to get it back to the original brick and wood. Right, Boyd?"

Nothing from Boyd.

Nell didn't even seem to notice. "I wanted to rename it, but Pat and Eric outvoted me. Probably for the best. The whole town knows it as the Dive Bar."

"You might have gotten haunted by the old man."

"Yeah. Andre Senior would not have been impressed."

On the other side of the room, I watched Vaughan mix a couple of bourbon and Cokes, passing them to Rosie. (Hey, I'd avoided looking at him for a solid thirty, forty seconds.) Joe tapped him on the arm, telling him something. Then, with a nod, Vaughan moved on to the next job. His lean angular face seemed fierce, determined. I felt for him. Learning a new trade was never easy—especially on such a busy night.

"Jesus, you've got it bad," said Nell.

I snapped to attention, spluttering, "What?"

"You keep watching him."

"I do not."

"Oh god, yes, you do," said Nell. "Tell her, Boyd. It's kind of nauseating."

Boyd didn't even bother looking up from the pot he was stirring.

"He saved my big butt yesterday. He's my friend and this is his first night on a new job," I said, trying my best to be nonchalant, noncrazy. "I want him to do well, that's all."

The redheaded woman raised a single brow.

"Fine." I took a deep breath. "Nell, I hate to be the one to have to tell you this. But your brother is hot. Like smokin' hot. Honestly, it's kind of impossible to have a vagina and not look."

She barked out a laugh.

Boyd frowned, continuing to cook. At least I'd gotten a reaction. I stirred my drink with the straw, chasing a cube of ice around the glass.

Hands always in motion, Nell moved on to the grill, tending to thick cuts of steak. "Has he said anything more about selling the house?"

Yikes, not safe territory. "You need to ask him about that."

"He's busy. I'm asking you."

"Yes. And I'm telling you to ask him." The woman could give me all the hard-eyed looks she wanted. I wasn't giving away a damn thing Vaughan had confided.

Lightbulbs suspended from the two-story-high ceiling turned on and filled the Dive Bar with a warm glow. I could have happily settled in at a corner table and read for hours. It just felt like a nice place to be.

Until it didn't.

A slick-looking man with a man-bun marched in, face crankier than thunder, his voice louder than all hell. "What the fuck, Nell?"

Unperturbed, the petite chef smiled. "What the fuck what, Eric?"

"He isn't working here."

"He is."

"No." The man, Eric, put a hella lot of emphasis on the word. "I'm an owner here too. You need to run this kind of shit past me, and I'm telling you no."

"Eric." The other waitress, Stella, hovered behind him, waiting. "Can I have a word with you?"

"Not now."

"It's important."

Eric didn't get a chance to answer, however, with Nell on the warpath.

"We hired Joe, your brother," she said.

"We all agreed to hire my brother. Only person I see supporting this decision is you."

Eyes as cold as the arctic, Nell picked up a particularly long dangerous-looking knife. "We need help. He needs a job. It's a win for everyone."

"We're doing fine. And that asshole can rot as far as I know." He moved forward, looming over Nell. It was kind of impressive how little fear he had for his life.

"He's. My. Brother."

"My brother helped us build this place. Worked day in, day out for next to nothing. Where the fuck was yours, huh?" he asked, jaw rigid. "Off banging groupies on the West Coast."

"Please. Like you wouldn't have been doing exactly the same given half a chance."

Behind him, Stella lingered, eyes hardening by the minute. The woman was not giving me happy vibes.

"Get rid of him," Eric snarled. "Now."

"No. We need him."

"Bullshit. I'll take over the bar with Joe."

"Don't do this, Eric," said Nell. "You want me to bring Pat in on this? Really?"

Eric's lips flat-lined.

"He'll have Vaughan's back. You'll be outvoted and you know it." She drove the blade of the knife deep into the cutting board with a loud *thunk*. Poor board.

The two forces of will faced off in silence. There was a world war going on between them. Death and disaster, lots of imaginary blood and bomb blasts. Boyd kept his head down and stayed the hell out of it. I did too.

To think I thought Coeur d'Alene was a quiet town. Nice people, not much drama. The longer I lived, the less I knew.

Only one person dared to break the stalemate. Stella visibly braced herself, shoulder back, head held high. "Eric!"

With a growl, Eric spun. "I said not—"

The waitress slapped him in the face. The noise was shockingly loud.

"Fuck you and your 'not now,'" she said. "I'm not wasting another minute of my life waiting on you."

Eric said nothing.

"Serious about exploring something with me, were you? Did you honestly think I wouldn't hear about you taking that skank to dinner last night?" Stella asked, rubbing her probably sore hand against the side of her skinny black jeans. "Well?"

His cheek ripe red, the man stood frozen. Busted. So damn busted.

"You lying piece of shit." The woman ripped off her neat black apron, shoving it into his stomach. Her teary eyes blazed with fury. "I quit!"

Holy hell.

For a minute, nobody moved. A Jason Isbell song started playing over the sound system. Slowly, the talk and sounds of eating and drinking started up again. The Dive Bar once more came to life. I'd been so caught up in the scene, I hadn't even noticed we yet again had an audience watching. At least they weren't interested in me this time.

A hand was at my back, a solid male body standing behind me. I didn't need to turn to know it was Vaughan. The sudden happy in my hormones was evidence enough.

"Tell me you didn't fuck another employee." Nell's voice was so deadly quiet I almost couldn't hear it. Her skin seemed snow pale, apart from the twin bright spots high on her cheeks. "You wouldn't, not after you promised. Not again, on top of everything else that's going on right now."

His hands curled into tight fists. "Nell—"

"Tell me you didn't."

Obviously, the man couldn't.

Breathing hard, Nell stared down at her chopping board. "Vaughan works here as long as he wants. I don't want to hear another word about it."

Apparently Eric didn't have a death wish, so he kept his mouth shut.

"Get out of my kitchen," she ground out through clenched teeth. "I'm serious, I don't want to even look at you again tonight. Get out."

"You need me here," he said.

"No." Furiously, she shook her head. "No, what I need is people I can depend upon to run a business. Not a fuck-up who can't even keep his dick in his pants during open hours."

No one spoke, the tension thick enough to choke on.

"Shit!" Eric slammed the apron onto the nearest flat metal surface and stalked out.

The restaurant was now completely full and I could hear someone calling for service.

Crap. Poor Nell.

"We need to get back to work," she said quietly, sending the staff on their way.

I couldn't just sit there. Not when I could help. Nell had been nice to me, plus there was the debt I owed her brother. So I picked up the apron Eric had just abused and shook it out. "I waitressed my way through college."

Nell just looked at me, mystified. She had the same beautiful blue eyes as Vaughan. Like a clear blue summer sky or your favorite jeans, which you'd washed a hundred times. But right now, those eyes seemed shaken, and her white face was a stark contrast to her bright red hair. She was a woman pushed to the edge, then given a little nudge over. God, did I know that feeling all too well.

While my fingers were busy with the apron ties, I took a deep breath. "Rosie can get me up to speed on the table numbering and the rest."

Vaughan's hand moved to the back of my neck, giving it a gentle squeeze. His thumb stroked over my skin, giving me goose bumps. It was impossible not to lean into him, to take a little more of what he was giving. All that heat and strength. The truth was, I liked his touch far more than I should have. Definitely far more than was wise. Also his smell. Man, he smelled good. Soap and him and sex. Though the sex was probably just my fevered imagination.

Then he was gone, heading back to the bar.

"You don't have to do that," said Nell.

"I know."

She blinked, frozen for a moment. Then the moment was gone. Loudly, Nell clapped her hands, getting back in the game. "We got a full house, people. Let's go. Boyd, how many times do I have to tell you to stop standing around gabbing? Work. Work!"

CHAPTER TEN

"Don't move an inch. I'm just going to run inside and grab my camera."

Looking amused, Vaughan straightened. He had been leaning over the front of the Mustang, doing deep and meaningful things to the vehicle's engine. I had to admit, the position did amazing things to his jean-clad ass. And the fact that he was sans T-shirt got me all a-tingle. The ink work on his arms made for an amazing display. The man was living art.

"Good morning, Lydia."

"Morning, Vaughan." I passed him one of the cups of coffee I'd made from the supplies Nell shoved at me the night before. Coffee, sugar, creamer, and containers full of restaurant leftovers, god bless her.

"Thanks." He took a sip, smiling at me.

"What?"

"You," he said. "Smirking and giving me crap. It's like you've freed your inner happy smart-ass self. Let it loose to run wild."

"Nah." I leaned a hip against the driver's side door. "That's just me complimenting your rear and practicing my come-on lines now that I'm swinging single again."

"I'm glad you felt my ass worthy of your attentions."

"No problem."

"And I want you to know, minute you give me the signal and lift-up your shirt I'll be more than happy to give your breasts all the best lines I've got."

"That's sweet." I took a sip of my coffee, trying to keep a straight face. In my infinite wisdom, I'd raised the subject of sex. Now here we were, my pulse speeding, heading straight toward a panic attack over the way he looked at me. How insane. I both wanted, and didn't want, his attention with all of my heart. "I'll give some thought to your shirt suggestion."

"Wish you would," he said. Oh, that sly little smile of his. It made my everything go weak.

I laughed, a little unnerved.

"Will you be falling for my flirting sometime soon?"

Whoa. I stopped, thrown.

"Not that I mind hitting on you, Lydia. Just curious," he said. "And I'm not being kind or trying to boost your self-confidence."

Ugh. "Am I that obviously neurotic and needy?"

He took another sip of coffee. "To be fair, the crap you've been through lately would make anyone doubt themselves."

Overhead, a bird flew by. How nice to just be able to up and disappear so easily. I wanted wings. Awkward conversation, shitty situation, I'd be out of here, suckers. Poof! Gone. They didn't even have to be pretty, any old pigeon wings would do.

"I guess so," I said, watching the bird disappear out of sight. "We're always hardest on ourselves, right?"

A shrug.

Right. As if this guy would be swimming in a sea of inner doubt. Beautiful. Talented. Loved by his family and friends. Imagine having the bravado to take to the stage in front of hundreds, no, thousands of people. It was up to schmucks like me to find their spines and get their shit together. Some people just naturally knew how to strut.

"I blame it on women's magazines and the media," I announced, setting my cup of coffee aside. "'Are you too needy? How to be more confident and look less like crap in seventy-eight simple steps! Only three hundred thousand dollars to a better you!' Well, thanks. I hadn't realized how everything about me was godawful until you pointed it out."

I gathered up my long hair, tying it into a loose knot on top of my head. "Every woman on earth should launch a class action against the mass media. Take it down."

Nothing from my friend on account of where his gaze was fixed. Yet again.

"Vaughan, I'm talking. Pay attention. My eyes aren't down there."

His gaze snapped back to my face.

"Thank you."

"That was a trap. You lifted your arms up," he grumbled, brows turned down. Never had a man looked quite so oppressed. "What was I supposed to do?"

"A trap? You think I'm trying to trap you?" I wrinkled up my forehead. "Vaughan, I'm genuinely beginning to get concerned about your breast fixation. Seriously. How can you function when any hint of tit sends your brain into a coma?"

"You were staring at my ass earlier. You don't see me telling you off." He cracked his neck. "And anyway, it's only happened with you. I'm fine around every other rack. I can discreetly appreciate and move on. Yours are different."

"Really?" I grinned, my stomach doing the strangest loop de loop.

In lieu of answering, he disappeared once more under the hood. In the distance, I could hear kids laughing and a car passing by.

The wind was blowing through the pine trees and a bird was singing. Man, this place was lovely. So relaxing. If I owned this home, I'd never give it up. They could bury me in the backyard, let me turn into fertilizer.

Vaughan glanced at me around the corner of the hood, immediately snagging my attention.

"I humbly apologize for objectifying you," I said. "I'll try not to do it again."

A snort.

Fair enough.

"What a lovely day," I said.

I couldn't have asked for a prettier picture. A big old tree shaded the driveway on the side of the house where he'd popped the hood. Stray rays of sunlight lit the golden red of his hair and the colored ink on his otherwise pale skin. I guess playing in bands, enjoying the nightlife, didn't make for a great tan. But it didn't matter. He didn't need one. Tall, lean, and firm in all the right places, Vaughan Hewson was a girl's wet dream. Luckily I respected him for his mind.

"My feet hurt from last night. It's been years since I spent that much time on them." I gave my Birkenstock-clad beauties a stretch. To cover the rest of me, I'd chosen denim cut-offs and an oversize tee. Comfortable was the look I was going for. "I've been thinking about your place some more, if you're still interested in selling it."

Nothing from beneath the hood.

"I know a good agent, Wes from Brewers Real Estate. He's a nice guy, not quite as cutthroat as the rest. I could give him a call, ask him to stop by if you like?"

I waited for a response.

"Up to you, of course."

The sound he made was far from happy. "Thought we were going to talk about this again when I was ready."

"I haven't heard from the Delaneys yet, but they're not going to waste time getting rid of me," I said, tone wry. "I don't know how much longer I'll be here and I don't want you getting ripped off."

He stopped, stared. "Thanks. If you could give him a call, that'd be good."

"Okay," I said quietly.

"It's just . . . it's hard to let it go."

"Yeah."

Wiping his greasy hands on a cloth, he turned to look at the house. "Always figured they'd be here. I'd come back for holidays and shit, and nothing would change. Dad would still be screwing up the Christmas lights and Mom would be going berserk over the pumpkins each Halloween. Nell and Pat would have a kid and it'd all be good."

"Sounds nice."

"Mm." He paused. "After I was over touring and had made some money, I was going to buy one of those places on the lake. Settle down."

"Here? Not out on in California?"

"Nah. In my head, it was always here." His hands twisted the cloth up into a tight ball. "I had everything figured out."

"You know," I said, trying to speak gently, "I've heard most people have three different careers over their lifetime."

"Do they?"

"Maybe playing in the band was just your first one."

"Are you serious? You want me to just give it up?" he asked, the volume of his voice rising. "Hock the guitars and what, get a job at Burger King making fries?"

"I don't want—"

"Because I can really see that working out fucking great, Lydia." He chucked the cloth aside, furious. "Good idea. Awesome."

"Vaughan." The muscles in my jaw ached.

"Want to know the difference between me and you, babe?"

I kept my mouth shut. Pretty damn sure he was going to tell me.

"Your dream was marrying some douche with a nice big bank account and hiding out behind the white picket fence for the rest of your life." The jerk towered over me, looming.

"That so?"

"Christ. You know it is." He laughed, spitefully.

Wow. Yeah. I had nothing to say in response.

"But my dream . . . mine." His thumb hit him squarely in the center of his chest. "It was a little bigger."

I had no words. None.

For a good minute I just stared up at him, amazed by his outburst, more than anything. There was no real reason why I should have been. He and I had now known each other for what . . . a bit under forty-eight hours? I'd known Chris for four months and been clueless. My track record for reading people was, after all, shitty.

"Okay. I'm sorry for saying something that upset you." I paused, taking a deep breath. "That was obviously insensitive of me, given everything you're going through."

Nothing.

"What I meant to say was that there might be other jobs in music that would work for you. That you might love as much."

Still nothing.

"I am not your enemy, Vaughan. I care a hell of a lot about you." My hands hung stiff by my sides. It was all I could do to resist strangling the idiot. "The way you just spoke to me is not okay. How dare you say that my hopes for the future are less important than yours. That I'm some money-grubbing bitch ready to spread her legs for a big house to play trophy wife."

"Lydia—"

"I'm not finished, you asshat."

The man looked down at me, eyes full of surprise, or bewilderment. His face was drawn, lips shut tight. Just as they should be. I stared at him, memorizing every detail for a later date, when I didn't want to burn him down or burst into tears. Stupid female emotions, always getting me into trouble when I wanted to be a hard ass. My butt wobbled, it always had and always would. Time to accept myself and all my flaws and move on.

"Actually, I am finished."

" 'kay."

"I'm going to get my stuff together," I said. "I think that would be best."

He had no comment.

I backed away, turned, and started walking toward the front door.

Most of my stuff was already packed into boxes. This shouldn't be too hard.

My foot hit the front step and I stumbled, losing my balance. I grasped at the old iron railing, fighting to catch myself before my face met the floor. Awesome. Such grace.

"I'm sorry."

I stopped cold.

Nothing more was said.

Slowly, I turned. He stood in the long grass, watching, waiting. Honestly, it was hard to look at him. The expression on his face and the way he held his body, the emotion in his eyes. My world was so colored when it came to him. Every detail so vivid and real. He shouldn't have that power. It would have been so much easier to leave him otherwise. I'd broken into his house, but he'd somehow broken into me, cracked me wide open, exposing me to so much more of life than what had existed before.

And to think I'd genuinely believed I loved Chris. What an idiot. I didn't have a fucking clue about love. I got like and lust, things along those lines. But the rest was an abyss, a big black hole, and I couldn't see the bottom. Couldn't even begin to fathom the depth of it. Inside me, there lived a big ball of emotion to do with my friend Vaughan. None of it was ready to be labeled. All I knew was, leaving him hurt.

"Is that it?" I knotted my fingers in front of myself, unsure.

One thick shoulder rose and fell. "Does there need to be more?"

"I'm not sure."

He took one step toward me, and then another. With him standing at the bottom of the stairs and me on the second, we were eye to eye. His hands tangled with mine, first one then the other. God, his skin was so warm.

Our bodies gravitated toward each other. The pull of one messed-up heart to another. I watched him warily, trying to hold something back for safekeeping. It didn't really work.

"You're right, I was an asshat."

"Yeah, you were."

A little nod. "I'm going to kiss you now," he whispered.

"Oh. Okay," I whispered back to him. I had no idea why we were whispering.

I didn't have a good reason not to let him kiss me. Well, there was always protection of the heart and all that. Really, though, given the grinder I'd already put mine through, it was a little late for that.

His lips brushed against mine. Such a soft touch. Up and down in the tiniest of motions, he grazed his mouth against mine. It was sweet, lovely, and a little weird. I'd never been kissed like this. Not by anybody. Every part of me yearned to press forward, to push for more. But at the same time, what he was giving me was so good. To rush him and his artistry would have been wrong.

His breath warmed my face and his fingers tightened around mine. I held perfectly still while he gently rubbed his lips against mine, doing what he wanted. The tip of his nose nudged my cheek, time and again, and my chest leaned against his. With what he was doing, I'd have been knocked on my ass otherwise. His kisses were hypnotizing.

When his lips opened a little, just enough to softly kiss my bottom lip, I swear I swooned. Over and over he kissed my lips, first the top then the bottom, the sides and the corner from where my smile started. No part was left untouched. My smile grew wider, my nipples hard and my loins Vaughan-addled. That's a medical term.

He drew back slightly, smiling too. "You forgive me?"

"I'd have forgiven you without the kiss."

"I know," he said, still speaking softly. "The kiss was more for me."

"Was it?" God, he was pretty. The prettiest man I'd ever met. "Do you believe in crazy at first sight?"

Lines creased his brow. "What?"

"I'm not down with the whole L-word and I don't think this, whatever this is, is that. So don't freak out and suddenly accuse me of being a stage-ten clinger or something, got it?"

"Okay." He looked amused.

"But what if there was crazy at first sight? Because I think we have a credible basis for that."

For a moment he just stared at me, obviously deep in thought. "I definitely thought you were crazy the first time I saw you, sitting in my shower in that dress."

"Mm-hmm."

"And you do drive me crazy, sometimes."

"Ditto."

His tongue played behind his cheek. "I might be a little crazy about you too."

"You definitely are about my breasts."

"Your tits are world-class," he said, hands flat on my back, pressing me harder against him.

"Thanks. I appreciate that."

"It's more of an all-of-you thing, though, on the crazy front. Just so you know."

I could only grin. "Yeah?"

"Yeah." He leaned his forehead against mine, getting closer. "What about you? I confessed. Come on."

"I came up with the idea in the first place."

"Doesn't let you off the hook."

I groaned. "Fine. I'm crazy about you too. Crazy in all the ways the word can be taken."

"We've only got a few days," he said, bringing all of the happy crashing to earth. Suddenly the sun didn't shine. The earth didn't spin. Everything was fucked.

No. I wouldn't let it be.

"I know. I mean, I know this isn't a permanent thing for either of us." Something inside of me screamed denial. "It's more of a crossing of paths on the great journey of life."

"Right." He kissed me lightly once more. "Doesn't mean I'm not crazy about you."

"I know."

"And about what you said," he started, gazing off over my shoulder. "I know you were trying to help. I'll think about it, okay?"

"Okay."

His hands rubbed my back, then he set me loose, exhaling hard. "Unless you want to go hit the mattress with me right now, I better take a breather. Go finish the car, start on mowing the lawn and shit."

I looked down. Yes, something was definitely hardening in the front of his pants. Huh. We hadn't even used tongue. And they said romance was dead.

Time on the mattress sounded great, but while we were short on time, I also didn't want to rush things. What if we had sex and then the build-up, the rush of all those good hormones and hopes and dreams through my, body was over? No. We needed to take it slow. Man, it was so hard to judge the ins and outs of this situation.

"I'll let you go do your jobs," I said in a rush, moving back from him a little.

"Okay."

"Oh, another thing I was thinking about, though." I put a hand on his super-hot bare chest to stall him.

He gave me a wary look.

"Relax. I was just wondering if you'd help me buy a car. You know about their insides, right?" I pawed at his chest in a totally nonsleazy subtle way. "I'm going to need wheels to escape this place."

"Sure. Be happy to, babe."

"Babe?" I looked at him down the length of my noise.

"Babe," he said, resolute.

Meh. Who was I to fight him? "Fine."

CHAPTER ELEVEN

Nell waltzed into the house late Monday afternoon, with Rosie the waitress hot on her heels. One carried booze, the other pizza boxes. Immediately my stomach rumbled in need. Pizza was just the best.

"Did I miss the part where you knocked?" Bent in half, Vaughan sat on the sofa, tying his shoelace.

"You're funny, little brother," said Nell breezily, dumping her box full of wine bottles on the kitchen counter. She was wearing a denim miniskirt and orange shirt. Rosie rocked a breezy blue maxi dress. Definitely not Dive Bar uniform.

"I'm serious," said Vaughan.

"I know. That's what makes it so amusing."

"What's going on?" I asked, stuffing crap into my handbag. We'd been preparing to head to work. Given the swift departure of Eric's waitress friend, Stella, I'd agreed to fill her shifts until a replacement was found. Or until it was time for me to leave town. Whichever came first. I was wearing my best black slacks and a matching Dive Bar shirt Nell had given me the night before.

"I'm giving us the night off." From a cabinet she pulled out three wineglasses, rinsing them beneath the tap. "Lydia, Rosie, and I are doing some girl time. Be a darling and go away, would you?"

"I really need to start locking the doors," Vaughan muttered, stretching out on the couch. "Who's running the bar?"

"Eric."

"And?"

"Just Eric." Nell beamed. It was an unnerving sight. "He'll also be tonight's waiter. Boyd has got the kitchen under control, but otherwise, Eric's on his own."

Rosie also grinned like a loon.

"Is that good for your business?" I asked without thinking, and accepting a very large glass of red. "Wait. Never mind. Forget I said that. I will not rain on people's parades with unnecessary practicalities they can figure out for themselves."

Over on the couch, Vaughan gave me a small smile, a look of understanding.

"O-kay. It's fine." Nell laughed. "We probably need a voice of practicality around here. But the thing is, sometimes, you just have to teach people a lesson. Either that or resort to homicide, and I'd rather not go to jail."

"Word," said Rosie, taking a sniff of her wine. "Ooh. You grabbed the good stuff."

"Of course I grabbed the good stuff." She turned to her brother and me, curiosity filling her eyes. "So what have you two been up to today?"

"Vaughan worked on his car for a while, then he helped narrow down some potential sets of wheels for me." I left out the part where my real estate agent pal had stopped by to take a look at the house.

"She wants a Prius." Vaughan snickered.

"They get good mileage."

"Lydia." Nell winced. "No. Just no. Okay?"

Even Rosie seemed mildly terrified by my taste in vehicles.

"Do none of you care about the environment?" I raised my shoulders, amazed.

"It's for your own good that we save you from this." Nell held her glass of wine high, toasting my lack of style, apparently. "You'll thank us one day."

"I doubt that." So this was what having friends involved. Maybe I should just get a pet rock or something. A plant, maybe. Anything incapable of answering back.

Once again the door swung open, this time care of the opposite sex. A tall dude with a massive beard and the sides of his head shaved walked in with a growler full of beer in each hand. Almost every inch of skin on him was covered in ink and a silver ring hung from his nose.

The instant he saw Nell, he stopped dead. "Shit."

"Pat," she said in a low careful voice. "I thought you were going to Whitefish."

"Changed my mind."

She nodded, gnawing at her lip.

"Hey." Joe walked in behind him, another couple of growlers in hand. Seemed everyone was planning a party.

Last came a slightly older guy. Not as tall as the other two, but built and very good looking, in an I've-seen-some-life way. Gray streaked his short spiky hair and the stubble on his jaw and cheeks. In one hand he carried a guitar, in the other he balanced a couple of big pizza boxes.

"Andre." In a rush, Vaughan got to his feet. "Fuck, man. Good to see you."

"Thanks for letting me know you were back." Andre thrust the guitar at Vaughan, all the better to grab the pizzas with both hands. "Joe had to tell me."

"Sorry." Vaughan took the guitar under one arm, holding it ready to play. Then he strummed a chord. "She still sounds sweet."

"Course she does. Martins only get better with age."

With a wry smile, he handed the instrument back, taking

charge of the pizza. "I don't want to go falling for something I can't afford."

Andre laughed, shook his head.

"Lydia," said Vaughan. "Want you to meet some old friends of mine, the one with the Gandalf-length beard is Pat. He owns that tattoo parlor next to the bar."

"Hi." I raised a hand in greeting and the man gave me a chin tip.

"And this here is Andre." Vaughan gave the man's shoulder a squeeze. "He's the one who taught me to play. Bought my first guitar off him when I was ten. He'd just opened his store."

"Yep," said Andre. "Took all your Christmas and birthday money."

"Typical." Joe set his growlers down on the dining table. "Ripping off small children. Should be ashamed of yourself. Bet you stole their candy too."

Ever so discreetly, Andre flipped him off.

"Oh, it cost me," agreed Vaughan. "That secondhand Epiphone had taken some hits, but you were right. She had a beautiful sound, did the job and then some. I've still got her."

"No shit?"

"Haven't played her in a long time. But I couldn't bring myself to let her go."

They both smiled.

"Anyway," said Vaughan. "I used to work in his shop sometimes after school and stuff."

"The music shop near the Dive Bar?" I asked, sipping my wine. Excellent quality, Rosie was right.

"That's the one," answered Andre, setting the acoustic down on a chair. He wandered my way, looking me over. "Good to meet you, Lydia."

Then he came closer, dropping his voice to a murmur. "Delaney's a dick. That was a lucky escape on your part. You can do a hell of a lot better, honey."

I huffed out a laugh. "Thank you."

The man leaned in, giving me a kiss on the cheek, smiling. Damn, he was smooth. He also wore a very nice aftershave.

"Hey," came a cranky voice. Vaughan was instantly by my side, shooting laser beams at his old friend. "Go easy, man. You only just walked in the door."

"I'm sorry, Lydia," said Andre. "Did I make you uncomfortable?"

"No."

The laser beams and frown turned my way.

"Good." After a pat on Vaughan's shoulder, Andre walked away. Next he went to Nell, kissing her on the cheek, and then Rosie. Clearly, it was just his way of being friendly with women he liked. As if I'd suddenly be catching the eye of every hottie.

"You have a lot of good friends in this town," I said, moving the conversation along.

A grunt.

"It's great to get to meet some of them."

"Yeah," he said. "Listen, Andre is a bit of a player and I don't want to see you get hurt."

I covered his mouth with my hand. "Stop right there. You think I'd take up with one of your friends?"

His worry didn't seem to ease.

"I wouldn't—especially after today," I lowered both my voice and my hand. "Remember the part where you kissed me?"

His gaze dropped to my lips. Ye gods, this man. "I remember."

"And the part after when we talked about crazy at first sight?"

"Yeah."

"That wasn't a commitment on either of our parts. I know that. But it was a statement."

His hand slipped beneath my low ponytail, thumb stroking the back of my neck. Shivers ran down my spine. Just that easily he got me all stirred up. Stupid me for not dragging him to the closest mattress earlier.

"Forty-eight hours," he muttered.

"What?"

"I've known you for forty-eight hours." He lowered his face, bringing us closer.

"That's right." This was a safe space. And it was beautiful. "Feels like we've covered a lot of territory in a very short amount of time. Kind of speed-friendship with the potential for benefits."

"Mm."

"And I just want you to know that I don't think less of you for driving a gas-guzzling environmental disaster of a car."

"Thanks, babe."

I screwed up my nose. "You caught me in a weak moment earlier. I didn't really mean to say you calling me babe was all right."

"No?"

"No."

"Sucks to be you." He placed a soft kiss on my forehead.

"Vaughan," said Joe, clapping his hands together loudly. "Still got that fire pit out back?"

"It's overgrown, but it's there." He gave the nape of my neck one last squeeze, then he took a step back. "You thinking we should get it working again?"

"You read my mind."

"Let's do it," said Andre.

Vaughan looked between Pat and his sister, neither of whom appeared to be particularly relaxed. Nell's smile seemed strained, the wine in her glass disappearing at lightning speed. A muscle jumped in his jawline. "Yeah, let's do that. Leave the girls in here to do their thing."

"Thank you, gentlemen," sang Rosie, the wine in her glass also greatly reduced. "My husband only agrees to baby-sit once every blue moon. I mean to make the most of it."

"Have fun." Vaughan picked up the growlers Joe had left on the table, then moseyed over to the big glass doors heading out back. "Grab some glasses."

"On it," said Joe.

"Coming, Pat?" Andre asked before going out into the early evening.

Without a word, the tattooist followed. Nell's gaze did too. There was love, in all its pain and glory, written over her face. In comparison, what I'd felt for Chris was laughable.

"We grew apart," said Nell, meeting my eyes.

"I'm sorry."

She shrugged and drained the last of her wine. "These things happen, right? Grab the bottle from the kitchen, would you?"

"Sure."

All three of us crowded together on the couch, topping off our glasses.

"Shit, I forgot. Pizza!" Rosie raced into the kitchen, bringing back one of the boxes. "Calabrese, tomato, and basil. My favorite."

"Nice." My stomach rumbled to life and I helped myself to a slice.

"Want me to heat it up?"

"There's no time for that," I said, taking a bite. "Oh. This is good. Really good."

"Sure about that?" Rosie laughed.

"You just wish you could talk with a mouth full of food, and still look this attractive."

That even made Nell snicker. Score.

"Made them for us before abandoning ship. I'm glad you like my cooking," she said. "Since I see my brother hasn't bothered to stock the house. You'll likely be relying on me for the duration of your stay."

"I'll go to the supermarket tomorrow," I said, pausing to gulp down a mouthful of the very good wine. "Vaughan's been busy."

"Wouldn't matter if he hadn't been," she said, swirling her glass of red. "He won't do anything that feels like settling in here. This place . . . it's just too hard for him. Too many memories, I guess. He'll be gone as fast as he can be."

"You really think he's going to sell it?" asked Rosie.

Nell lay her head back against the top of the couch, staring up at the ceiling. "All he ever wanted to be was a guitarist, play in a band. He needs the money."

"Shit," whispered Rosie. "I'm sorry."

I ate more pizza and drank more wine. My heart hurt for her, but there was nothing I could say.

"It's like I lost him when I lost Mom and Dad. Now Pat's gone too." Nell sniffed, quickly wiping at her eyes. "Fuck. Sorry, girls. Didn't mean to get all weepy on you."

"It's okay," I said, touching her elbow. "You're safe here, Nell."

"What she said," echoed Rosie, rising to grab an old box of Kleenex from the corner. I really did like her. She was good people.

"I'm the hard-core bitch," said Nell. "I'm not allowed to cry."

"We all cry sometimes. It's no biggie."

"My period's due any day now. Let's blame it on that."

"Done." I smiled.

Rosie shoved the box of tissues at her, then ran off to the kitchen to grab another bottle of wine. This night was going to get messy. Everyone needed to cut loose now and then.

I couldn't help but wonder if this was the only end result of love. Feeling lost, hurting, clinging onto what was left of your life? Thank goodness I hadn't gone through with the wedding. And thank god this thing with Vaughan had an end date. Otherwise, who knew what might happen. I could wind up broken, left in an even worse state than after Chris's betrayal. Because Vaughan could do that. Forty-eight hours in, and already he stirred up feelings I didn't want to mention. We were a train wreck waiting to happen. But, damn, it'd be hard to avoid going down that track. Even if I'd regret it for the rest of my life.

"Considering we work in the same building, Pat's gotten amazingly good at sticking close to the tattoo parlor and avoiding me," she said. "I haven't seen him in weeks. I think that's what caused our split."

We kept quiet, letting her spill. Sometimes, that's just what a girl needs.

"When he took over the parlor it was shit. A total mess. He worked his ass off to get it to where it is today and I supported him. I thought when we opened the bar that it was my turn, my thing. I figured he'd understand. But it didn't work that way." She held out her glass and Rosie filled it up again. "We were hardly ever seeing each other and we just . . . we drifted. One day he got up and said, I don't know why we're even bothering. What can you say to that? How the fuck are you supposed to react? It was like every bit of emotion had drained right out of him. His body was there, but his head and his heart were on another planet."

Her mouth opened, but for a moment nothing came out. Nell looked ruined. Christ, if this was marriage, if this was trusting another person body and soul, it scared the living shit out of me.

Suddenly, her chin lifted, her shoulders squared. "Like I'm supposed to smack him around the head with our marriage certificate? I told him if he didn't want to be there then he should go. I wasn't going to stop him. Fuck, I didn't think he'd actually leave."

Outside there was shouting, laughter. It seemed so out of place. Wrong. But I guess life went on, even when it shouldn't.

Nell flipped her hair back, licked her shining lips. "Anyway . . ."

"I'm sorry," I said, not that it helped.

She turned her splotchy red face my way, tears trailing down her cheeks. "Can't you just accidentally get pregnant and make Vaughan stay in Coeur d'Alene? I want some family around."

"Um, no. Sorry."

She barked that signature laugh. "Fine. Ruin everything, Lydia. See if I care."

"Gosh, Lydia," chided Rosie with a smile. "She's not asking for much."

I laughed and drank more wine. Everything would make more sense inebriated. I just knew it. And boy, was it going straight to my head. I guess having eaten only a piece of pecan pie today wasn't the best way to start a night of wine drinking.

"I'm not being funny."

"I know," I said. "I'm a selfish ho."

"Yes. You are." Nell blew her nose and refilled her glass, attempting to pull herself together under our watchful eyes. "You should just let me do what I want with your uterus."

The woman was nuts. Children weren't even on my radar yet. Let alone with Vaughan.

"Your brother and I are just friends, Nell," I said.

Both women laughed so hard it was a wonder they didn't fall off the couch. I stoically ignored them as best I could. Female friends, so overrated. Though also kind of wonderful in all the ways. Damn Coeur d'Alene for getting so great just as I was about to leave.

"A toast!" Rosie held her wine glass high. "To bullshit and broken hearts."

"Ha. Nice one." I grinned.

"Here, here," said Nell, drinking deep.

"To bullshit and broken hearts," I said. Then I drank too.

Hours later someone knocked on the door. Hours and hours and many bottles of wine and slices of pizza later. Nell slowly got to her feet and stumbled on over to answer it. I'll admit, it kind of surprised me when the person didn't just charge inside the same way everyone else did.

"Oh. It's you." Nell turned around and returned to the couch.

Behind her was Eric, his anger from last night missing. Well, mostly. His lips were pressed tight together, but his eyes were completely devoid of the fire and rage. "You've made your point."

"Glad to hear it," said Nell, picking up her wineglass.

"It was a shitty thing to do, leaving me to run the bar on my own," he said. "But I get why you felt the need."

Nell just watched him with eyes slightly glazed.

"We're lucky we weren't nearly as busy as last night. As it was, we had a few complaints about the slow service. More than one table left without tipping."

"Hmm."

Eric studied his shoes, and shoved his hands in the pockets of his pants. He looked like a schoolboy called to the principal's office.

He really was a good-looking man, I thought, as I eyed his long dark hair and sculpted face. Some expensive underwear company could have put him on a billboard. He didn't dress casual like the other guys. He wore a white button-down shirt that was rolled up to his elbows, and nice black trousers instead of jeans.

"Where's Vaughan? I better talk to him," he said. "Set things right."

"He's busy," blurted out Rosie, sitting up straight, all of a sudden at full attention.

"We can tell him." Again, Nell clambered to her feet, red-tinged eyes suddenly far more open. "But I appreciate you offering to smoke the peace pipe."

"No, I've been thinking," said Eric. "There's something I want to say to him."

"But—"

"Vaughan!" Eric craned his neck right and then left, checking out the hallway and the dining area. "Hey, Vaughan, you got a minute?"

"Eric, don't." She grabbed at his arm, yanking him toward the door. "Later. Talk to him later."

"Relax, Nell. I'm not going to cause any trouble."

The kitchen door flew open, banging against the wall so hard you could hear the glass shudder. Though it wasn't Vaughan who stood there, fury etched into the skin of his face, above the mammoth beard.

"What are you doing here?" Pat growled, taking several large steps into the room.

Nell released Eric's arm, taking a hasty step back. "Patrick . . ."

"It was a work thing," said Eric, tone calm, placating, even. "I just stopped by to tell her something. I'll leave now."

"Shit," Andre mumbled, looking far from happy. The other guys had come inside too, Vaughan hanging back by the dining table, confusion in his eyes.

But Joe hustled ass around the room, getting over to his brother's side, pronto. "Come on, Eric. Let's go. Catch you guys later."

"What is this?" Vaughan stepped up beside Pat, brows pulled in so tight they almost touched.

"I just wanted to say I'm fine with you working at the bar," said Eric. "It's fine with me. That's all I came here for."

Nell stood at the edge of the room, wringing her hands, looking like she'd bolt at the first opportunity. I set down my wineglass. Whatever was going on, the party was most definitely over.

"Pat," said Vaughan. "Man?"

Pat just stood there, steaming. And I'd thought Vaughan's laser beam eyes were impressive. He had nothing on Pat. With the way Pat was glaring at him, Eric should have turned into ashes. Dust.

"Don't," warned Nell, eyes silently pleading with her ex. "Do not bring my brother into this."

"Everyone fucking knows." With some mumbled expletives, Pat offered her a bitter grin. "Did you really think he wouldn't find out eventually?"

"Find out what?" asked Vaughan, voice beyond tense. "Nell?"

"They screwed," said Pat. "Your sister and him. Can you believe that shit?"

"What the fuck?" said Vaughan, eyes huge as he turned to his sister. "Nell?"

"Don't you look at me like that, Vaughan. You weren't here, you have no idea what this has been like for me." Fists tight against her stomach, Nell struggled to stay calm. "It only happened a few weeks ago. Pat and I have been separated for over a year. I am not a cheater."

"Sorry," muttered Vaughan. "Didn't mean to accuse you of anything."

Nell just shook her head. "And you . . . you were at the goddamn Iron Horse every night tapping all that ass, weren't you, Pat?"

His jaw trembled with rage.

"You hypocritical bastard," she said.

"I didn't fuck your friend, Nell!"

"I made a mistake. I got drunk, and I made mistake." Again, her eyes welled with tears.

Hand outstretched, Eric stepped forward. "Pat—"

"I don't want to hear a single thing from you." Beneath his faded black shirt, Pat's shoulders heaved. "Not a single damn thing ever again."

Mouth hanging open, Vaughan didn't seem to know where to look. All of his family and friends gathered around him and now this. What should have been a positive experience had hit the wall.

"I trusted you," snarled Pat. "I trusted both of you."

"Enough," said Vaughan, shoving a hand through his hair, obviously struggling. "Leave, Eric. Now."

"Christ." Eric hung his head, giving a harsh laugh. "I came here to smooth things over with you. To bury the hatchet. This is such bullshit."

"Man, c'mon." Joe grabbed at Eric's shoulder, but he shook it off.

"Bullshit is it?" Pat took a step forward. "You fuck my wife and that's bullshit?"

"You know what I don't get," said Eric. "You walked out on her, man. So why are you so bitter about this? Got some regrets, Pat?"

"Stop it." Nell groaned, tears coursing down her face.

"She wasn't your wife," continued Eric as if he hadn't heard. "You heard her. You two had been separated for ages. It isn't like you've been waiting for the divorce to come through before moving on, is it? More like making up for lost time if you ask me."

"Both of you assholes, shut up now," yelled Vaughan. "You don't make my sister cry. Not here, not in this house."

Lip curled, Pat glared at Eric. Neither of them moving.

Vaughan took a deep breath, visibly reaching for calm. "I think it'd be best for now if both of you left."

A sobbing sound came from Nell and she turned her face away, obviously distraught. Funnily enough, the fury in Pat's eyes faded when he saw her in that state. But I don't think Eric noticed at all, cruel gaze and handsome face warped with anger.

"You know, Pat, I thought you were crazy sticking with the one woman all these years," said Eric, holding his face up. His smile was more of a sneer. "But now I understand. Fuck me, if Nell isn't the hottest piece of—"

With a roar, Vaughan suddenly launched himself at the man. Fists flew, sickening thuds. "You don't talk about her that way!"

Feet kicking, voices shouting, wood splintering as the coffee table exploded beneath the brawling men. Things moved impossibly fast. Someone was screaming. Nell, I think. It was all too much for my drunk dazed mind to comprehend.

Rosie grabbed my arm, hauling me as best she could over the back of the couch. I scrambled to keep up. To get to safety. The two men were like a hurricane, destroying everything in their path. Warm blood splattered my face, then I was up and over, falling onto the floor, crawling away to stand by Nell.

Both Joe and Pat entered the fray. I think Joe tried to tear the men apart, but Pat seemed to have lost his senses. While trying to land a punch on Eric, he clipped Joe's arm. Joe defended his brother. Of course he did. The couch was shoved back, sliding toward us. I put out my hands, pushing back before it made impact. Rosie grabbed Nell's arm, dragging her into the hallway.

Fuck. I'd never seen a fight before. Not like this.

I wanted to heave. And Vaughan was in there, caught up in that mess. The thought of him getting hurt made me want to do something extreme. God knows, he'd stood up for me more than once.

"Don't," said Andre, pulling me farther back before I could do something stupid. Probably unnecessary, my feet were stuck, frozen. The rest of my body was pretty much stuck too, deep in shock.

On the floor, the four men fought it out. I could only see blood and violence, Vaughan and Eric still struggling on the floor. In the hallway, Nell gave into the impulse to puke. The sound and smell made me swallow hard. I took deep breaths.

Time seemed to be messed up. Because it didn't feel like that long until I heard sirens fill the air.

"Thank god," I said, sagging against Andre.

His arm tightened around my waist, his head leaning against mine. It wasn't sexual in the least. We both needed the comfort.

"It'll be okay," he said. "They've all been friends for a long time. They'll work it out."

"You really believe that?"

He puffed out a breath. "No."

CHAPTER TWELVE

I stood at the foot of Vaughan's bed, slowly looking the half-naked man over. Moonlight shone through the open window, a summer breeze toying with the curtain. The things he did to me. All the emotions and effects of just being near him. Crazy. It was crazy.

"What?" he asked, voice husky.

"Just thinking." I smiled.

"About?"

"How hot you look lying on your bed with a bag of frozen beans stuffed down your jeans to ice your bruised balls."

One side of his cracked, puffy lips started moving upward. Then stopped. "Ow. Thanks."

"Is there anything else I can get you?"

"No." He patted the mattress beside him. "Sit with me awhile?"

"Sure." I sat by his side, trying not to move the mattress too much and aggravate his sore bits. Kind of hard considering the beating he'd taken.

"Can't believe Eric kneed me in the groin," he said, sounding wounded. "Even for him, that's low."

"You did attack him first."

"Mm." He sighed. "He had no business talking about Nell like that. I don't care what's gone down between them or how long I've been away. I'm still her brother. No way could I just stand by and let him say those sorts of things."

"I get that you needed to defend your sister."

He made a noise. God only knew what it meant.

"I thought it was nice of Officer Andy not to throw you all in jail."

Vaughan snorted. "He would have if Nell hadn't been here. Schmuck. Couldn't believe the way he was crawling up her ass."

"It's just as well she could talk him into walking away."

He watched me from his one good eye; the other was hidden beneath an ice pack. Shadows and lumps marred his beautiful face and one side of his ribs.

"I better let you get some sleep."

"You okay?" he asked.

I halted, searching for the right words. Thing was, there were none. "The fight scared me, Vaughan. Hell, it terrified me. You could have been seriously injured."

"Lydia," he said, then stopped. With various pained noises he moved himself over, making more room. "Lie down."

With nil grace, I did as asked, kicking off my shoes and lying down on the bed beside him. Head on the pillow, I immediately started to yawn. It had to be three, four in the morning at least. Any alcohol-induced happy buzz had worn off hours ago. Soon enough the sun would be rising. What a night.

"Hey." He hooked my pinkie with his, holding on tight. "Thanks for worrying about me."

"I was worried about all of you."

A pause. "That's not what you said."

"Yes, it was."

"No. You said, you could have been seriously injured. 'You' meaning me," he said, carefully turning his head to face me.

I just sniffed tiredly.

"You were worried about me."

"Whatever."

Shadows shifted across the ceiling, dark and mysterious. Outside, with the exception of the occasional horny bug sending out its booty call, silence reigned. Everyone was asleep. Or at least everyone in our little corner of the world.

"Is that why Andre had his arm around you," he asked out of nowhere. "Cause you were scared?"

I rose up on one elbow. "You and Eric were trying to kill each other and you still somehow managed to notice this?"

No answer.

Amazing. The man was simply amazing. I lay back down, resumed staring at the ceiling. My ribs felt a size too small; all the important organs in there were overexcited. I tried not to smile, but failed.

"You going to say something?" he asked eventually.

"You like me." The knowledge sank deep, soaking into my bones and settling. With it came a strange sort of calmness, a rightness, even though I should have been freaking right out about how transient we were. Sensibility dictated I keep him at arm's length. Sense wanted to stick its hand down his pants, bury its nose in his neck, and get something going. Now.

"Didn't we cover this already?" He gave my pinkie a squeeze.

"I don't know. Somehow it feels more real now. Or maybe I wasn't listening properly before." I grinned. "Or maybe I'm just having a moment."

"You're always having moments."

True. "Deal with it. If you hadn't gotten involved in the fight we could be getting biblical."

A long and loaded moan. "Do not talk to me about sex right now."

"I'm just saying . . ."

"Well, don't."

"Fine. I won't." I shut my eyes tight, took a great big breath then slowly let it out. Disappointment. It sucked. Things low in my belly leading to my loins were aware they'd been very badly treated.

Completely denied.

Christmas lay right beside me, but I couldn't touch my present for fear of hurting him further. I might just beat up Eric myself. Slap him around the head a few times with a handbag, something like that. It would be fitting.

Vaughan's hand slid over mine. Care of the calluses on his fingers from playing guitar, they weren't soft. The skin there was harder, jagged, even. But I didn't mind. He could touch me as much as he liked. Hell, mood I was in, I'd tape myself permanently to his side if I could get away with such a thing.

"Did you hear from the real estate agent?" I turned my hand over, palm side up. All the better to catch his fingers with mine and hold on.

"He's bringing through some people tomorrow. Guess the trashed sitting room isn't going to look so great." He swore softly.

"It's fine," I said. "Nell and Rosie and I cleaned up the worst of the mess. If they ask, he'll say you're a minimalist who doesn't believe in having much furniture or something. It'll be fine."

A sigh. "Yeah. Well, it'll have to be. Thanks for helping out."

"No problem." I gently lifted his hand to my lips and kissed it, careful to avoid the two cracked knuckles. "Can I ask a personal question?"

"Shoot." He didn't even hesitate.

"What's the deal with Eric and you? Why did he react so badly to you working at the bar in the first place?"

The groaning was back, but it soon turned into laughter. The sound was not a happy one. "Thought you'd have asked about that before now, actually. After that damn scene at the bar last night."

"I didn't want to pry."

Without a word he lifted my hand to his lips and kissed it. Oh, god. I was melting. All they'd find of me come morning was soppy goo on the bed and it was all his fault.

"I like you, Lydia."

"I like you too, Vaughan. Now give me the gossip."

His laughter turned to an altogether more acceptable sound. "Eric was in the band all during high school. Helped me put it together, actually. We were tight back then. His parents only live a street over, so we pretty much grew up together . . ."

"What happened?"

"Same things that's happening now. He fucked it up with the band. He was always screwing around, never taking the group seriously. All he had to do was learn how to hit the fucking drums in time, but was he able to do it?" He held my hand to his chest, heart pounding away against the back of my hand. It felt strong, good, like the man it lay within. "Not a chance. I warned him, if he didn't get his act together then he wasn't coming west with us after graduation. Guess he didn't believe me. Time came and I had to tell him he was out. He didn't take it well."

I sucked in a breath, blowing it out between pursed lips. "Hell. That must have sucked. Now I know why you were nervous about showing up to work at the Dive Bar."

"Yeah." He said no more.

We lay in silence, holding hands, ever so slowly dozing off to sleep. Despite my busy mind, exhaustion called to me loud and clear. Sheets and pillow smelling of Vaughan, the heat of his body right next to mine and a cool early morning summer breeze blowing in through the window. My own personal paradise. God, if anything I was overtired. The weight of my body seemed to have tripled, and yet, it felt light as a feather at the same time. Like I could feel myself sinking through the mattress and floating off into the ether, attached to the earth only by Vaughan's hand. I wanted to float there forever, having sweet dreams.

I wondered how Chris and Paul were doing, living it up in Hawaii. Interesting, the thought could almost drift through my brain without me wanting to go into a berserker rage and set fire to shit. Almost. The time Chris and I had spent together, the wedding that never was, all of it just kind of free-fell through my mind.

Beside me, Vaughan's bare chest rose and fell in perfect rhythm. All of his immaculate ink no more than a blur in the low light. The eye that I could see was closed, his poor battered face relaxed.

"I didn't love Chris like I should have," I whispered. "I think I was just lonely and all the attention . . . I don't know, it went to my head or something. But it wasn't real."

He didn't move. Nothing changed. The night went on.

I stared back up at his bedroom ceiling, my old friend. It made as good a witness to my confession as any. "In two and a half days I think I've honestly come to feel more for you than I ever felt for him. It's different, though. I thought I knew exactly how life would be with Chris. What we'd do, how we'd be together. He fit into this mold that I thought I wanted and understood, and you don't."

I rolled my eyes back, moaning at my own drama-itis. Nothing made sense. Everything perplexed me. Vaughan Hewson had my vagina on insta-dial if he could just figure it out. Pathetic, crazy, and all the rest. Hang my sad sore heart to dry and be done with it already. Gah.

"I guess what I'm trying to say is, I wouldn't give up a second with you for all the months of being lied to and manipulated by him, as insane as that sounds. That's all. The end."

There, it was out there, floating around in the universe. The truth as I knew it released.

God, it felt like some mammoth weight, some big cumbersome

bastard, had been lifted off me and thrown into the abyss. Down and down into the darkness.

Let the new day begin and all of yesterday's crap go. I was done with it. It hurt, it cost me, and I was done with it. I'd lived, I'd learned, et cetera.

Wisdom came at a bitch of a price. But I'd paid it and now I'd move on.

"Babe," said a voice in the darkness, grasping my hand.

"I thought you were asleep," I said, voice weirdly clogged. I guess throwing off your emotional crap into the depths of space took a toll on your nasal cavities. "Are you in pain? Do you need me to get you something?"

"No. Just stay with me."

"Okay."

Silence.

"Are you drunk?"

"No," I said, feeling myself inside and out. "No, I don't think so. I think it wore off a while back."

"'kay."

Silence.

"Lydia, the band breaking up, having to come back here . . ." His breathing in the darkness sounded so loud, profound, even. The silence broken and my secrets revealed. Man, it was so always the way with him. I couldn't hide if I tried.

"Yeah," I asked, urging him to go on.

"Meeting you makes it almost worthwhile."

Almost. But his pain, his dreams had taken a decade or more than mine to grow and die. Our situations weren't the same. That was the truth.

"Thank you," I said, holding on tight to his hand.

"Go to sleep, babe. We'll deal with it tomorrow."

"Okay."

CHAPTER THIRTEEN

Men were the weirdest.

We'd been scheduled to work from noon until nine the next day. As soon as we entered the Dive Bar, Vaughan oh so casually headed behind the bar, moseying up alongside Eric, who was chatting with his brother, Joe. It was ridiculous. Five rounds with Godzilla couldn't have made the three men any prettier. Busted lips, black eyes, grazed cheekbones, they had it all. Ninety-nine percent of their faces were colored black and blue.

The men all looked at each other . . . and nothing.

Absolutely nothing.

They did the manly chin-tip thing then got to work. If the fight had been between women, I'm pretty sure hostilities would have carried on for months. Which just goes to prove my point regarding women being the superior species, and having more commitment to things in general. We stick.

Today, the chalkboards hanging on the walls of the Dive Bar were all about tacos. The menu options were always based on whatever Nell happened to be in the mood to cook. Some staples were always on offer, such as steak, mac n cheese, sliders, and fries covered in every good thing you could imagine. Stuff like that. But outside of those, what might be available was a constant gastro-nomic mystery.

Got to admire a woman who respects Taco Tuesday, though.

Scrawled across the boards were shredded beef, chili lime chicken, spicy shrimp, and roasted sweet potato with black beans. Yum. I was getting high just off the smell. The Dive Bar was fast becoming my happy place.

I filled my tray with a combination of margaritas, a couple of Coronas, and a shot of Herradura tequila with a slice of lemon on the side.

"All good?" asked Vaughan.

"All good." I looked between him and Joe, smirking just a little. "How's fight club going, boys?"

"Can't talk about it," mumbled Joe.

I laughed and lifted my tray, heading over to serve the order to a group of older couples. They were on their second round of drinks—smiling, relaxing, and just plain having a nice time.

"You were right about the shrimp," said one woman. "It's got a definite kick to it. But the chicken is amazing."

"It's great, isn't it?" I handed her one of the Coronas while her partner got busy sucking down the margarita. "I wish I could cook half as well as Nell. I can't pour milk on cereal without burning it."

"Ha! You and me both."

I grinned. "Can I get you anything else?"

They responded with a chorus of no's and not yet's.

With a nod, I wandered off to check on my other tables. The lunch rush had dwindled and we'd moved into the hang-out-and-drink phase of the afternoon. At one table, a dude read a book with coffee and cake in front of him, at another, a group of girls around my age gossiped and giggled over many glasses of wine.

"Later." Joe passed me by, hands in his pockets, heading out into the street. He'd finished for the day.

"Bye."

Despite the revelry-turned-chaos of last night, today was turning out to be a good day.

. . . And I spoke too soon. "Hi, Betsy."

"Liddy." The Delaneys' real estate receptionist sneered more than smiled, looking me over with not even a vague sense of delight. "My, how the mighty have fallen."

"Mm. I don't see it that way."

"Good for you." Oh, the lack of sincerity in her words.

The woman was around my age. Much more country club than I'd ever be. When I used to work with her, it had crossed my mind a time or two that she and Chris would have made an excellent couple. I could just imagine them posing in matching Christmas sweaters and shit, wearing white linen. They fit. Luckily for Betsy, she'd been in town a hell of a lot longer than me and must have been in on the whole "Chris is gay" secret. Though I doubt it would have stopped her from nabbing the name or the money, if he'd been interested. Maybe admin level had been too low for Chris to go.

Who knew? And, turns out, I didn't care. Yep, my level of fucks given had definitely dropped. Go, me.

"What are you grinning about?" the woman snapped, probably dismayed by my lack of butthurt.

"What can I do for you, Betsy?"

She sniffed, head jumping up so far it's a wonder she didn't get whiplash. "Mr. Delaney asked me to deliver this to you."

A large envelope was shoved at me. "Thank you."

"Don't mention it. Anything that gets you gone. Well, I have to go. Some of us have actual important work to do." Another round of sniffs and doing her best to look down at me. Whatever made her happy. "I hear you're living with the neighbor, some failed musician wannabe."

"Did you?"

"A bit low, even for you."

For the life of me, I couldn't recall what I'd done to piss the girl off so badly during my four months at the agency. Our interactions had always been polite, friendly, even. I didn't need to be universally loved. But if I was outright hated by someone, I should know why.

Maybe she was just Team Delaney through and through. Good for her.

"Is that him?" she asked, pointing toward the bar.

"Yep." He'd tamed the usual mess of his golden-red hair into an old fashioned combed down style. Which he rocked. And the width of his shoulders stretched his plain black T-shirt just a little. God, his poor face, all gray, black, and blue. At least he hadn't been too badly hurt. Something about the tattoo on his neck worked for me. I wanted to kiss it and lick it and do all sorts of things. Things requiring an X rating.

"I can't tell you how great he is," I said, not bothering to face her. My view was far too good. "Vaughan is . . . he's awesome. And it's not just the hot body and his whole tattooed rocker bad-ass vibe. Because let me tell you, most of the time the man is a total pussycat. The sweetest guy I've ever met. Loyal and supportive, open-minded, totally trustworthy. We can talk for hours about nothing, just hanging out together. He has his cranky moments, but hey . . . don't we all? Not to mention he's sexy as hell. I'm too much of a lady to discuss what he's got in his pants, or how he can make me feel without even bringing that into play. But when the guy can light you up with just a kiss, not even any tongue, you know you're on to a *good* thing. Know what I mean, B?"

Betsy stared at me, mouth open. I'm reasonably certain a bug flew in. Oops.

"Anyway," I said. "I better get back to work. Oh, did I mention how much I'm enjoying waitressing again? It's different when your friends are involved and you're actually invested in the business emotionally. When you truly believe in the quality of the product, you know? Everyone's working together to achieve the same thing. None of the be-the-shark bullshit, constantly trying to outdo everyone else and get the best sales figures. Plus, you should see the leftovers I get to take home. Nell truly is the most talented chef."

And still, she stared.

"Anyhoo. Didn't you say you had to go?"

"You're ridiculous. A complete joke," she spat, turning on her heel and stalking out. Goodness. And her heels were a good four inches. That was one impressive skill.

"Buh-bye!"

"You okay?" a deep familiar voice asked me from behind.

"Yep. Want to go out with me tonight after work, Vaughan?"

First, a gentle tug on my ponytail, then his lips brushed my ear. Christ, I liked that. Goose bumps ran riot down my spine. It was all I could do not to give a happy-girl moan.

"You asking me out on a date, Lydia?"

"Yes," I said. "I am."

"Babe, I'd love to." His hand rose to the back of my neck, stroking, drawing me closer. Hot damn, did he have the moves. The man turned my mind to mush.

"Something you need to know," he said. "Before tonight."

"What's that?"

"I put out on the first date," he told me with a perfectly straight face. "That okay with you?"

"Oh, I'm counting on it." My face might have been aflame, but then so was the rest of my body. "I mean . . . it would have been so awkward if you expected me to respect you for your mind or something. Yikes, how embarrassing. Between you and me, I'm really only interested in getting into your pants."

The corner of his mouth twitched.

"I'm sure you're a nice guy and all but, priorities, you know?"

"I know." The man's smile would have made a nun think twice. I never stood a chance. The way it lit his eyes seemed more magic than biology. "All right then."

"We're all set?"

"We are indeed."

No chance of containing my grin. "Until tonight, Mr. Hewson."

I was not standing idly by eyeing Vaughan's ass as he strolled back to the bar when the stranger approached. Deep inside my brain all sorts of things were happening. Work-related things. I swear. Sort of.

"Excuse me?" A neatly dressed young Asian man with a hipster mustache flashed me a friendly smile. "Miss Green?"

All happy thoughts fled as I snapped to attention.

"Lydia Green?"

"Who's asking?" I replied with my best fake smile.

He pulled a business card out of his shirt pocket, presenting it to me with a flourish. "Brett Chen. I'm a freelance reporter. I was wondering if we could talk about your recent split with Christopher Delaney and the wedding you walked out on last weekend."

"No, thank you." I held his card back out to him.

He ignored it. "As you'd be aware, the Delaneys and their real estate agency are well known throughout the area and have strong connections to some key political figures. But I believe that a sensational story such as yours could have a much wider reach. A national, if not an international one."

"Wow. The opportunity to have strangers all over the world sticking their nose into my business." I waved the business card beneath his nose, growing impatient. "No."

"The money involved could be big, Lydia."

"No. Again."

Frustration furrowed his brow. "As I told Mr. Ray Delaney, I'll be going ahead with my piece with, or without, your cooperation. But I'd very much prefer it was with."

I crumpled up the jerk's business card and about-faced, heading for the counter.

"The police report states you hit Mr. Christopher Delaney. Would you like to comment on that?"

"Nope." Behind the counter was a bin, and in went the journalist's card. I huffed out a breath, avoiding his eyes. "Please leave. I'm not going to answer your questions."

"Multiple sources have confirmed that Chris Delaney is currently in Hawaii with his best man, Paul Mueller." Chen faced me across the counter, going nowhere, apparently. Dammit. "There's been much speculation that Mr. Mueller and Mr. Delaney are in fact secret lovers. Is that the reason you refused to go through with the wedding?"

"No comment."

"Why are you no longer employed by the Delaney Real—"

"No." I held onto the edge of the counter, fingernails pressing into the old wood. On the other side of the room, Vaughan served a customer. I couldn't hear anyone in the kitchen behind me. But I also didn't want to start crying for help, causing problems for Nell. This guy had to give up and go away eventually without me getting vocal and disturbing our customers. He had to.

"Lydia, is it true there was a video of—"

"No."

"What the fuck is this?" Eric stood beside the reporter, his bruised face lined with annoyance. "Who are you? No, don't answer that. I don't want to know. Just get out."

Mr. Chen's mouth worked, his eyes suddenly anxious. "But if I could just have a minute with Miss Green."

"Miss Green clearly wants nothing to do with whatever you're selling. Get out."

"But—"

"Management reserves the right to refuse anyone entrance to the business premises. From this moment on, that's you," said Eric, going toe to toe with the man. And winning. "You're harassing a member of my staff. Leave now or I'll be forced to remove you."

"Call me, Lydia," he said, slapping down another business card. "Opportunities like this only come along once in a lifetime."

"Get out," growled Eric.

Flashing a final covetous look my way, the reporter did as told.

Damn. Chin tucked in, I tried to calm both my breathing and my temper. What a bastard. A story bringing attention to the whole damn disaster was the last damn thing I needed.

"You okay?" asked Eric, rounding the counter.

"Yeah. Thanks. I could have gotten rid of him myself, I just didn't want to cause a scene."

A nod.

"What was that?" Vaughan stormed up to us. "Babe, who was that guy?"

"Some reporter." I swiped the second card he'd left, letting it join the first in the bin. "Doesn't matter. Eric got rid of him. Thank you again for that."

"Thanks, man," said Vaughan.

Eric nodded, heading back into the kitchen.

"Hey." His finger curled beneath my chin, raising it gently. "Okay?"

"Just angry." I crossed my arms, pressing my lips tightly together. "*Opportunities like this only come along once in a lifetime.* Like I should be grateful that the guy I was about to marry was a closet homosexual and using me. It was so much damn fun finding out the first time, let's go through it again! Asshole."

He gave me a small smile.

I groaned. "Sometimes it feels like I'm never going to put it behind me."

"It only happened on Saturday." He trailed his fingers over my cheek, smiling more broadly. "Today is Tuesday. This shit is going to be behind you, it's just going to take a little more time. Three—four days . . . is not so long."

I destroyed him with my very best death glare. "Stop being reasonable, Vaughan. Who even asked you?"

He sighed, then came around the counter and planted a kiss on top of my head. I leaned into him, taking much more comfort in his presence than I should have. Soon he wouldn't be there. I needed to learn how to stand on my own. Deal with my own crap. But, gah. Soon was soon enough to stand alone.

"Forget about that asshole," he said, rubbing my back, kissing my cheek. "Think about what makes you happy, like our date tonight or something."

"Okay."

"I better get back over there."

"Thanks." My hand somehow managed to curve over his ass as he turned away. There may have been a subtle squeeze involved. Like a girl could always be held responsible for what her fingers did. Please.

"I felt that."

"I don't know what you're talking about."

"Later," was all he said.

Later.

I couldn't wait.

CHAPTER FOURTEEN

Later turned out to be closer to midnight than nine p.m.

Rosie's baby caught a bad cold so she couldn't come to work. Nell also wasn't feeling fantastic and had to be sent home, leaving Boyd to deal with the kitchen alone. On top of this, several large parties turned up without a booking, and we were packed.

Eric took turns waiting tables and helping Vaughan keep up with orders behind the bar. By the time we finished cleaning, I was dead on my feet. But fighting it for all I was worth.

"How you doing?" Vaughan asked, revving the Mustang's engine. "Still want to go on that date?"

"More than anything."

"What are you thinking?" He drove off slowly into the dark. We were pretty much the only vehicle in sight.

"I want the full Vaughan Hewson Coeur d'Alene seduction experience, please."

"That so?" Curiosity lit his eyes.

"Yep." I linked my fingers, stretching my arms out low in front of me. Every muscle in my shoulders and back were in a state of deep crankiness. I couldn't really blame them. "Just like your sister teased you the other day. I want to be taken to some secluded spot by the lake, and for you to play me emo tunes."

He laughed.

"What happens after that?"

"Ah." He rubbed his chin. "I'd dare you to go skinny-dipping."

"Makes sense."

"After that, we'd screw on the beach. Sometimes that part was rushed. Depends how bad the bugs were."

"Ouch"

"You're telling me." He gave me a quick grin before turning his gaze back to the road. "Hard to really enjoy things when mosquitos are making a meal of your ass."

I snorted. "I can see how that would be difficult."

"Hmm. Then I usually rushed to get the girl home before curfew. Sometimes helped her climb in a window or whatever."

"Romantic."

"I always thought so," he mused, face cast in shadows. "Never got any complaints."

The world seemed empty, peaceful. There continued to be next to no traffic. We pulled into the bungalow's driveway and Vaughan turned off the engine. For a moment we just sat in silence.

"Thing is, I'm not eighteen anymore." He turned his head, watching me in the near dark as I watched him. "I want better for you. I can do better."

Without another word, he opened his door, climbed out. I sat, watching him walk around to open the passenger side door, and offer me a hand. Guess chivalry wasn't dead.

"Thank you." I climbed out, taking my bag with me. The large envelope Betsy had delivered still hadn't been opened. Some jobs needed time and space. I got the distinct feeling reading over the settlement from the Delaneys would be one of those.

Instead of letting go of my hand, he led me across the lawn and up the front steps. To think only three days ago I'd stood here, listening to Samantha call me every name under the sun while Ray talked to his lawyer on the phone. Amazing how fast things could change. The last few days Vaughan had been busy, cutting the grass and beating the overgrown front garden back into submission, getting the place ready for sale. Under the moonlight everything appeared even lovelier, every edge softened, the old house was a thing of magic. A lover's delight.

Keys jangled, then the front door opened and inside we went. He didn't turn on any lights. The door closed and he pressed me back against it, the smile at his lips only just visible. "I know you asked me on a date, but do you mind if maybe I take over?"

"Depends. What did you have in mind?"

"You got to know?"

"Yes," I said.

"Control freak." He laughed softly, relieving me of my handbag and lowering it onto the floor.

"I gave up control to Chris. It didn't work out so well."

"I know." He exhaled hard. "But I am not that piece of shit. I'd never deliberately do anything to hurt or humiliate you."

My fingers flexed, tightening my hold on both his hands. A dead giveaway for the rush of emotions surging through me, from the intensity of his words, the sincerity in his eyes. Fear, lust, and everything in between filled me to flooding.

I tried to calm myself. Casual sex with a friend, nothing more, nothing less. Just scratching an itch.

Yeah. Right.

"You okay?" he asked.

"Yes. I just . . ." I licked my lips. "I'm fine."

He said nothing.

It'd been months since Chris had attempted any real touching and it had not ended well for anyone. Sex before him had been one long-term boyfriend in college (who got a job in Greenland after graduation) followed by many hookups. Some yay, some blah.

Much the same as everyone else, I'd imagine. This was just one more. No big loved-up joining of private parts requiring poetry, mood lighting, and classical music. Declarations of commitment not required. Fun sex. The end.

"We can always do this another time," he said, drawing back a little. "That was a long day, I—"

"No," I blurted out, not sounding desperate at all.

"No? You sure?"

I released his hands, grabbing hold of his T-shirt, holding on as if my life was at stake. Or at least my sex life. He was mine, for the moment, and I wasn't giving that up.

"Babe?"

"I want you."

"I want you too," he said, groaning as I pressed myself against him. He felt so good, strong and sturdy. Also, the man smelled fucking great.

If only I could imprint myself in his skin, hide away in his arms for a good long time until things felt safe again. Instead, I flattened my breasts against his chest, wrapped my arms around his neck, getting as close as I could. Stubble gently scratched my face and fingers dug into my ass, holding me closer, encouraging me further.

"I really, really want you," I said. "Not later. Now."

"Fuck. Lydia."

I knew exactly what he meant.

"Your skin's so pale." His voice made gravel sound smooth. "How do you feel about biting?"

I blinked in surprise, pulling back so I could see his face. "Biting?"

"Yeah."

"Um. I've never tried it."

"Just little bites. Nips. Nothing to hurt you, I swear. I'll behave."

"Th-that's what you like?"

"I like you." He leaned closer, almost bringing our mouths together. "Question is, do you like me?"

"You're my favorite person on the planet," I told him honestly.

"I am?"

"Yes." Dazed, I stared up at him, his eyes and mouth both so enthralling. My heart pounded and the air grew thin, every inch of my skin electric. I was more than alive and beyond awake, despite the overly long day. Desire is such a disease. It'd completely taken me over.

"Thanks, babe. I like you a hell of a lot too."

"Not just my breasts?"

He chuckled, low-down and dirty. Warmth swelled to alarming levels in my chest. My heart needed to calm the heck down. My loins felt about ready to burst into spontaneous combustion. The man had started a fire in my panties only he could put out.

To think, if I'd married Chris, I'd never have had this again. Seeing my needs reflected in someone else, being so in tune with another human being. Amazing. I might have spent my whole life having average sex with someone who wasn't really into it, and all for the sake of security. To have a home.

"What are you thinking about?" Vaughan's hands slid over my arms, untangling me from him, easing me back.

"Nothing."

"Try again."

I groaned, my face blazing to life. "I'm just grateful to have this time with you. I thought my life was ruined, that I'd made all these bad choices and messed everything up. But being here with you, things feel a long way from bad."

"Good." He kissed my forehead, smiled. "Let me tell you a story."

"Now?"

"Yeah. Right now." Then he went down on one knee, picked up one of my feet and eased off the very sensible black flat I'd been wearing all day. Excellent, my foot odor would knock him dead. Very sexy.

"When I was fifteen I started seeing this girl who was a couple of years older than me, a senior." He calmly set my shoe aside and reached for my other foot, baring it as well. Hair slid forward, hiding his face, and he pushed it back as he stood. "She was a cheerleader. Had a hell of a lot more experience than me, which wasn't hard, 'cause I had none."

"She was your first?"

"She was." Fingers worked at the button on my pants, the zipper. The cooler night air hit my exposed skin, raising gooseflesh. Thought probably, it was just him. Hot hands slid over my hips as he eased the material down. Down over my thighs, down until they lay on the floor and I stood there in a not so sensible pair of black lace panties.

You never could tell when swanky underwear would be needed. Best to be prepared.

I stepped out of my work pants, pushing them aside with a toe. "And?"

"And I had issues meeting her expectations." He stroked my neck, running his fingers around the neckline of my work T-shirt. "Kept getting overexcited and coming too soon."

I grinned.

"She liked me, but ah . . . she was starting to get a bit angry about it." One finger wandered, drawing a line down the middle of my tee, pressing in between the divide between my breasts. Of course he had my nipples' undivided attention. Hell, he had my whole body's attention, apart from my brain. It was swimming with happy hormones, drowning in them.

"Huh," I said, because I'm an intellectual genius like that.

"Not that I wouldn't finish her off. She showed me how to give her a hand-job, told me how to use my mouth." He gripped the hem of my T-shirt, the backs of his fingers sliding over my stomach, toying with me.

My insides tumbled and twisted. My panties were wet.

"Now that I think about it, she was seriously bossy. But I learned *a lot*."

Up went my T-shirt, exposing my matching lace bra. Then away it went, flying off into the darkness.

"Christ," he said.

All of a sudden light flooded the room, blinding me. Bright patterns danced before my eyes, making me blink like crazy.

"Sorry. I needed to see." Vaughan's big hands slid up over my rib cage, stopping beneath the band of my bra. His eyes were as big as . . . well, my boobs.

"Okay. You've seen now." I fumbled my hand along the wall, trying to feel out the light switch. Darkness was good. Why, it hid all manner of things. The bulge of my tummy and the dimples on my thunder thighs. Darkness and me were great friends.

"It's staying on."

"But atmosphere!"

"Babe." He caught my hand, kissing my knuckles. "It's staying on."

"Talk about bossy," I grumbled.

He leveled me with a look. Or he tried to.

"It's just that I would be more comfortable—"

Before I could even finish the thought, he whipped off his shirt, dropping it on the floor. Next his feet got busy toeing off his shoes while he tore into the buttons on his jeans. With a hand pressed against the wall for balance, his socks were gone, and then so were his pants. Hey presto, the man stood before me in no more than a snug pair of blue boxer briefs, which happily left little to the imagination. He was so pretty. When it came to Vaughan Hewson, words were insufficient. I could spend all day trying to describe every curve and plane, each subtly delineated muscle. His long lean body was pure poetry. Poetry or porn, maybe both. My brain and vagina were still at war over that one.

"That was fast," I said.

"Now we're both almost naked. Feel better?"

I shrugged, my greedy gaze roving over his body. Me in the light made for not much happy. But him in the light made for fucking awesome. Odd how every bit of moisture evaporated from my open mouth. Though to be fair, the wetness was desperately required elsewhere.

"Lydia," he remonstrated, going so far as to actually tut at me like I was some kid.

"What?"

Again, he dropped to his knees. His head almost, but not quite, level with my breasts. Lips an unimpressed line, he stared at my stomach. Fair enough. My belly didn't do much for me either. Not that I'd put a ban on cheesecake and start jogging. Let's not go crazy.

Instead of expressing concern regarding my Body Mass Index or some such, he pried away the hands covering my stomach, holding them captive with his own.

"Don't do that," he said quietly. "You're beautiful. Every bit of you."

Oh.

Lips placed tender kisses across my middle, his tongue sneaking out and flicking over my belly button. I gasped, sucking myself in as much as I could.

"It tickled," I said when he gave me yet another look.

A brief smile.

"Are you going to finish your story?" Anything to distract him from my body issues was a good thing.

"Yes." He stood once again, rubbing his fingers over the palms of his hands. "Where was I?"

"Her, starting to get a little angry. Me, breasts."

"'Course." With a hand beneath each, he took their weight, lifting them gently. "Fuck."

I had nothing.

"Think I should just follow you around all day, holding your tits like this." He nuzzled my neck, the side of my face. And all the while his hands worked, massaging lightly, thumbs playing with my nipples. "You'll never need a bra again."

"That should work well." It grew harder to breathe for some reason. Like my lungs were indisposed or out of order.

"I think so." He groaned, pressing his cock into my hip. Big, hard, definitely turned on. And lord, so was I. At the feel of him, everything low in me went nuclear. Red lights flashing, sirens wailing. The way he was touching me, pressing himself against me. The wonder in his eyes and admiration in his words. It was all too much, but I never wanted it to end. My whole body burned bright. I could light up a city. Nothing else existed beyond him and me.

"Can't stop touching you," he said.

"Please don't."

"Why the hell haven't we been doing this before now," he whispered in my ear, breathing heavy.

"Because we're idiots?"

A pained laugh. Then he nipped at my neck, the sting a startling thing. But his lips sucking, tongue licking the slight pain away was so sweet. I went up on my toes, trying to escape his eager mouth, yet keeping a death grip on his arms in case he tried to go anywhere.

Fuck me. Confusion ruled my mind. There were too many sensations, both sharp and sweet. Firm lips and a wicked tongue. The licks grew longer, slower, as he dragged his tongue up my neck.

Soft soothing kisses lined my jaw, the edge of my lips.

"See? Not so bad," he mumbled, rubbing his nose against my cheek. God, I wish he'd get closer. Inside me would be good.

"No. Not so bad."

"Mm."

I eased my feet back flat upon the floor, wound my arms around his neck. His hair was better than mine. Soft and silken. Bet the man only washed it with soap or something too. How unfair.

"Do you have a condom on you?" I said, threading my fingers through his hair, stroking the back of his neck, touching as much of the man as I could.

"Went and got a box on my break. A big one. I stocked up just for you."

"Excellent."

His hands slipped behind my back, fiddling with something. Then the weight of my breasts shifted, the straps of my bra loosening. "So . . . my story."

"Yep?" How he expected me to concentrate on anything, I have no idea.

"I kept coming too soon and it was pissing her off."

"Understandable," I said. "Can I just quickly say how much I'm enjoying hearing about one of your ex-girlfriends right now?"

This time he nipped where my neck and shoulder joined, biting down harder, holding on longer. When he eased the wound he spread his lips wide, sucking on a larger area, drawing hard. Hands spread across my back, he held me against him, leaving no space between us. Blood rushed through me, loud behind my ears. My nerves fired, half in heaven, half in hell. All of me confused as shit.

The man was part vampire and I had the worst feeling I liked it. A lot.

"That one's going to leave a mark," he reported matter-of-factly.

As if he weren't affected. Like his cock wasn't prodding my stomach, hard as stone.

A smartass reply would have to wait, however. I was too busy just breathing.

Vaughan eased back, searching my face for something. When he didn't find whatever it was, he slid a hand down between my legs. He pulled aside my panties and slid a finger carefully into me. Though there was no real need to be careful. Lubricant factories would have been envious. The state of my underwear was a damn disgrace.

"Hot and wet," he said.

I frowned. "Was I not supposed to be?"

"Just checking." Once, twice, he kissed my lips. Quick, inconsequential things. Nothing like what I hungered for. The devouring I was after. He made a happy humming sound, keeping his finger in place. "I got worried when you didn't say anything. Had to know if it was working for you."

"That makes sense."

"Hmm." His thumb slid up into my panties, sliding dangerously near my overexcited clit. I gasped, tightening my hold on his hair. The man winced, but didn't complain. And let the record show, he was breathing every bit as heavily as I was.

"Should we have a safety word or something?" I asked, trying to thinks straight, to be practical.

"Sure. If it makes you feel better."

"Okay." The finger inside of me swirled around, pumping in and out, doing everything good. Every muscle down there contracted in glee. I could feel my pulse hammering between my legs. "Oh god, that feels good."

"What's your safety word, babe?"

"Keep doing that or I'll kill you?"

"What this?" The clever finger teased my entrance, spreading the wetness around.

"More."

"Soon," he said, slowly withdrawing his hand from my panties. Dammit.

I gave a sad, pitiful kind of moan. "No. Now."

"So, she tells me I have to start thinking of something else when we're having sex." He pressed his thigh between my legs, keeping a constant pressure against my nether regions. Those being all of my fun girl bits, currently in desperate need of attention. It was impossible not to push back hard, even though it eased the ache only a little. His story eased nothing at all, and was quite frankly a distraction.

"I have to keep my mind busy while we're doing it, she says." He held my hip with one hand, sliding the other between my breast and bra cup, easing the material down. "She asks me what I like. I say, I really like Fender guitars."

"Mm-hmm," I said, trying to stay polite.

"So I have to think about Fender guitars."

"Fender guitars. Right."

"Are you paying attention?" he asked. His thumb rubbed over my hard nipple, making everything that much worse (better). Hell, the way he looked at me with such hunger. I didn't know how much more I could take. The heat of his skin and the scent of his sweat, everything about the man made me insane. Insatiable. Whatever.

"What? Oh, yeah. Mostly." I rubbed myself against his leg, beyond caring what I looked like. Only getting off mattered. "And?"

"And." His hand grabbed hold of my ass, pulling me more firmly against his leg, grinding me against him. Meanwhile his other hand was performing awesome feats with my left breast, rolling and lightly pinching the nipple. Fingers grabbing hold of me a smidgeon harder than necessary. It was strange. With him, I liked that edge.

"Damn, you're wet. The smell of you is killing me. I could eat you fucking whole."

"In me now. Oral later."

"Later," he agreed. "We need to move this to the bedroom."

"No time."

"Shit." He focused on my lips, alternating nips with kisses. But his hands kept doing good things too. Wonderful, amazing things. And seriously, enough was enough. Time to move onto the actual penis-in-vagina part of the show.

I shoved my hand into his boxer briefs, sliding the palm of my hand over his dick. Soft, smooth skin over the most perfect hardness. It was official. My hand was in heaven. Seriously, who'd have thought salvation lay hidden in Vaughan's pants? Not me.

I wrapped my fingers around him, stroking reverently.

With a groan, his head fell forward, resting against mine. Precum dampened my fingers, encouraging my hold, increasing my rhythm.

"Do not make me fuck you against this door, Lydia."

Everything inside me squeezed tight. "God, that sounds good. Let's do that."

"Shit."

I slid my free hand into the back of his hair, pulling his mouth down to mine. The time had come to take what I wanted. Everything I wanted. And hell yeah, I was all over that.

With a growl, he attacked my mouth, kissing me ferociously. We each used our lips, teeth, and tongues. Desperate to get into each other any way we could. Wars had been less messy. His tongue tangled with mine, giving me a taste of him. But it wasn't enough. It could never be enough.

Hips working, he fucked my fist. His cock growing harder and thicker. Much more of this and I'd come on his leg, he'd come on my hand. What an awesome idea. The thought alone nearly got me there.

So close.

Then in an almighty rush he pushed back, out of my grip, away from my mouth. Slightly dangerous, though I guess the man knew what he was doing. Maybe. Without his thigh propping me up, my ass almost hit the floor. My back started sliding down the door, knees wobbling. It took a while for me to stand back up.

"Vaughan?"

Hand wrapped tight around his cock he stood, hanging his head. "Wait."

Bra straps were sliding down my arms, the undergarment slowly falling off. I helped it along, well past caring about the whole body image thing. "But—"

"One sec." He grabbed his jeans, rifling through the pockets. Out came a condom packet and he tore into it like a man possessed.

Yes. YES.

I shoved down my panties as he did likewise to his boxer briefs. It could have been a race judging by the determined set of his mouth, the fierce look in his eyes. With movements swift and sure, he donned the condom. Then he came at me. For a moment, I almost felt fear. Sweet and Fun Vaughan had long left the building. This man was someone else completely. I tried to back up but there was nowhere to go.

Our bodies collided, hitting the door. Hands grasped my face, maneuvering my mouth, holding it in position for a soul-searing kiss. Then he gripped my thighs, urging me up, taking my weight and wrapping my legs around him. It all happened so quickly. With one hand to my ass, he reached down between us with the other, moving his cock into position. The blunt head immediately started pushing in, parting my flesh, becoming one with me. All I could do was hold tight to his neck and take him.

Slowly but surely, he filled me. Only when his hips were flat against me and we were skin to skin did he pause. His lips brushed over my cheek, placing open-mouthed kisses along my jaw.

"Okay?" he asked, his body shaking with the effort to hold back, to wait for my reply.

In answer I turned my head, meeting his mouth with my own, kissing him stupid. And so it began. I can't say I know exactly what it feels like to be nailed to a door. But the way Vaughan did it made for one hell of an experience.

He pulled back before driving deep into me, thrusting hard and sure from the beginning. There was no going easy. No gentle buildup. We were both too far gone for such things. Our skin slapped hard together, his balls tapping my ass. The thick length of him plunged into me time and again. With our teeth knocking together, we had to stop kissing before someone got hurt. Sweat slicked our skins and the sounds of our panting filled the room.

In all honesty, we were kind of feral. Animalistic. Definitely dirty.

Fingers dug deep into my ass cheeks as he angled us right. So his pelvis kept making contact with my clit. Again and again, he hit my sweet spot, pushing me closer to the edge, sending me out of my mind. Electricity raced through me, blood rushing, every nerve singing. I'd never been so strung out, everything tensed from top to toe, desperately in need of release. The strength of him holding me, the way his muscles stood out in stark relief. The scent of sex and sweat. It was all good and right. Even the occasional edge of pain. Vaughan pounded me into the door, stretching me, filling me beyond what I thought I could take.

Then his fingers tightened, gripping my butt cheeks bruisingly hard. Somehow, he changed what he was doing slightly. The angle or the manner of god only knows. But his hips smacked into me as he thrust hard, grinding his pelvis against my clit. Pressure built to the breaking point at the base of my spine, every muscle in me contracting. Once, twice, three times he did this and then my world turned to white.

Stars. Fireworks. Every part of me convulsing like I was shaking apart, exploding. Soon, there'd be nothing of me left. And still, he held me tight. My spine hit the door, making it rattle, its hinges squeaking. His body moving in mine, our body parts entangled to the point I didn't think we'd ever part.

Until he made this noise, a guttural yell. Twice more he filled me. Face buried in my neck, he came.

CHAPTER FIFTEEN

"Hope you're happy with yourself," grumped Vaughan, lying on his back, staring at the bedroom ceiling.

I hid my grin against his side, breathing him in. Turns out, the man smelled even better the morning after hot sex. I wanted to lick him from top to toe, then come back for more. Instead I yawned, cautiously stretching. Certain things hurt in the very best way. After months and months of neglect, joy had finally come my vagina's way. "I honestly don't think I could be happier."

A grunt.

"Thank you for all the effort. I really appreciated it."

"You went straight to sleep."

"I know," I said. "But it'd been a very long day and I'd just come hard enough to cause myself actual neurological damage."

Another grunt.

"Now that I think about it, it was probably closer to a coma than sleep."

"Babe, you're not funny." He slipped an arm around me despite his lack of amusement, fingers stroking the side of my breast. Of course. Such a tit man. "It was supposed to be romantic."

"It was."

He raised his weary head. "Lydia, you've got bruises down your back from me banging you so hard against the front door. I might not have a lot of experience in this area, but I'm pretty fucking sure that's not romance."

This from Mr. Bitey himself. The dude was serious.

Stripes of sunlight shone through the gaps in the curtains. Just enough to illuminate the unlit candles scattered around the room, the vases overflowing with wildflowers. An unopened bottle of champagne sat in a bucket of long since melted ice. I'm certain the fresh sheets were Egyptian cotton. I wanted to roll around on them with Vaughan until the world went *boom*. What a perfect way to make my exit.

I wiggled closer, holding on tight. Acting like a limpet sometimes is soothing, don't question it. "I do appreciate you going to all this trouble. Thank you."

With a sigh, he laid his head back against the pillow. "I'm going to owe Joe for years for doing all this while we were at work."

"You certainly went all out. The room looks amazing."

"Yeah." His frowny face turned sheepish. "Actually, I just gave him twenty and asked him to grab a bunch of flowers and a couple of candles. I had no idea he'd do all this."

"Huh. Who'd have thought Joe would have the soul of a romantic."

All the flowers and the clusters of candles, the bubbly on ice and awesome sheets. Amazing. The big blond bear of a bartender knew how to woo.

He patted me on the arm. "Got to use the bathroom."

I set him free and slowly sat up, holding the sheet to my chest. A fine position for watching all of the goodness that was Vaughan Hewson rise from the bed. The pale skin and ink work on his back, his broad shoulders and firm ass. All so good. He shoved a hand through his shaggy golden-red hair and yawned long and loud, wandering out into the hallway in all his naked glory. "I should get a haircut."

"No," I commanded, a bit too forcefully considering the temporary nature of our relationship. "Get one when I'm gone."

He laughed and went to heed the call of nature. I needed to do some of that and teeth brushing too. Also, my hair felt remarkably similar to hell. I should probably fix it sometime. Funny, with Chris I'd been all over my presentation. Constantly checking my hair and makeup to the point of OCD. Not just at work, as per the usual, but all the time. Yet here I sat a thoroughly rumpled mess and quite relaxed about the whole thing. Strange how easily the woman I'd been with Chris had dropped away. I could kiss Paul for sending the video and stopping me from making the biggest mistake of my life. Kiss him and hit him too. The rage hadn't completely abated.

"Hey." Vaughan sat at the end of the bed, gently pulling at the sheet.

I held it to my chest, keeping things covered. "Hey."

"You're frowning."

"I was just thinking about Chris. How badly I let him mess with my head."

He nodded, giving the sheet another surreptitious tug.

I held on tighter. "You know, it wasn't just him. It was their whole world. Everything was image, all the time. The right hair, the right clothes, the right labels. And I let myself get sucked into that. I bought into it."

"You were looking for happiness, Lydia. How do you know whether something works unless you give it a try?"

"Maybe."

"I'm looking for happiness." He pulled at the sheet.

I clutched it against my chest. "Are you?"

"Oh, yeah." The sexy bastard gave me a slow smile. "No work today. We're free to do what we want."

Instantly, my sex fired up, knowing exactly how and what it wanted. But Practical Lydia got to my mouth first, the cow. Some habits are hard to break. "I thought you said you were going to fix the kitchen door and do some more work on the Mustang, start on the back garden. And I should really go over the paperwork from Ray and look for a car."

Brows drawn down, he gave me a disappointed look.

"Maybe?"

"Babe." Vaughan shook his head, pulling a little harder on the sheet. "Those things are work. They won't make us happy."

"No?"

"No. But fucking will."

"True. Okay then." I grinned.

The crazy man launched himself at me. My back hit the mattress and I was covered, the long length of his body suspended over mine. Luckily, he'd caught himself before impact. We both had enough bruises. Skin is our largest organ and he played with mine like a maestro. While I laughed like a lunatic, squirming beneath him, he nuzzled my neck, stubble tickling every damn sensitive spot. The heat of his body, the feel of his hair brushing against me, all of it fed the fire building between us. Slowly, he worked his way down to my breasts. All of my girl parts still sore from the night before were wide awake and wanting more. Squadrons of butterflies took flight in my stomach. The man was a whole-body experience, awesome and addictive. I couldn't see how I'd ever get enough of him.

A day in bed with Vaughan sounded like heaven. His cell phone buzzing away on the bedside table, not so much.

"Shit," he muttered, reaching over and lifting it to take a look at the screen. "It's Nell. I better answer or she'll keep calling."

I cried on the inside, my craving for the man making me weak.

"Yeah?" he answered, lying on his side next to me. The corners of his mouth turned down. "We're still in bed. What do you want to talk to her for?"

Nell's voice sounded small and far away. As much as I liked the woman, I did not want to talk to her right now.

"Fuck's sake." He held the cell out.

I took it. "Hi, Nell."

"You need to get your own phone," she said.

"I know."

"And what are you doing in my brother's bed?"

The brother in question pushed aside the exceptionally fine top sheet and started kissing his way down my torso once more. Licking here, nibbling there. What a nice man. My heart beat double time, flooding me with even more happy hormones. I caressed his hair, then pushed him in the direction of my pussy. In a friendly manner. You know. He laughed and shook off my hold, sharp teeth snapping at my fingers. Christ, he was cute. And hot.

"You don't really want me to answer that question," I told her.

Nell groaned. "Well, whatever you're doing, cut it out. I need you at the bar."

"What? No," I said, voice panicky. "I can't. I have the black plague."

"Good one," murmured Vaughan, moving ever closer to where I wanted him. Needed him.

"Take an Advil," said Nell. "Rosie's caught the puking bug off her kid and Joe's helping his dad with a building job. We're booked out for lunch. Masa can't handle it on his own."

"Who's Masa?" I asked.

"One of my waiters, he just got back from holidays. Goes to the local tech college. You'll like him."

"Great. But what about Eric, can't he help?"

"Eric's behind the bar," she said, obviously growing impatient. "Come on, I'll cook something delicious just for you."

"Nell . . ."

"Look, I know you'd rather do stuff in bed with my brother, but I need you. Please, Lydia?"

GAH. "Fine. Let me take a quick shower then I'll be in."

"Thank you." She hung up in my ear.

People were the worst. I dramatically flung my arm over my eyes, quietly crying. Okay, so they weren't real tears. The sadness, though, was unfeigned.

Vaughan took this opportunity to bite my thigh, sinking his teeth into my flesh and holding on. It hurt. "Ow."

"That's for not putting your happiness first." He kissed the sore spot a time or two. Then he licked it. "And that's for helping my sister. I'll make it feel better when you get off work."

"You better. Jerk." I put his cell back on the bedside table, climbing off the bed. "Keep biting me like that and I'm going to buy you a teething ring."

"Your skin's so pretty, I can't resist leaving my mark on you. It's your own fault." Not even a hint of remorse from him. "Go on. I'll make coffee, you shower."

"Thanks. Can I borrow your car?"

"I'll drive you in, pick you up when you're finished." Arms wound around me as he hugged me from behind, pressing himself against my back. I'd forgotten how nice having a hot and horny male around felt. This one in particular worked for me big-time. Huge.

"Are you sure?"

"Gives me a chance to pick up some strings from Andre. Run a few errands."

"Cool." I ran my hands over his arms, enjoying the feel of him, of being with him.

He lined up the length of his cock with the divide between my butt cheeks, rubbing himself against me. Whoa. What an interesting sensation. My spine stiffened then relaxed, getting into the feeling. He rumbled a low noise of approval in my ear.

"We don't have time," I said, getting turned on once again. I was a wet and wanton, swollen mess. No way could Nell cook me anything delicious enough to make up for losing out on bed time with Vaughan. Impossible.

"I know." Big hands gripped my hips, pulling me firmly back against him. "Fuck, that's sweet."

"Vaughan." The feel of him hardening, lengthening, made breathing difficult. Thinking was pretty much right out.

"I like your ass, babe. I like it a lot."

"Thought you were a breast man."

His hot mouth pressed against my neck, lighting fires wherever it went. One hand splayed over my belly, the other playing with a nipple. He continued to rub himself against me, making everything that much worse. Or better. Both, maybe.

"So did I," he said. "But I pretty much want to kiss, lick, bite, and fuck every bit of you."

Oh, god. My knees shook.

"Shit. Nell's timing sucks." He groaned, stepping back. "Go shower."

"Right." My weak knees wobbled. "Go make coffee."

"Yeah."

I stumbled toward the door. Then stopped, befuddled in body and mind, but curious about something. "Hey. You never did finish that story last night."

With a pained face, he held his cock against his stomach. "What?"

"The one about the girl and you coming too soon."

He half smiled. "Ah, yeah. So she tells me to think about something else that I like while we're fucking. To take my mind off of being inside her and everything. Next time we're doing it, I think about Fender guitars. I think about them good and hard. I tell her my plan so she knows that I'm trying."

"And?"

"I lasted. She came shouting, 'Yes! Fenders!'" He smiled. "Woke up her parents. I've never climbed out a window so fast in my life."

Quietly, I laughed, shaking my head. "Great."

"Mm."

"Why were you telling me that?" I leaned against the doorway, watching him. Carefully, slowly, he sat on the edge of the bed. "I mean, it's a great story. But why last night?"

"I don't know." He sighed. "To get you to relax, to take your mind off worrying about your body."

"Oh."

A shrug.

"Thanks."

"I didn't like you trying to hide parts of yourself from me." Vaughan stared at the wall. "I'm not like that asshole, picking and choosing which bits of you suit him and expecting you to change the rest. I'm into you, Lydia. All of you."

My heart felt huge. Out of control.

"It worked," I said, voice thick with emotion despite my best efforts.

He turned his head toward me.

"I'm standing here naked, not covering anything. That's not usually me." I shrugged, nervously laughing. Somehow having my pale wobbly ass and bumps and bulges on display hadn't sent me running for cover. Yet. A miracle, really. The earlier tug-of-war with the sheet had been more about fun than anything else. "I don't know . . . I guess I trust you. I mean, I must."

Nothing.

Not a goddamn thing.

Ouch. When would I learn? Baring your soul sucked. I looked at the floor, the wall, at everything but him. It didn't even make any sense; I mean, so he'd told me a silly story. So he'd been kind, understanding. He was always being kind and understanding. This was nothing new. That he'd then screwed me senseless, giving me the best sex of my life thus far, meant we'd had a great night. But not some life-altering, perception-changing, stars-aligning experience. I just happened to be going through a growth period and he just happened to be a part of it.

That's all.

When would I learn? Just because my vagina was having fun didn't mean my heart had to get all clingy.

"Babe," he said. "Look at me."

Reluctantly, I did.

"Thank you."

I nodded.

"I've said it before, but . . . I'm glad you're here."

"Me too." The smile on my face felt foreign, wrong. Time for a reality check. Things that shouldn't really mean anything were beginning to feel big and important, and that was neither necessary nor good.

Just friends having sex. Nothing more.

CHAPTER SIXTEEN

"What do you know about book work?"

I untied my apron, throwing it into the laundry hamper. "Inputting accounting data into a computer, you mean?"

"Yes."

"A little. I can type. I'm familiar with the basic programs."

We were out back in the small cluttered office, the lunch rush having finally eased. My fellow waiter, Masa, a young Japanese dude studying at the local tech college, had indeed been a delight. Working with him was fun. The Dive Bar might be a little light on staff right now, but those that were here were solid. Even Eric proved to be more than competent, keeping up with our drink orders while carrying on a conversation with a couple hanging at the bar.

"Why are you asking me this?" I inquired, schlepping myself over to the only spare chair in the room. "God, my feet hurt. You're good with knives, chop them off for me. I don't want them anymore."

"Stop being a whiny little princess."

"Seriously, they ache. If I keep doing this, I'm going to have to invest in better-soled shoes."

Nell's head shot up. "You're thinking of staying?"

"What? No." My stupid mouth opened, closed. "No, of course

not. I don't know where that came from. I already have a career, I'm a real estate agent."

"No, you're not. You got fired."

"Thanks," I replied drily. "Actually, I need to read over the settlement from the Delaneys tonight. Get that sorted out."

"So you'll be receiving a payout?" She set her elbows on the table and clasped her fingers together, watching me with bright beady little eyes. "How much, do you think?"

"Hopefully enough to buy me a decent used car and help me resettle somewhere else." I crossed my legs, getting comfortable. "I honestly don't know what it will be. I'm a little afraid to look. My savings are not immense."

"You have a job here, a place to stay."

"Nell, these are just emergency measures. You'll find a new waiter and Vaughan will be gone soon, the house sold."

She flinched.

Regret flooded me. "I'm sorry."

"Don't be. It's the truth." Her shiny red hair had been pulled back into a bun. It still seemed too bright against the pale of her cheeks, the shadows under her eyes. It was concerning.

"You're still looking a little off. Do you think you might have caught whatever bug Rosie's family has going around?"

"Maybe." She scrunched up her face. "I'm just so damn tired lately. Everything's getting to me."

"You've been dealing with a lot."

"Mm. Eric's apologized and is carrying his weight again, but Pat still won't step foot in the place. I don't see that changing anytime this century."

All I could do was frown on her behalf. Men sucked so bad sometimes.

"I just wish I had the money to buy him out," she said, squeezing her eyes shut for a moment. "My share of the tattoo shop doesn't account for half of what I'd need. Going all out setting up this place is biting me on the ass."

"If you hadn't you wouldn't have the booming growing business you've got. The investment was sound."

"Yeah. Just a shame my marriage wasn't." Her eyes were glossy with tears. "I'm so proud of this place, Lydia. I can't lose it."

It was a hard situation. False promises wouldn't help, so I kept my mouth shut.

A heavy sigh. "At any rate, how would you like some more work? We had a great bookkeeper, but she retired last Christmas. I was hoping between all of us we'd be able to keep on top of this, but it's not happening. Joe's got the computer and program all set up, ready to go. What do you say?"

I pinned my lips shut, considering the consequences. More money. Less time with Vaughan. A very sad thought indeed.

"It'd probably only take you a day or so to get us up to date," Nell wheedled, flopping back in the seat. "And you'd be sitting down the entire time. I guarantee it won't hurt your feet at all. Please, Lydia?"

"You already used 'please' on me today."

"Pretty please?" The face she made was truly pathetic. Some sort of cross between a hound dog and a depressed redheaded sloth. It wasn't pretty. "I'm willing to beg. Kissing your smelly feet I draw the line at, but begging could definitely happen."

"*God*. Fine," I said, slowly rising. "But you start looking for a new bookkeeper."

"Absolutely."

"And a new waiter."

"Yep."

"I mean it, Nell." I waved a pointy finger at her.

"I know you do." She smiled beatifically.

I didn't trust that smile one bit. "I have to go meet Vaughan."

"Speaking of which." She delicately scrunched up her nose, eyes alight with mischief. "Can you please use more concealer on the hickeys next time? Either that, or ask my bro to stop using you as his chew toy. You're bringing down the class of the place with your kinky sex play. It's not okay. We're a serious, well-respected establishment."

"Oh, yeah," I said sarcastically. "Playing punk music all day definitely reinforces that image."

"It was Boyd's turn to pick the music. He says he chooses punk to soothe the ghost of Andre Senior."

"Do you really think the place is haunted?" I asked, curious. No ghost had ever crossed my path, but you never did know. There was a lot in this world I could neither explain nor label.

Nell just shrugged. "Might be. The old man was definitely married to the place. He hardly ever went home, ask Andre Junior about it. His mom was a model, always traveling for work. Eventually she met someone else and settled in New York. Andre traveled back and forth a bit, but he basically raised himself."

"Tough childhood."

"Yeah. Andre Senior loved this place so much it didn't leave much room for anything else."

"Some people shouldn't have kids," I said, sounding more than a touch bitter. Memories poisoned my present, the same as they ever did. "Self-absorbed assholes, it's ridiculous."

"Yes."

"It's not like you have to. There's no legal requirement to reproduce. But people with no real intention of actually bothering to be a parent keep doing it just the same."

No response apart from a sad smile.

"Anyway." Ugh. The lid on my emotional shit needed fixing, pronto. "I better go."

"Thanks for coming in again, Lydia. You saved our asses."

"Sure." I pasted a smile on my face and made for the exit.

"And thanks for listening to me whine."

I stopped, then retraced my steps, sticking my head back into the room. "Ditto, Nell."

The smile she gave me made a lot worthwhile. It was nice having a friend.

Outside, the afternoon sun beat down, baking the top of my head. An occasional car swept past and a few shoppers lingered. Mostly, however, it was quiet. As if the whole area had fallen into an afternoon lull. Siesta time. I shook off the lingering remnants of my bad-parenting rant. Seeing Vaughan would work wonders. I swear my body started tingling at just the thought.

A sign sat out on the hot sidewalk advertising how Inkaho would be open until eight. Distantly I could hear the buzz of the tattoo needle doing its thing. I hadn't seen Pat since the night of the great fight and I certainly didn't stop and wave through the front window. God knows what I'd say to the man.

While the Dive Bar shone like new and Pat's tattoo parlor appeared to be well maintained, the Guitar Den was of a simpler style. I stepped inside, grateful for the chill of the air-conditioning. Gray industrial carpeting that was worn down to next to nothing covered the floor, beneath a large battered metal and glass shop counter. Amplifiers were all over the place, a drum kit sat set up in the back, and the walls were covered by every kind of guitar—the bulk of which I knew nothing about.

A portrait of Bill Murray hung behind the counter. An interesting choice of patron saint.

From deeper within the shop came voices, the sound of music. I followed it into an open area hidden behind a wall of amps. It was a secret garden made for six strings. Sort of.

"Hi," said Andre, leaning against the end of a ceiling-high rack of guitars. How the man managed to look dapper in a bright red vintage Hawaiian shirt I had no idea.

Some people are simply born cool. I wasn't even remotely one of them.

"Hi, Andre."

"Check this out." He jerked his chin in the same direction the music was coming from.

Vaughan sat on a low stool, playing an acoustic guitar, while three kids of varying ages stood watching. Their faces were rapt. I completely understood why. Vaughan with a guitar in his hands would enthrall anyone.

He was magic.

The precision of his fingers and the dance of muscles in his arms. Jaw set and eyes distant, he wove the music out of thin air, filling the shop with its beauty. It wasn't anything fancy, full of finger picking and over-the-top showmanship. Just a simple old soft rock song. By Dylan, I think, though I'd heard it covered a million times. The care Vaughan gave it, however, the heart, made it special.

"C to G," said one of the kids, who looked like she was in her early teens.

"That's right." Vaughan smiled as he kept on playing.

"Then D," added another, pointing at the bottom strings.

"Yep. You got it."

The third remained silent, staring at his fingers.

"He's good with them," I said quietly to Andre.

"No, he's fucking great with them," he whispered back. "This has been going on for over an hour now."

"Really?" I stared at the group in awe.

Andre slipped his hand in mine, drawing me back so we wouldn't disturb them with our conversation. He led me over to the counter, giving my fingers a squeeze before letting go.

"The kids belong to the owner of the hair salon across the road," he said. "She's been over twice to check on them, wants to sign all three up for lessons with him. Already bought a half-size guitar for them to use."

"Don't you do lessons?"

His smile slipped a little. "Honestly, I'm not that great with children. Older teens, adults? Fine. But kids under sixteen generally have a two-second attention span. Annoys the living crap out of me. Plus they never practice."

I laughed. "Did you tell her Vaughan was only visiting?"

"Yeah. She said I need to talk him into staying."

In a swarm of noise and movement, the kids ran past us and out the door.

"Don't run!" Andre swiftly followed them, swearing under his breath. "Use the crosswalk! Hey, are you listening to me?"

A hot rush of summer air blew in then the shop door swung shut again, the bell above the door jangling. Andre's voice faded into the distance, still shouting orders at the kids as he escorted them across the street. Out of a shop across the way came a woman with bright blue hair. All three children basically fell on her, their excitement obvious even from a distance. She hugged them back with exuberance. Nice to see someone engaging with their kids, being affectionate.

An arm slipped around my shoulders, a familiar body stood at my side. Worn jeans, a pair of battered green Converse, and a tee. (Today's was the Clash. He would have enjoyed Boyd's punk music.) It was Vaughan's usual wardrobe, and damn, he wore it well. Ray-Bans sat on top of his head, holding his beautiful hair back out of his face.

Even fully dressed, the man made my mouth water. What he did to me undressed was best not mentioned in polite company.

"How was the bar?"

"Fine," I said, reaching up for a quick kiss. Being able to do such a thing? Best. Feeling. Ever. "Rosie had accidentally overbooked but I moved some tables around, asked a couple of people if they didn't mind sitting at the bar. All fixed."

"No one gave you any shit?"

"Nope. Just don't ask me where those bloody body parts in the Dumpster out back came from."

"Got it." He stole another quick kiss.

"I hear you've started giving guitar lessons."

He huffed out a laugh. "Unintentionally. It was actually kind of fun."

"I saw. You had them in the palm of your hand."

"Yeah?" Getting closer, he rubbed the tip of his nose against mine. The man was a perfect mix of hot and sweet. "I think I'd rather have you in the palm of my hand."

My mouth opened but nothing came out. Tongue-tied. Brain dead. Cock struck. He made me all of those things and more. Standing so close, looking at me like he was, the man rendered me next to useless.

"What do you think, Lydia?"

"I can't."

A frown. "You can't what?"

"Think."

His smile was pure carnal pleasure.

The doorbell jangled again and Andre entered, all smiles. "Those kids are your new biggest fans. You should have heard them going on about you."

Vaughan moved back a step. Thank god. I got the feeling mounting him on the shop counter in the Guitar Den might be a no-no. Public place, children had recently been present, et cetera.

"They're great kids," said Vaughan.

"No," corrected Andre. "*You're* a great teacher."

With a laugh, Vaughan moved his hand to the back of my neck and started rubbing. Sore muscles eased. Even my feet stopped hurting, mostly. I leaned into his touch, urging him on. Any and all contact with the man made things better.

"I'm serious," said Andre. "You've got a gift, Vaughan."

"No. Just a little more patience with children than you do."

Andre cut the air with his hand, suddenly serious. "Bullshit."

"Man—"

"I didn't need it, so I pretty much let the teaching side of the business slide. But it wouldn't take much for you to build it up again," said Andre, hand outstretched and expression earnest. "Soundproof room's out back, it's all there. Move back here and teach guitar. You can make decent money doing something you like."

"Come on."

"Don't tell me you weren't enjoying sharing the music with those kids. I saw your face."

The fingers fell from my neck and Vaughan turned away. "It was fun, sure. But it's not what I do."

"It could be."

"No." Vaughan shook his head. "Listen, I called Conn earlier. You're not going to believe this, but Henning Peters wants to work with us. Isn't that fucking amazing?"

"Impressive."

"Right? Apparently he saw us play last year and liked what he heard. Thinks we could write some good stuff together," said Vaughan. "And get this, he's got record companies already lined up wanting to hear his next project."

"Is that what you want, to be someone's project?"

"Hell yes. Henning's on the verge of going big and we'll be right there with him. Come on, Andre. This is an amazing opportunity, you know it." Vaughan's grin was big, huge. "All I have to do is survive financially until we've got enough songs ready then we are going to make a shitload of money."

"That's what it's about now, the money?"

"It was always about the money."

"No, it wasn't," argued Andre "When you left here, you wanted to share your music. You wanted to play guitar, write songs and get them out there, perform live. That's what drove you."

I hung back, keeping quiet. Awkward. It seemed being caught in difficult situations was my lot these days. I only wish I knew how to help. Other than keeping my mouth shut and staying out of it, of course.

"Christ," breathed Vaughan, laughing softly. "Ease up, Andre. I'm still doing what I love."

"Then why are you so fucking unhappy?"

Vaughan's face was blank, empty.

"I've known you almost all your life. You put on a good show, but you're not fooling everybody."

"We've been going through some shit, that's all."

Face lined with frustration, Andre shook his head. "I'm not talking about *we*, about the band. I'm talking about *you*."

Nothing.

"Heading back out to the coast is not the only option you—"

"Are you insane?" Vaughan took a deep breath, visibly searching for calm. "This is the biggest opportunity of my life. I'm not stopping now."

"You played to crowds of thousands, got albums out there, songs on the charts. Sure as hell, you got further than I ever did," said Andre with a self-deprecating smile. "If your parents were alive, they'd be ecstatic."

"It's not enough."

"When something is no longer working, changing your plans is not giving up. It's not failure."

"Maybe not for you. But for me, it would be. Especially with Henning now in the cards. I'm not staying here, I've moved on."

For a moment Andre said nothing and the silence stung. But his next words, and the tone of his voice, was far worse. "Yeah, Vaughan, you moved on, and you left a hell of a lot of people behind."

Everything stopped as if someone had pressed "pause."

The two men just looked at each other. Then a car zoomed past, the doorbell jangled, and a customer entered. Nothing had changed. Angry words didn't stop the world from turning round.

"Just do me a favor," said Andre. "When you go back to the coast, call your sister occasionally. Maybe even Pat now and then, okay?"

A nod.

"Thank you."

"Lydia and I have plans," said Vaughan, reaching for my hand. He squeezed my fingers tight, his grip sweaty. "I'll catch you before I go."

"All right."

"It was good to see you again, Andre," I said, offering a brief smile.

"You too, Lydia." He stepped forward, giving me a quick kiss on the cheek. "Take care."

We were out of the shop, down the street, and into the Mustang in under a minute. Two steps for every one of Vaughan's, I almost ran to keep up, puffing all the way. He didn't talk until the key went in the ignition, the engine revving, loud and proud. Slowly, his shoulders descended, the walls came down. But they didn't disappear. Not really.

Not for him and not for me.

"Sorry about that," he said, gaze firmly on the road ahead.

"It's fine."

"Better get back, finish that work on the house."

"Right." I fussed in my seat, gripping the handbag in my lap.

Someone once told me that when people pass in assisted care facilities it's common for men to be found holding their penises. Women, however, grab hold of their handbags. Our money, our identities, our lives, are stuffed into those things. All of the bits and pieces we've collected over the years. Everything we might need to make it through any minor, or major, emergencies.

Men are so much less reliable than handbags.

"I need to read the documents from the Delaneys," I said, putting my priorities back into place. "I should pack my stuff properly too. Nell and I just threw everything into boxes. It'd be horrible if more got broken in the move."

A grunt from the man temporarily at my side.

CHAPTER SEVENTEEN

"Hey."

The man lying spread-eagled in the backyard raised a hand, then let it fall back to earth.

"For you," I said, passing him a beer.

"You're an angel." The sweat on his body glistened in the moonlight. Dark wet tendrils of hair clung to his face. He chugged a good three-quarters of the beer in four, five seconds max. It was impressive. Very manly.

Just as well I'd brought out a six-pack.

The scent of cut grass filled the air. Every bush had been neatly trimmed. Instead of an Idaho Amazon, the backyard now resembled a neat suburban garden with an awesome stone fire pit at its center. I sat on one of the surrounding rocks, sipping my beer. Stars twinkled overhead. The moon shone. Soon enough, Vaughan finished off his beer and I passed him another.

He sat up, elbows resting on his knees. "You going to say something?"

"About what?" I asked, looking round. "The garden? Great job."

"I meant about the fight with Andre."

I raised my brows, taking another sip. "No."

Nothing beat ice cold beer on a summer's night. I'd showered and changed into a loose cotton dress. After the dust of the garage and repacking almost everything I owned, it was necessary to clean up. Wet hair sat up high on my head in a topknot. All the better for adding a bit of bounce to it tomorrow. It also left my neck exposed to the beautiful cooling nighttime breeze, a definite bonus. It felt so good after the heat of the day.

He looked at me, then he looked around. A process he repeated quite a few times, occasionally stopping for a mouthful of beer.

"I don't know you, Vaughan," I said, when I couldn't take the silent questioning any longer. "Not really. And you don't know me."

His brow furrowed.

"What Andre said was enough to send you spiraling into some sort of frenzied gardening bender. I'm not going to add to it."

"The yard was just a job that needed doing," he mumbled around the top of his beer. "No need to make it a big deal."

"Right. Just a job that needed doing . . . for seven hours without a break."

One shoulder lifted. "That's how long it took."

"In your underwear."

"It got hot." He took another mouthful of beer. "Thanks for putting out the bottles of water earlier."

"No problem."

For a while, we drank in silence. Up high the tips of the old pine trees swayed in the breeze like they were waving at the stars. Someone somewhere played Simon and Garfunkel a little louder than necessary. Otherwise the night was peaceful, nice.

"Good thing about the fences," I said eventually.

"Hmm?"

"Otherwise the neighbors would have had a wonderful time watching you trim the hedges in your boxer briefs."

He snorted. "True. Those fences aren't tall enough to keep out runaway brides, though."

I breathed in through my teeth, making a hissing noise. "A nasty invasive breed. I'd be surprised if anything could stop them."

He motioned to the neat line of hedges with his half-empty bottle. "This is how Dad used to keep it, all neat and tidy. Then Mom would plant flowers everywhere she could fit them. They'd be spilling out all over the place. Total chaos."

"Yeah?"

"I'm pretty sure she did it just to drive him nuts." A ghost of a smile crossed his face. "Every year she'd do a different color. All white flowers one summer, all yellow the next, and so on. Want to hear another of my embarrassing stories?"

"Hells yes."

"One year, I accidentally broke a lamp. I was throwing a ball around inside the house, completely against the rules," he said. "Anyway, I blamed it on the dog. This yappy ball of fluff Nell had begged them to buy her for Christmas. She even called the stupid thing Snowball."

"What happened?" I asked.

"Well, Mom knew I was lying about the lamp, but she couldn't prove it."

"What about your dad?"

A laugh. "He hated the dog too. Gave me the benefit of the doubt."

"Poor Snowball."

"Mm. He had to spend more time outside after that," he said. "Nell wouldn't talk to me for weeks and Mom was definitely not impressed."

"I bet. You sound like a terrible child," I joked.

"Hold on, I'm not finished." He turned my way, his smile definite this time. "So I was having a water fight in the backyard for my eighth birthday party. Had been planning it for months. I'd stockpiled all these water balloons and me and Eric spent weeks building these giant forts out of cardboard boxes. It was going to be excellent. Absolutely no girls allowed."

"And?"

"Mom planted pink that year. And not just light pink, oh no. Big bright pink flowers everywhere. They were hanging in baskets and filling pots. She went berserk with them, far worse than normal." He paused, drank. "You couldn't come out here without being struck blind by it all. It looked like a flock of flamingos had exploded."

"Oh, no," I cried out dramatically. My senior year drama classes were finally proving useful, thank god. "Your poor burgeoning masculinity and street cred. Gone!"

"Right? I was completely humiliated." He stretched out his legs, semi-reclining back on his elbows. "Eric wanted to dig them all up right before the party and try blaming it on Snowball. But I really didn't see how that could work twice."

"Probably a wise call."

A nod.

"You mom sounds awesome," I said with no small amount of wonder.

"Yeah. She was."

With no ace parenting tales of my own to share, conversation lapsed again. This time, however, it didn't feel awkward. We were just two people hanging out, star gazing on a summer night. It was all good.

"I do know you," he said quietly. "You're wrong about that."

My gaze jumped from the stars to him. Both equally stunning. His eyes shone in the moonlight, which was singularly useless. I couldn't read him at all. I needed more light to see his expression, so I could figure out where this was going.

"You've done nothing but show me who you are since I met you," he said.

And that right there was the problem. "I'm not sure it's fair to judge me on recent events. The last few days have quite possibly been among the most bizarre and traumatic of my life."

"Lydia, you've broken into my house, punched a lying asshole in the nose, stayed with me when I didn't want to be alone, stepped in to help my sister's business, forgiven me when I behaved like a dickhead, cleaned me and my house up after a brawl, and pushed me into having rough sex with you."

". . . yeah."

"Yeah," he repeated. "I like you. But more than that, I trust you."

"Wow. That's what you get from all that?"

"That's what I get."

I raised my brows, looking away. It was a lot to take in. More than I needed or less than I wanted, I couldn't quite decide. Confusion of the heart is a bitch. Assuming *like*, the same as *love*, came from the vascular muscle, of course. *Crazy* obviously came from the head and the loins.

So while the sane part of my head was saying things like "it's only temporary" and "take it easy," the crazy part was shouting "ooh look, it's Vaughan, he's so pretty and shiny and makes you feel good" and "jump on the man, for fuck's sake." And that part was much, much louder. Crazy was a bit of a whore, god bless her.

At any rate, my body was at war. Chocolate chip cookie dough ice cream would hit the spot. Insert heavy sigh here.

"What was that for?" asked Vaughan.

"Ice cream."

"Right. We don't have any." A pause. "I think there's some of Nell's flourless chocolate cake in the fridge. Will that do instead?"

"I suppose so." God, life was so hard. I took a swig of beer, firmly pushing all my deep and insane thoughts aside. Enough already. "Do you feel any better now that you've done the garden?"

He took his turn releasing a heavy sigh. "Honestly, I don't know. Being back here . . . Andre was right. It is fucking with me."

I kept quiet, letting him work it through.

"I keep expecting to see Dad come out of the garage. Hear Mom yell at me from the kitchen about something." Light glinted off his bottle as he held it to his lips and drank deep. "Away from here, I could just ignore their absence. Pretend they didn't die in that car crash, like the funeral was just some shitty dream."

In a sudden burst of rage he surged up, throwing the bottle of beer at the back fence. It didn't shatter and break. There was no satisfying smash of destruction. The bottle just hit the fence and fell behind the bushes, landing in the dirt with a soft thud. Such a weak, useless response.

"Fuck!" Vaughan lay back down, staring up at the night sky. Pain and anger flowed off him in waves, filling the darkness.

No light was needed for me to feel it. And it hurt.

"Babe," he said, voice guttural. He lifted his hand, beckoning me forward with his fingers.

I set my drink aside, going to him without thinking. The man just had that kind of power over me. "What can I get for you?"

No response.

"Vaughan?"

I knelt at his side, better able to see him up close. Sweat or something else dampened his face. Dirt and grass stained his beautiful body. The man was a mess. He sat up, grabbing hold of my face and bringing his mouth to mine. Hot wet kisses and frenzied hands. The taste of him drove me wild. It all happened so fast it was dizzying. First his thumbs stroked my cheeks, hands holding me in place. Then he had one arm around my waist and a hand gripping my thigh, maneuvering me over him. Knees pressing into the manicured lawn, I found myself straddling him before I even knew what he wanted.

Luckily I'd worn a dress.

Touching the man made me high. All that bare skin and violent need, just for me. He fed me passionate kisses, making my insides melt. My thigh muscles quivered, the feel of him hardening against me was breathtaking. Immediately my girl parts kicked into gear. They knew how superb it felt to have him inside and wanted him to make a return visit.

If he needed it, I'd fuck the fear of death out of him, chase away the hurt of old memories.

If he wanted it, I wouldn't think twice.

Fingers pushed down my panties. Not that they could go far. He kneaded my ass, still kissing me senseless. I ground myself against him, panting. So good. His tongue in my mouth, his breath in my lungs. Making out like crazy in the backyard of his childhood home. I couldn't care less if anyone could see.

"Lydia." He pressed kisses across my cheek, then down along my jawline. Teeth grazed across the sensitive skin of my neck.

Goddamn vampire.

Meanwhile, his hands had apparently tired of feeling up my ass. One dug into my hair, while the other tugged my underwear aside. Fingers slipped in between the lips of my pussy, trailing lightly back and forth in the damp, teasing me. Everything low in me tensed, a vibrant sensation racing down my spine. I didn't know whether to move or stay still. The pad of his thumb decided it for me, drawing circles around my clit. It dipped down into the moisture lower then returned with a vengeance.

"Look at me," he muttered.

The thumb brushed over my sweet spot, making me shiver. Crap, that was good. If he'd just keep going a little longer, pressing a little harder . . .

"Open your eyes, babe."

The fist in my hair tightened sharply, stinging my scalp. It was completely unexpected. My whole focus had been on my pussy, where it belonged. My eyelids flew up, mouth open. "V-Vaughan."

"That's it." The lines of his face stood out starkly, his eyes huge and hypnotic. He nipped at my bottom lip, then kissed it better. "Don't leave me now."

"No." I shook my head emphatically. Our time wasn't up. Not yet.

"Need you here," he said, still manipulating my clit with expertise. His clever thumb never stopped, touch varying from light to hard, teasing to almost rough. How he knew where the all-important line between pleasure and pain lay, I had no idea. I guess Fender girl had taught him. If the woman ever crossed my path, I'd kiss her. My hair stood on end, sweat was beading on my back. He could have been writing the American Constitution down there. I didn't care. So long as he didn't stop.

"Need you right here," he said, staring deep into my eyes.

I nodded, beyond words.

Then he moved his thumb away. It was the saddest thing ever. The back of his hand brushed against me, doing something. Without his interference, my underwear slid back over, a line of elastic dissecting my swollen labia. Not cool.

Before I could fix it, his fingers returned, pulling it back out of the way. The smooth broad head of his cock dragged across my clit, between the wet lips of my sex. And yes, hells yes. The moment I could, I slowly pushed down, taking him inside. My eyes rolled back into my head it was so good. Delicious, glorious, and all these things and more. I'd never felt anything like it. His hard cock sliding into me was pure bliss and I never wanted it to end.

I whimpered and moaned like a wanton hussy.

He swore up a storm.

If any neighbors, astronauts, or heavenly deities were out there watching, they had to be jealous as hell.

His free arm slid around my waist, holding me to him in an

almost brutal embrace. Like I had any intention of trying to get away. The feel of him stretching me, filling me up inside, was just too fine. Every vein in his dick seemed tantalizingly magnified. My back arched, pelvis trying to rock but not getting far. Interior muscles clutched at him in pain and pleasure. I ached inside and only he could make it better. In frustration, I twisted against his hold, writhing on him.

It was sweet torture.

"I need to move," I pled, pressing my mouth to his face, kissing every inch of skin I could reach. Stubble scratched my skin, but no matter. "Vaughan?"

The controlling bastard tugged on my hair, turning his face to claim my mouth again. I kissed him as savagely as I could muster. Tongue stroking over his teeth, then tangling with his. Teeth grazing his firm bottom lip. Liquid copper hit my taste buds. I must have reopened his busted lip. Oh well.

"You going to fuck me, dirty girl?" he asked, voice guttural.

"Yes," I hissed back at him. Partially plotting his death, but mostly just orgasms.

"How hard?"

"Hard. I promise, so hard. Let me go, Vaughan."

"Say please."

Bastard. "Please."

"Do it."

His arm relented, setting me free. And I grabbed hold of his shoulders, using them for leverage as I rose and fell on his cock. I might not make it into the Kentucky Derby, but I did ride Vaughan into the ground.

Literally.

Grass and dirt were pulverized beneath my knees as I pounded myself down on him. I clasped at him with my insides. His moans were music to my ears. Skin slapped against skin, sweat poured out of both of us. Nothing mattered. Only feeling him inside of me and coming. Hands gripped my breasts, squeezing and molding them over the fabric of my dress and bra. It wasn't enough. I took control and pushed him back, angling my body forward. All the better to grind my clit against his pubic bone.

Yes.

A groan was torn from my throat. Nerve endings sizzled, hot pleasure pouring through me. It kept on building, getting bigger and higher and even more amazing. His hand cupped my face, trying to move with me, to keep the contact. His gaze swallowed me whole. All the time I kept moving, fucking him hard like he wanted. Like we both wanted. The muscles in my thighs screamed bloody murder. But the light inside me grew hotter and brighter until it became a flash fire.

I saw nothing and felt everything. My whole body gripped by the shattering pleasure. I came and came until there was nothing left. The ringing in my ears went on for a while as I fell limp against him. His hips bucked against me, still shoving his hard cock in deep. Hands gripped my hips viciously tight. Then he came too, exhaling hard, chest rising steeply against mine. Strong arms clasped me to him.

The night pressed in around us once again. Just doing its thing.

Vaughan's heart beat hard beneath my ear, the heat of his body keeping me warm. I don't think I needed anything else. At least, not right now.

"Hell of a set of lungs on you. Neighbors are going to think I was trying to kill you," he said.

"You basically were. It was terrible."

He snickered. "Babe, you came so hard you nearly broke me."

"Whatever." Who even had the energy to fight? I'd worn myself out fucking.

Then I felt it. A thick liquid oozing out of me. The dreaded sperm.

"We didn't use anything," I whispered.

"Shit."

The poor baby was seriously pissed off. Red-faced and wailing, shaking his tiny fists at the world. His mother didn't look much better, pale and worn out. Given that they had such tiny lungs, infants could unleash an extraordinary amount of sound. An unfortunate thing for this hour of the night. For any hour, really.

"He's teething," the woman said, having caught me staring.

"Oh."

Drool covered the baby's chin.

"I guess that would hurt like a bi . . . bad thing."

"Hmm," said the woman, rubbing his little back.

Her gaze moved back and forth between me and the man loitering behind me, all tall and covered in tattoos, as we waited. Strands of freshly washed golden-red hair clung to the sides of his face, the color brilliant beneath the harsh lighting. His eyes were glued to the selection of denture accessories on the wall. He should have just stayed in the car. I told him he didn't need to accompany me into the twenty-four-hour drugstore. The drive had been awkward enough. Amazing sex shouldn't come with bad consequences. A few bruises, grass stains on my knees? Fine. Fear of pestilence, disease, and childbirth, not so fucking much.

"You have any of your own?" she asked.

I blinked. "Children? No. No-o-o."

The man behind me shifted uneasily.

"Not yet. One day, maybe," I babbled on, feeling just a wee bit self-conscious. "In the future, you know. There's no rush. Not that your little boy doesn't look lovely. He's just wonderful."

The baby bawled on.

"And becoming a parent, a good parent, it's a big deal. A lot of work."

No one else said anything.

"Vaughan," the woman said with a sudden smile. "My god, that is you. I'm Nina Harrison, we had English together senior year."

"Nina," he said, voice stilted. "Hey."

"How are you? I heard you left for L.A. with your band straight after graduation," she gushed. "How's that going?"

The muscles in his neck moved. "Ah, yeah. Good."

"Actually, I heard one of your songs on the radio a couple of years back. It wasn't bad!"

"Thanks."

"Ma'am. Your order's ready." The neat white-clad pharmacist nodded my way and sat a small box on the counter. "Side effects and more information are listed on the brochure inside the box. And please remember, it may delay your menstruation cycle by a couple of days. If you're over your usual menstruation date by more than two weeks, you might want to try taking a pregnancy test."

"Okay." My hand shook as I picked up the package and handed over the cash. "Thank you."

Nina stared at us, her mouth a perfect O. Like she'd never had unprotected sex. Puh-lease.

I charged toward the exit. Vaughan mumbled a goodbye and followed. The minute he unlocked the passenger door I jumped in, grabbing my bottle of water. Out came the post-coital contraception pill, then down my throat it went. Done.

Vaughan just looked at me, his face a blank mask. He was good at that. I'd seen it a couple of times now, but it was still impressive.

I on the other hand gave him my best plastic professional smile. "All good."

A nod.

"I am clean, I promise," I recited for the tenth time in the past few hours. "I had a test after college just to be safe. But I've always used protection."

"Yeah, me too."

"We've both been vigilant. This was just an anomaly." It was embarrassing, really. How foolish I'd been, first with the wedding that wasn't, and now with Vaughan. I frowned out at the glitter and glare of the drugstore's neon sign. A dancing bottle of drugs waved its arms back and forth. What the ever-loving fuck? "If I hadn't forgotten to take my pill on Sunday we wouldn't have even had to worry about rushing to the pharmacy like this."

"It's fine," he said.

"It's good that we did this. You can't be too careful."

"Yeah." He paused, shook his head. "I'm sorry, Lydia. I should have thought, I just got—"

"It's okay. We're both adults, Vaughan. We were both there."

He opened his mouth like he was going to say something. But he didn't.

With a turn of the key the Mustang's engine roared to life, same as always. Such an ostentatious hunk of metal. Much too loud for the middle of the night.

I thought again about how muscle cars, tattooed men, and other wild cool things weren't my thing. I craved stability. A sensible, settled life. The whole Chris thing had been a mistake, yes. Obviously. Next time I'd take things slower. Not get so carried away. Whatever the future brought, this temporary time of insanity was at an end. Dirty and crazy were not for me.

"I think I might test-drive a Prius tomorrow," I said, decision made. "One of the used car dealerships has a four-year-old model for sale."

Another nod.

We didn't talk again until we were back at his place. Even then, it was just a quiet good night as he disappeared into his bedroom, closing the door.

Me and my annoying ovaries were shut out.

Nausea and cramping made it difficult to sleep. So I sat up and read through the settlement offer from the Delaneys' lawyers. In fact, I read through it twice. Then, just for kicks, I read through it a third time. It took that long for the shock to die down.

CHAPTER EIGHTEEN

"Do I look like someone who wants to spend the rest of tonight crapping myself?" The cranky man shoved the antipasto platter into my hands. "I told the waiter I needed gluten free. I was very clear about it."

"I apologize for the mistake, sir," I said. "Let me get that fixed right away for you."

"Thank you," he ground out, his expression far from appreciative.

Whatever.

I hauled ass to the kitchen, where Boyd raised an eyebrow at me. "I need a new antipasto gluten free, please."

He nodded and got busy. Or rather, as the only chef in the kitchen tonight, stayed busy. Nell had called in sick after vomiting all day, the poor thing. Luckily the Dive Bar was only half full tonight.

God, I hoped I didn't come down with her virus. The morning-after pill had messed with me enough.

An almighty clatter came from the front counter. I spun around to find Masa standing there, a tray full of glasses shattered at his feet. Ice cubes, lemon slices, and straws, all spread out across the floor.

"Crap," I muttered.

Masa just made a small sound of despair and dropped to his knees, to clean up.

I grabbed the dustpan and brush, then joined him down there.

"I'm sorry," he said, hands moving frantically. "This won't take a minute."

"Slow down. You cutting yourself on broken glass won't help anyone."

He didn't say anything, but he did calm down. A start.

"What's going on with you?" I asked, carefully scooping up the remains of a beer bottle.

"What? Nothing," said the young man.

"Try again."

He just sniffed.

"Masa, you served mint to the woman with mint allergies, got the gluten-intolerant guy's order wrong, and told Boyd that the vegetarians at table eight wanted the chicken satay pizza instead of the margherita. And the list goes on."

He looked at me, dark eyes swollen and red.

"You're clearly upset and distracted," I said. "Talk to me."

He hung his head. "My girlfriend dumped me."

"Oh no. I'm so sorry."

"She's been fucking her tutor for months behind my back." Masa's chin wrinkled, his jaw rigid. "They're in love, apparently. She texted me just before work, told me all about it."

"What a bitch."

From over behind the bar, Eric watched us as he poured another beer. He made no move to come over, and communicated nothing with his gaze. So be it. Broken hearts were serious shit. Someone had to act before Masa accidentally set the place on fire while serving Bombe Alaska, or something.

"Clean this up, then head home," I said, handing Masa the dustpan and brush. "I'll make sure Eric's okay with it."

"Are you sure?" He looked worried. As he probably should be.

"Yeah. The dinner rush is almost over. I can finish up here."

"Thank you."

"No problem." I smiled and got back to work.

Gluten-intolerant dude didn't leave a tip and cleanup took a little longer than normal, but there were no more complaints or catastrophes. I'm pretty sure I spotted the reporter who'd wanted the scoop on my botched wedding lurking out on the sidewalk at one stage during the night. So long as he didn't actively get in my face, however, I was willing to ignore him. For now.

The Dive Bar felt different after closing, all shadows and quiet. A change from all the bright light and music of business hours. It was nice.

Vaughan was missing in action when I woke this morning. When it came time for me to head in to work, Boyd drove up in a late-model Jeep and honked the horn. I guess Vaughan organized the ride for me. It's not like Boyd was talking. Ever. I was about to start walking since I didn't have a phone to call a cab—an issue I'd dared raise with my driver. Boyd kindly stopped at a phone store, allowing me to race in and purchase a cell.

Ah, technology. I didn't actually miss it, but in this modern world of constant communication, it was a necessity. The first thing I'd done was leave a message for my folks. Not that I really expected a reply before the annual Christmas card. Communication wasn't their strong-suit. As parents, they fundamentally sucked. It was just a fact of life. People were who they were, yada yada. Hormones and social expectations had a lot to answer for when it came to population growth.

I could still hear Boyd banging pots and pans around in the kitchen. Assuming he was my ride home, I'd be waiting for a while. Which was fine. I'm sure I could find something to do here. Maybe I'd go ghost hunting for Andre Senior Scare the crap out of myself down in the dark basement. To my knowledge, I'd never been in a haunted building before. It could be fun. A once-in-a-lifetime experience.

"Lydia, think it's time we talked," said Eric from the bar.

Ruh roh.

"All right." I wandered on over, untying my apron as I walked. If I was about to be fired for telling Masa to go home, at least it would be in comfort. I climbed onto one of the stools, giving my poor whiny aching feet a break. Actually, they weren't so bad today. Guess I was getting used to being on them all the time.

Eric set a drink on the bar, served in one of the chunky pretend-cut-crystal, vintage-style glasses. I loved them. He clinked his matching drink against mine, then took a sip. It was an amber liquid. Scotch, judging by the smell. A spiral of orange rind and cubes of ice swam around inside.

"It's an Old Fashioned," he said with a smile. "Ever had one before?"

"No." I took another sniff then dared a sip. Scotch and sweetness and something else I couldn't recognize. Not bad. "Nice. Thank you."

A nod. "You told Masa to go home."

"Yes. He wasn't feeling well and we weren't crazy busy, so . . . given Rosie and Nell have got this virus . . ."

"We sometimes get large groups coming in late. Friends and other people in the area who know we're not going to turn them away."

I took another sip of my drink.

"You really think you'd have been able to handle it on your own?" he asked.

"Having to apologize for the service being a little slow would be preferable to having a customer get puked on, I think." I didn't bother crossing my fingers to protect against the lie. Masa could be sick too. You never know.

Eric coughed out a laugh. "Fair enough."

Phew.

I took another sip of the Old Fashioned, trying to appreciate the scotch. Doubtless it was the top-shelf good stuff. Aged for three hundred years or something. But it was pretty much wasted on me.

Eric's green eyes studied me from across the bar. His dark hair was tied back and he was wearing a crisp black button-up shirt with rolled-up sleeves. Vaughan wasn't classically handsome, more of a custom job. Starkly unique and beautiful with his long lean body and angled face. Eric, however, was pure pretty. You could see how growing girls went from obsessing over ponies to boys like him in the blink of an eye. They were both lovely and just a touch wild.

"Saw you reorganized the front desk," he said. "Cleaned up the reservations book."

"We were quiet this afternoon."

"Mm." He did some more drinking. "Nell says you're just passing through. That this isn't your usual line of work. But if you were thinking of staying, we could definitely use someone to be in charge of the restaurant section."

"Oh."

"Nell's got the kitchen under control. There'll be a new assistant starting next week to help her and Boyd out. And between me, Joe, and Vaughan while he's here, the bar's fine," he said. "We need a manager, or maître d'–type person, to keep the restaurant floor running smoothly, though. The job's yours if you want it. A month on trial then we consider permanent, discuss suitable money and the rest. I don't know what you earn selling houses, but we'd make it worth your while."

Huh. My eyes felt very wide. "I was not expecting that."

"You were good with the angry customers tonight. Calmed them down without us losing business," he said, then nodded to my glass. "Drink up."

I drank up. Given my mostly empty stomach on account of the earlier nausea and cramping, it was going straight to my head. "There are people with far more experience managing a restaurant out there."

He stared at me for a moment then got busy grabbing a couple of bottles off the wall, pouring out shots into a cocktail shaker. "When we started this place, we just wanted to earn a living and have somewhere to hang out with our friends. Nell wanted to run her own kitchen, cook what she liked. I'd worked behind a few bars, figured it was pretty much just more of the same. We were naive as shit."

While he spoke, he worked, mixing up something new. I watched, fascinated. Ice went into the cocktail shaker along with the alcohol then on went the lid. Silver flashed back and forth before my eyes as he shook the concoction. Next, out of one of the fridges below the endless shelves of bottles behind him came an elegant frosted martini glass. In went the liquid, poured through the cocktail shaker's strainer. The drink was off white, cloudy. Eric pierced a single red rose petal, then the fruit of a lychee, with a little stick of bamboo, tied with a knot at one end. He carefully added the garnish.

"Try that instead," he suggested, sitting the fresh creation in front of me. "Might be more to your taste."

"Thank you." First I studied it from various angles. The cocktail was a work of art. If I had my new cell on me, I'd have taken a picture. Not that anyone currently cared what I was drinking for dinner. "It's beautiful. I don't think you'd get that at your normal dive bar."

"You'd be surprised." He smiled. "But we're not your normal dive bar. Drink."

"Right." I carefully raised the glass to my lips. Ice cold and syrupy sweet. It definitely had lychee liqueur in it and vodka. This mix tasted like heaven served up in a swanky glass.

"Lychee martini."

"Whoa. Eric, I love it. I want to bathe in it from now on," I said, only partially joking. "What are you, some kind of clairvoyant mixologist?"

He laughed. "No. I just know women."

I snorted. "Don't they all."

We shared a smile. Though in all honesty it was probably closer to a smirk on both our parts. The battle of the sexes waged ever on.

"How's things going with Vaughan?" he asked, downing his Old Fashioned. And yeah, my currently nonexistent relationship with my temporary landlord was so none of his business.

"Banged any waitresses lately?"

"No. You're not interested in me." The man made flirty eyes at me. You had to give it to him, he had the sexy heated promising looks all locked up. A total professional man whore. "Sadly."

I drank my drink and otherwise kept my mouth shut.

"I'm having to go further afield to find new partners." He reached for a bottle of scotch. Top shelf. What did I tell you?

I still had nothing to say.

"Getting back to my point," he announced. "Nell and I didn't know a shitload about running a place like this. Pat wasn't much better. They'd been running the tattoo parlor for a while, but that didn't involve working as closely with suppliers, managing stock to the same degree. And none of us are really great at schmoozing. But you are."

"Really? You seem like a people person."

One side of his lips kicked up. "Hmm."

"Eric, this is all very interesting. And for the record, just as I told Nell, I think this business is solid and has a good future ahead of it." I took another sip of my stiff drink. This conversation needed it. "But I don't see me as being part of that future. I have other plans."

"Starting somewhere else selling houses."

"Yes," I said. "It's what I know."

"But is it what you love?"

I shrugged.

He shrugged right back at me.

I drank.

"Well, that's a shame." A new Old Fashioned sat by his hand, but he started in on making another cocktail just the same. "Good staff's hard to find, especially people who fit in here. Someone we can pretty much all get along with. This work, dealing with people all the time and more than occasionally taking their shit, isn't for everybody. I told Nell I'd try and talk you into staying. Consider yourself talked to."

"Okay."

"Drink up," he repeated. "Boyd will be in the kitchen for a while. I'll make you a Caipirinha next. See if you like that one too."

Oh boy. Hangover, here I come.

Thursday had morphed into Friday by the time I stumbled in the door. Vaughan sat on the sofa, the lone piece of furniture left in the living room since the sad demise of the coffee table and an old sitting chair during the men's epic battle. Men were such idiots. Meh to them.

"Was starting to worry about you," he said, strumming away at the guitar on his lap. Andre had been right, Vaughan had gifts. The way he played, his ability to bring out the most amazing beautiful sounds from this instrument, was just one of many.

"Hey." I plonked myself down on the couch beside him, head only spinning a little. Regular glasses full of water and a bowl of gnocchi with this incredibly delicious cheese and spinach sauce care of Boyd had helped mitigate the booze. A little, at least.

Vaughan picked up the notebook and pen I'd partially planted my butt on, setting it down on the floor. He did not have his happy face on. Thankfully, he didn't have his blank face on either. His lips were a flat line, his gaze troubled.

"Let me guess, Eric invited you to stay back and sample his wares." He resumed playing his guitar quietly. "Nell said that's how he operates."

"We had a few drinks," I admitted.

"Did you fuck him?"

"Do you care?"

He licked his lips, wrinkles crossing his brow. "Guess I do or I wouldn't be asking."

Grace be damned. I flopped back on the sofa, leaning my head against the cushion and closing my eyes. "Is it the penis that makes you all such abhorrent shitheads? It must be. That bit of anatomy is the one real point of universal commonality between you all, isn't it?"

Nothing from him.

I opened my eyes, rolling my head in his direction. "Do something for me?" I asked.

"What?"

"If you honestly believe there's a chance I had sex with Eric tonight, be a good boy and shove that guitar where the sun doesn't shine."

His expression hardened. I daresay it matched mine. We were two angry emotional people. One of the main problems with being female, however, is our propensity for tears. Even when we'd rather not, those sucker glands get all worked up, squeezing out the salt water, making us look and feel weak when we'd rather be going medieval.

"Night." I struggled to my feet, subtly wiping my face with one hand. Or apparently not so subtly because he immediately followed.

"Lydia, wait," he said as his strong arms turned me, hauling me against his body. I face-planted into his chest, sniveling all the while because I'm cool like that. If only we'd kept our pelvises separated. We got along well before sex became part of the equation.

"I'm sorry," he mumbled.

"You shut me out last night."

"I know."

"You disappeared on me today without a word."

"Yeah."

"Then you have the gall to act all entitled and pissed off over Eric?"

He rubbed his face against my hair, squeezing me tight. I had to turn my face sideways to breathe. Even then, his octopus hold made it tricky.

"Who gains entry to my pants is none of your business," I said, stomping one foot. The foot did not appreciate it, but bad luck. "There's no commitment here."

"I know, I know." A pause. "But you didn't sleep with him, right?"

I kicked the man in the shin with everything I had. All of my pent-up rage and drunken anger. Bastard was lucky I didn't try and break his nose. Then I shoved him off.

"Shit, Lydia."

"Good night."

I tried to strut to my room with style, but I'm reasonably certain I flounced. It felt like a flounce. All loose limbs and dubious morals. Slamming the bedroom door shut was also quite juvenile, but whatever. I kicked off my shoes. It took several attempts. I only fell over once, though. Go, Team Lydia!

I dealt with my black skinny jeans while still on the floor.

Because let's be honest, odds were I'd wind up back down there anyway. And go, brain, for being coherent enough to work that one out. My drunken ass was on fire, I tell you. On fire!

"What are you doing on the floor?"

I looked up to find *him* standing there. Uninvited. Ugh.

"Go away," I said.

Chances were, if I attempted the removal of my work shirt and bra, I'd somehow manage to take out an eye. Best that I quit while I was ahead.

Now, time for some rest. I climbed up onto the mattress and stretched out on my back.

"Seriously, how awesome are beds? Beds are just the best."

"Are they?" he asked.

"What are you still doing here?" I threw my pillow at him. Which he caught and replaced on the end of the bed. Pity, it was the only pillow I had and the bottom of the mattress was like miles away. Oh well, I'd just have to sleep without it. "Go away, Vaughan."

"Christ, you're plastered," he muttered. "Again."

"You and your friends are a bad influence on me."

"Right." He cocked his head, giving me a long hard look. Idiot male. "Are you going to throw up?"

"No."

"How many drinks did you have?"

I held up three fingers.

"He make you cocktails?"

"Yes." I sighed and closed my eyes, linking my fingers over my belly. "I'm not plastered, just tipsy. I drank lots of water, paced myself, and ate. Go away."

Instead of hearing the door clicking shut, I felt the mattress shifting beneath me. Mostly on my right-hand side. I opened my eyes and sure enough there he was, sitting next to me.

"I had a lot of stuff to do today," he said. "I wasn't avoiding you or anything."

I scoffed.

"All right, I was avoiding you a little."

"No shit. Well, now I'm avoiding you a lot," I said, reclosing my eyes. "Go away. And turn off the light on your way out, please."

Callused fingers stroked my arm, the touch lingering, loving, even. I slapped madly at the hand, doing my best to chase him away. Except of course this was Vaughan so that didn't quite work. Next thing I knew he was crouched over me, swift fingers tickling my ribs, under my arms, my belly. Everywhere, the bastard. I wriggled and squirmed, getting nowhere.

"Do not tickle me! Leave me alone," I bellowed. "You suck."

The tickling continued.

"Get away from me, Hewson. I don't even like you anymore."

He lay his long body down on top of me, effectively thwarting my ability to fight back. Of course, the feel of him rubbing himself against me woke up my inner horn dog. The desire to arch into him, to stick my tongue down his throat and get me some was mighty. But no! My girl parts would not be so easily swayed. No sex for him.

By god, the jerk was heavy. Elephants, the *Titanic,* think that kind of weight range.

"You're squishing me!"

Warm lips pressed kisses all over my face. "Do you forgive me?" he asked.

"No. You're the worst. I'll never forgive you."

I beat at him with clenched fists, as best as I could. Unfortunately, not only was he heavy, he was strong. The asshat caught my wrists, pressing them down above my head. But I wasn't done yet. Oh no. Like some fearsome, deadly, half-drunk creature, I waited for my chance to strike. Then . . . my sharp teeth bit hard into his hot salty skin, holding on. A full frontal attack on the base of his thick neck.

Hahahahaha.

"Ouch," he bitched.

A hand held the back of my head, almost cradling it, but this was war so it couldn't be that. Regardless, I bit on.

"Fuck, babe." He wrapped my hair around his fist and tugged hard. "All right, you've made your point. I already said I'm sorry. That's enough."

I released the hard flesh between my teeth. Victory was mine. Plus, my jaw was starting to ache.

"Am I bleeding?" he asked, trying to look at the wound.

"No. You're going to have a doozy of a bruise, though." I relaxed back against the mattress, taking a deep breath. At some stage he'd taken most of his weight on one knee. So I actually could breathe freely now. "I told you not to tickle me. And if that was you trying to start something, think again. I can get myself off just fine without your help."

A grunt of much unhappiness. Then he climbed off of me, collapsing onto the bed at my side, making the mattress shake. For a while, we just lay there in silence.

"I thought about you today," he said eventually.

I didn't know how to respond.

"I am sorry about leaving you alone last night. I just . . ."

"You just what?" I asked when it became clear he wouldn't be finishing the thought on his own.

"It was serious, going to get the pill."

"Yes, it was." With a heavy sigh I rolled onto my side, facing him. There might come a day in a thousand years or so when the sight of him didn't move me. I doubt it, though. He addled my brain and made the butterflies inside me come to life. What effect he had on my heart, I didn't even want to ponder.

"I think it shocked me." There was such honesty in his eyes, in his unguarded expression. "I've always been careful about protection. Always. Dad lectured me constantly about it and growing up, I saw friends become fathers way ahead of their time. Then there's all the STDs. But last night with you . . ."

"You were upset, Vaughan."

"Yeah." He stared into my eyes, giving me a sad smile. "You look tired. Lie down, I'll get the light."

I didn't ask him if he was staying or retreating to his own room. Being needy annoyed the crap out of me. We didn't have that kind of relationship. He rolled off the bed and flicked off the light. Then he wandered out into the hallway. One by one, the other lights in the house disappeared and full darkness crept in. Heavy footsteps came my way and then the mattress squeaked as he sat at the end.

That wasn't relief rolling through me. It was something else. Something complicated and beyond my control.

The palms of his hands slid up over my bare legs, all the way up to my panties, where they lingered with obvious intent.

"Vaughan."

"I want to get you off." He traced delicate lines over my stomach, making my muscles clench with need. "Please."

"I don't know . . ."

"Just you. Nothing for me," he said, hooking his fingers in my underwear and slowly dragging them down my legs. "Let me go down on you, Lydia. I want to make amends."

"I'm not sure making someone perform oral sex should be used as a method of punishment. The ethics are a bit icky." Yeah, I was fighting him hard.

Gently, he pushed my legs open, kneeling between them. "Babe, licking your pretty pussy is a treat. Not getting a piece of you afterward is the punishment."

I laughed. "Treat. A piece of me. You make me sound like pie."

Without further ado, he licked straight up my center. From my butt to my clit and back again. An amazing rush, a whole new kind of intoxication, raced through me. My spine arched, jaw falling open. "Fuck."

"You're sweet enough to be pie," he mumbled, fixing his mouth to my labia and softly sucking. His nose nuzzled the area around my clit, hot breath stirring over all of that delicate flesh. Every ounce of blood in me rushed to the call of his mouth. My head spun, my body light, incandescent. He sucked and licked and savored me like a feast.

It was breathtaking.

The man knew his stuff, driving my excitement to scary heights. First softly grazing his teeth over my mound, then circling my clit with the tip of his tongue. Long licks between my lips, over and over again as his hands held me open. He followed no set pattern, I didn't know what he'd do next. A tender wet open-mouthed French kiss to my opening. Or giving my clit a tongue lashing. Maybe even teasing over my asshole with a light finger. Nothing was off limits in his pursuit of my pleasure.

Had I been mad at the man? I couldn't remember.

Surely it was all some silly mistake. No one with a mouth so talented and blessed could possibly have behaved like a thoughtless bastard.

A finger eased into me and bent a little, taking on the shape of a hook. It was the only way he could have reached the pertinent areas. Carefully the pad of his finger rubbed over the back of my clit, massaging me inside. My poor wet swollen pussy never stood a chance. The orgasm nearly knocked me out. Bright lights bursting inside of me, a pleasure so keen it was almost pain. I came hard and fast, gasping his name, clinging to the bedsheets as the world turned upside down. It took a fair while for things to come right again.

Someone was mouth-breathing seriously loud. How uncouth.

Muscles kept twitching, inside me, in my thick thighs. Poor shell-shocked things. They'd probably never be the same. He'd broken me for all others. I was sure of it. And I didn't even have the energy to care.

He wiped his face off on the sheet and then pulled me into his arms, spooning me. Getting comfortable and settling in for the night. The scent of my come still lingered on him. His lips were still damp as he kissed my shoulder, the back of my neck. I don't know if I'd ever been with someone quite as raw. Not vulgar, just open, relaxed, and matter-of-fact about sex and into all of my body.

"Apology accepted," I said.

"Good."

"Be warned, though, I'm practicing to become a better feminist." I rolled onto my back, staring at his luminous eyes in the dark. "The whole Chris thing was a kick to the clit, but I'm working hard to set myself straight now. I own this body. My fate is mine."

"Okay," he said slowly, meshing his fingers with mine. "Where is this going?"

"I just want you to know, I will not be falling slave to your devil dick and demon tongue. No matter how good they are."

"Hmm." He rubbed his mouth against my shoulder. "Is that your way of saying you like how I fuck?"

"Yes. Basically."

"Well . . . I'm glad," he said eventually. "And I'd like you to know that I consider myself a feminist too. You are more than my equal. But with all due respect, I think maybe you should consider getting some sleep now. This body that you own is probably going to feel bad in the morning. I'm a little worried that you're fated to have a hangover tomorrow."

Sadly, the man made sense. I snuggled into him, closing my eyes. "I'm going to miss you when you're gone."

A squeeze and another kiss to the back of my neck.

"The town was so pretty as Boyd was driving me home. We went by the scenic route through downtown."

"Downtown's in the opposite direction," he said with a smile in his voice.

"I know, but Boyd didn't seem to mind and I just felt like seeing it. All of the lights and the trees, the water. It's all so beautiful, you know?"

"I know," he said, sounding a little sad.

"I started wondering what it will be like when the trees change color, when it snows."

"Cold," he deadpanned.

"You don't say."

A snicker.

"At any rate, I got thinking and . . . I'm not sure I want to leave after all." I tried to organize my thoughts in a straight line, but my brain was all orgasm- and alcohol-befuddled. It wasn't easy. "See, part of me wants to spend the rest of my days at least two states away from the Delaneys at any given time. But the other part of me is all 'you take your problems with you wherever you go.' The truth is, my issues aren't really about Chris and company, they're about me not being happy with my life and making bad choices. That's not going to change just because my address does."

Nothing.

"What do you think?"

He sighed. "Honestly, people have long memories. There's a lot to be said for starting over somewhere new."

"My parents had that attitude and it never quite worked for me. And here . . . I'm finally starting to feel like I've found the place where I belong."

Vaughn didn't answer and a sneaky unwelcome little voice suggested he didn't want me here. However he felt about the place, it would always be his hometown. He had family and friends here, a history. For certain at some time in the future he'd be back around and if I was still here . . . well, running into ex-lovers could be awkward as hell.

"You don't have to make any decisions right now," he said. "Rest."

Everything was quiet for a good long time before I heard him speak again. My mind was on the edge of sleep, so it might have even been a dream. A delusion.

"I'm going to miss you too," a voice whispered.

CHAPTER NINETEEN

Friday morning, Vaughan sat out on the back patio steps, basking in the sun, playing his guitar. No shirt on, which was definitely my preferred attire for his upper body. Same went for the lower. A pad and pen were at his side, like last night. I remembered it all . . . vaguely.

Did he really say he was going to miss me? Maybe he had and it didn't mean anything major. You could run out of ketchup and miss it without a crushing sense of deprivation overwhelming your life. It was, after all, just a condiment. I might well be the current pick of the condiments in his life. But he'd still eat a hamburger without me.

A terrible analogy, I know. But quite possibly true.

At any rate, I couldn't think about it right now. Literally couldn't. Any usage of the brain was bad. Inside my skull, things throbbed and hurt. I threw down two Advil with a bottle full of water and made a cup of coffee while trying not to think of anything. Only, trying not to think of anything was just as bad as focusing on something, and the malevolent organism in my head took it as a declaration of war.

Pain, so much pain.

Maybe not drinking anything with an alcohol percentage for a while was the way to go. Also, Eric must die. Enablers were bad, evil people. The world must be purged of them.

I hid behind my sunglasses, sitting at one of the few remaining dining room chairs (several had fallen during the great fight) and listened to him playing through the open kitchen doors. Thank god for coffee. Coffee understood. Coffee was my friend.

Merrily, the drugs were at long last beginning to kick in when he noticed my presence.

"Morning." He shifted his position, all the better to see me. Unfortunately, I wasn't a good view.

"Hi."

"How you feeling?"

"Like Long Island Iced Teas are not my friend."

He inspected me over the top of his sunglasses. "Shit, you were drinking those? No wonder you were smashed."

"One Old Fashioned, one lychee martini, one Caipirinha, and one Long Island Iced Tea."

"So you had four cocktails," he said. "Last night you told me three."

"Did I? Huh."

He gave me a look that was most dubious.

"I've decided I have no further statement to make about last night."

"Have you now?" His tongue played behind his cheek. No idea what expression filled his eyes; he'd retreated back behind his shades. Probably for the best.

He gave up the sun and came inside, carrying his guitar in one hand and a pad and pen in the other. All of it got dumped on the kitchen table.

"Working on a new song?" I asked.

"Yes," he said, sitting down across the table from me. "It's called 'You Say Funny Shit When You're Drunk.'"

"I like it. Sounds like a winner."

"Yeah. It's going to be by the Devil Dick and Demon Tongue

Band." He took off his sunglasses, placed them on the table. "What do you think?"

"That's the name of the new band? Sweet."

"Classy, right?"

"Totally." I suppressed my smile, just barely. Funny bastard. I swirled the dregs of my coffee around in the cup. "Do you have any plans for today?"

"No, nothing today." He stared out the open kitchen doors at the world beyond. The large broken panel of glass had been replaced sometime yesterday. "I, ah, I accepted an offer on the house."

My face froze. "You did?"

A nod.

"Wow. That was fast. I guess I shouldn't be surprised, it's a great property."

High up on the wall, the kitchen clock was ticking. I don't know if I'd really noticed it before, but now . . . damn, it was loud.

"You're happy with the price?" I asked.

"Very."

"Great." I smiled, trying my utmost to be happy for him. Just like a friend would be. "That's . . . that's really great."

Odd how he didn't smile back. Instead, he kept staring out at the backyard, face betraying no emotion. It was his parents' place. Whatever his issues over accepting their death, giving up his child-hood home had to hit hard. All those memories.

"When are you thinking of leaving town?"

"Henning and Conn want to get started putting together the new material soon as possible." He grabbed at the back of his neck. "So early next week, I guess."

"That soon?"

"Yeah." His gaze zeroed in on me. "Is that a problem for you, with your stuff and all that, Lydia?"

"No." I looked down, trying to get a handle on . . . well, me. It felt like my little world had been turned upside down and been shaken to shit. The perfect scene in the snow globe was a blizzardy mess. What the hell was my problem? None of this should be a surprise. "No. I'll get storage sorted out in the next few days. Not a problem."

"So you're still thinking of staying?"

"Maybe." It was my turn to look away, to avoid his eyes. Such a perfect shade of blue. I'd just have to avoid looking up at the sky for the rest of my life so as not to be reminded of him. Completely doable. "So, early next week. What are you thinking, Monday, Tuesday?"

"Something like that."

I nodded and tucked my mass of bed hair back behind my ears. Then I messed it back up again because exposing myself right now was plain dumb. "Well, it's great that you got a big offer on the house right away. Just great."

"Mm."

"I should go shower. Make some small attempt to look less like the undead."

"Hey," he said. "Did you want to go check out some cars today?"

"Yes, that would be good. Thanks." I rose, my legs feeling bizarrely flimsy, weak.

The great thing about crying in the shower was that with all of the noise and water, there was no real evidence.

No one need ever know.

"See, babe. Isn't this nice?"

I gave him an unimpressed look. Not an easy feat, given how good he looked. With the window down, his golden-red hair blew wild in the wind and a toned inked arm leaned on the door frame. He was like an ad for the good life.

"Come on, you have to admit this is a great car."

I didn't have to admit a damn thing.

"Lydia, this is the right choice," he said smoothly. "Comfortable interior, high safety standards, handles well in wet weather and snow, and it even has a small sunroof just for you."

"You're being condescending. Stop it before I hurt you."

"I know you like that piece of shit Prius and the *cute* little MINI Cooper." He reached out, slipping a hand behind my neck and massaging gently. Dude was lucky I didn't bite off his limb. If he wasn't so good with his fingers, I would. "But the WRX will work out far better for you, I promise."

"I didn't even want to take it for a test drive. You and that idiot ganged up on me."

"Babe."

"It's true. You know you did."

"I had no idea Mitch even worked there," he said with a laugh. A devious one. "Is it really so bad that me and my old friend want you to have an awesome car at the best price possible?"

"It is a good price."

"It's a fucking amazing price and you know it. You're supposed to be test-driving it, not me." He pulled into a gravel car park in a secluded spot by the lake, switched off the engine. "Fastest line-built vehicle on the market, Lydia. You know you want to try it."

"It probably got thrashed by its previous owners."

"No way would Mitch sell you something that'd been treated bad. I'd come back to Coeur d'Alene to kick his ass if he did, and he knows it."

"God, would you stop talking about leaving?" I snapped. And immediately regretted it.

Vaughan cocked his head.

"Sorry." I took out a deep breath, let it out slowly. "Apparently, I'm Ms. Bad Attitude today. Let's just enjoy the here and now. Okay?"

He slowly nodded his head. Then he gazed back out the

windshield at the sparkling blue water. "You wanted the Vaughan Hewson Coeur d'Alene experience."

It took a moment for my poor brain to catch up. "This is where you brought your dates when you were in school?"

"Yes, it is."

"Nice. Very nice."

"Far enough out of town, away from the lights. The whole sky would be full of stars."

"Mm." I smiled wistfully. "Sounds romantic. Too bad it's daytime."

"No one's around."

I turned my head so fast we both should have gotten whiplash. "What?"

"No one's around."

"Ha." I smiled, raised my eyes to the heavens. "God, I thought you were serious there for a minute."

"I am." He was? Shit. He was. Beautiful blue eyes all intense and heated, looking at me and licking his lips like I was definitely at the top of today's menu.

"Oh."

He tucked a strand of hair behind my ear, trailing his fingers down my neck. Toying first with the spaghetti strap of my blousy white top and then with my bra beneath. The man had moves. But also, he basically had me on a leash, the bastard. Mind, body, heart, and soul. Not that I'd ever tell him. Immediately my breathing picked up pace, my skin grew all shivery.

"Lewd acts. Exposure." I giggled hysterically, sounding a lot like an idiot. "I'm pretty sure there are laws protecting public places against that. Especially in broad daylight. We better not."

"We're not going to get caught."

"But we might."

"We won't." He slipped both straps off my shoulder, exposing more skin. In the smoothest of moves, he unclipped his seatbelt and then moved directly on to releasing mine. But the man wasn't done. Oh, no. There would soon come a day when he would be done with me, but it wasn't this one.

"Hold on." He twisted and rose up. With a knee on his seat, he reached right across me. Things were fiddled with on the side of my seat, and all of a sudden the back was way back and I was staring directly up at the beige car ceiling. Out the open window, a tree swayed overhead. Green leafy branches rustled in the wind. Lots of nature. Now and then the sun broke through, a dazzling shaft of light from the heavens above.

Did the sun have to be so bright? We were going to get caught for sure. Also, cellulite did best under soft or no lighting. Try as I did to accept my body, this sort of shit remained a concern.

"Um," I said, because my brain was still in genius mode. "I'm not sure this is safe."

"Car's stationary and I've got a condom in my back pocket. We couldn't be safer." Without further ado, he climbed on top of me, his hips situated between my legs. An elbow to my side near the top of the seat took the bulk of his weight. Still, the feel of his body on mine sent tremors of excitement racing through me. Red alert, illegal and possibly embarrassing, but very good times ahead. I gripped the sides of my chair like I was on a roller-coaster and a loop de loop was coming up. Yet all the while, my vagina prepared to party like it was 1999.

Fuck. I was so confused. "We have a bed at home. I mean, at your place."

Low laughter from the deviant. "Yeah, but I have you all turned on right here. Why wait?"

"I'm not really turned on."

"Nipples."

I looked down. They were indeed twin hard points, all too

obvious beneath the thin cotton of my top. Talk about betrayal. "They know nothing."

"Hey. You really want me to stop?" He stared deep into my eyes, seeing the panic in my soul. I could feel it, his understanding, his concern. And not just over the public exposure sex thing. Let's be honest here. My current freak-out had way more to do with the creeping dread of him leaving and the fear regarding the state of my muddled heart.

"Babe?"

His face was so close. Lips just barely touching mine, the heat and beauty of him setting me on fire. I could feel him hardening against my stomach, reacting to me. My need fed on his, growing by the moment.

"Say the word," he continued. "You know I'll do whatever you want."

I wanted to call bullshit on that so badly. Or better yet, tell him exactly what I wanted. Just as soon as I figured out exactly what that was. . . .

Instead I craned my neck, kissing him gently, sweetly. Over and over with lips closed, then with them open just a little. On this went until his tongue eased into my mouth, taking me over. We kissed in slow motion as if we had all the time in the world. The palm of his hand molded to my breast, squeezing and teasing the sensitive flesh. My hands meanwhile slipped beneath his tee, exploring his back. Stroking his smooth skin, coming close to getting off on the feel of him. The ridges in his spine and the hard planes of his muscles. All the while, he moved against me, rubbing his hard dick over my pubic bone, stroking close to the top of my sweet spot. I angled my hips, trying to get more.

Shit, it felt good. So good. But it wasn't enough.

"Vaughan," I panted, slipping my hands down into his jeans, squeezing his firm ass cheeks. "No underwear?"

"I wanted to be prepared."

I grinned as he lightly bit my earlobe, then licked my neck.

It could never get old, being with him. Every intimacy we shared added to the familiarity of his body and his ways. The thrill of being with him, however, never waned. Given time, it might change and grow. But never would it disappear. Some things just were absolute.

I slipped my hands between us, unbuttoning his jeans and lowering his zipper. Demure, I was not. Or at least, not once we got going. Getting that item of clothing right the hell out of my way. Hot velvet skin over rigid flesh. He was a tactile heaven. My fingers brushed over the rounded head, thumb searching out the join in the ridge of his cockhead and massaging just beneath.

He groaned into my neck, shoulders heaving. "Fuck, that feels good."

Ah, the power of getting your hand on a man's cock. It was mighty. "Does it?"

"Mm."

A hand pushed up my chambray skirt, exposing my dimpled thighs. Screw any anxiety. I was too caught up in the goodness of touching Vaughan to care. He slipped a finger into the leg opening of my panties, tugging at the material.

"Why the fuck are you wearing these, Lydia?"

"Because I'm a fool?"

He chuckled.

"I didn't know what you were planning," I complained.

"Assume I always want to fuck you. That would be safest."

His mouth covered mine and he kissed me deep and wet. Mutual masturbation worked well. I fondled and caressed his cock, doing my best to drive him insane. While he did likewise, curling in his fingers and sliding his knuckles through my wet slit. Every muscle between my neck and knees tensed, it felt so good. The boy gave me bliss, pure and simple. Then he broke the kiss and licked the pad of his thumb before going to work on my clit. God, he was good at this, his touch just right. His hand stretched the elastic in my panties, making room for him to play. Happy chemicals made my head spin round, my whole world was in a daze. I almost forgot to keep stroking him. Sad, because the feel of him thickening in my hand was sublime. Not something I'd ever want to miss.

"Cum on me." I nipped at his lips.

"That what you want? You want my cum on your soft skin?"

I nodded my head, milking him harder with every stroke.

"No. Not this time." He pulled his hand out of my panties, a crying shame. Then he drew the condom out of his back pocket and ripped it open with his teeth. I made a truly sad sound when he pried my fingers off of his cock and rolled it on.

"Scoot your ass down a little," he said, drawing me closer to the edge of the seat. "Why couldn't you want a bigger car?"

"Why couldn't you cum on me?"

The sides of his lips hitched up. He pulled aside my stretched underwear and carefully lined his cock up with my opening. In one smooth thrust he filled me, both of us moaning. Loudly.

"Oh god." My eyelids fluttered, my insides doing the same. Indescribable. That's what having him inside of me felt like. Every good thing, everything bright and shiny. But more, so much more. And the way he looked at me, studying my every expression, gauging my every move. I don't know why, but having such total committed focus from him nearly undid me. I almost cried for the second time today.

"That's why I couldn't cum on you," he whispered in my ear. "Because I needed to do this."

I had no words. Happily, none was required.

Slowly, deliberately, he made love to me. Crammed into the passenger side of a test vehicle which now definitively must be mine.

Of all the places to have a meaningful moment. He rocked in and out of me, taking his time, building the passion between us. Our connection was absolute and always would be. No matter where he went. No matter what he did. I'd lost a part of myself to him that I'd never get back. Hell, I gave it, even knowing it wasn't smart and I might regret it one day soon.

Hearts are so stupid.

Gradually he increased his pace. My legs were wrapped around him, holding on tight. Sweat soaked both our skins. We moved as best we could, reaching for the peak, clinging together. It went on and on, and yet was over all too soon. I angled my hips up, taking him deep. He plowed into me with great purpose. One hand tangled in my hair and the other taking some of his weight. The sound of our frantic breathing, of our bodies slamming together filled the small space.

And still it surprised me. My orgasm ripped out my lungs. I silently cried out, my cunt clutching at him as my heart skipped a beat. My whole body shook beneath him as he groaned my name, pressing his cheek bruisingly hard against mine. Apparently, the French refer to an orgasm as the little death. However, that didn't cover it. Try the mass murder of all of my hopes and dreams. It shouldn't have felt so astonishingly mind-numbingly superb to fall for a man who'd never be mine. But it did.

Love sucks.

CHAPTER TWENTY

Strange things were afoot at the Dive Bar the next day. Saturday, the anniversary of my botched wedding. Hooray.

Nothing of any great interest had happened after our sexcapades in my new car. We went back to see Mitch at the dealership, who gave our skewed clothing dubious looks. He visibly relaxed after I told him I'd be buying the vehicle. Vaughan had gone quiet, but then so had I.

We went to work. And when we got back to his house exhausted after a long night, we went to sleep, together in the same bed.

But back to today.

Brett Chen, the reporter, lounged against his car parked opposite my place of work. He pulled out his Canon and started snapping photos of Vaughan and me as we were walking inside.

"Talk to me, Lydia," he yelled from across the street. "I've got a big-name magazine taking the story. Nationwide distribution. A lot of money."

"Asshole," I muttered, keeping my sunglasses on and my face down.

"Time to give Officer Andy a call," said Vaughan. "Get rid of this guy."

"I'm not sure legally there's much he can do. Anyway, the

reporter's not going to get what he wants," I said without slowing down. "Let karma take care of him for profiting from people's heartbreak and misery. I've got better things to do with my time."

"This is the third time he's been here in almost as many days. Taking your picture without your permission. The idiot's practically stalking you, babe."

I shrugged, reached out and gave his fingers a squeeze. We stepped into the bar and I headed straight for a small table at the back. Poor Betsy, the Delaneys' real estate receptionist, did not look like a happy girl. Boo-hoo.

"I've been waiting for you for nearly twenty minutes." She sniffed, pushing back a half-drunk cup of coffee and rising out of her seat. "The brew here is godawful. Are the papers all correctly signed? I don't want to have to come down here again just because you can't read."

God, what a bitch. The papers were signed, all right, but she could figure that out for herself.

In lieu of conversation, I tossed the large envelope containing the Delaneys' settlement contract her way. Betsy dived for it. making a weird gasping noise. Indignation burned bright in her beady little eyes. Before she could rip into me for lack of care or whatever, I got the hell away from her. I had things to do. It was time to make over my life. Minus the bullshit this time.

Saturday was a big day. At only twenty past twelve, most of the tables were already filled. I called out greetings to Rosie and Masa on the restaurant floor, Eric behind the bar, and Nell and Boyd busy at work in the kitchen. Then I continued on my way to the back office.

The big blond bear, aka Joe, sat in front of the computer, engrossed in whatever was on the screen.

"Hi," I said, dumping my handbag in the corner. "Nell wanted me to start on the bookkeeping."

Startled eyes glanced up at me and his fingers froze on the keys. "Ah, hey, Lydia."

"Are you working today too?" Three people behind the bar seemed excessive but whatever.

"No," he said. "I just needed to use the computer. Mine's playing up. Be out of here in a minute."

"No problem. I'll go grab a cup of coffee."

The deer-caught-in-headlights look faded, transforming into something else. He cleared his throat, gaze returning to me every few seconds. Whatever was on that screen, Joe did not want it to be seen. Probably porn.

"Would you like one?" I asked, taking a step toward the table.

His whole body tensed as if he was preparing to jump up and cover whatever it was. "One what?"

"Coffee."

"No," he said. "Thanks."

"Okay." I gave him a brief smile, strolling toward the door. "Back in a minute."

His chin jerked, eyes stuck to me like I might vault over the desk and launch a violent invasion of his online privacy at any moment.

Very strange.

When I came back with my coffee, Joe had disappeared out the back door. Nell had left a list detailing what kinds of expenses belonged in which category. Beyond that, it was pretty basic. I worked away at the piles of receipts, banking records, and invoices. Inputting all of the information—business name, items in question, their price, etc. Gradually, the backlog began to dwindle.

The best part of doing this particular job (which no one else wanted to do) were the excellent service and gastronomical benefits. Rosie or Masa regularly delivered coffees, bottles of sparkling water, a delectable Vietnamese-style chicken salad for lunch, and an amazingly good steak with a baked potato and all the trimmings for dinner. I had no idea what they did to the cow to make the meat so tender. Daily massages. Weekly pedicures. Whatever it was, it worked. Best steak ever.

"How's it going?" Nell collapsed into the chair opposite my desk, face still pale and shadows beneath her eyes. She looked only marginally better than the other day.

"I'm slowly beating the accounts into submission. Should you be home in bed?"

"Probably." She cracked the lid on a bottle of apple juice and gulped some down, then set it on the table. "I'm heading home soon."

"Good." And here came the nervy part. "Nell . . ."

"Yeah?"

I rubbed the tip of my tongue over my teeth, trying to think of the best way to say what I needed to say. Fear and excitement stirred inside of me, speeding my heart and making my hands shake. No matter how I tried to calm myself. "Not to sound like some psycho corporate spy out to infiltrate you."

She raised her brows in question.

"But while I was going over the figures, I went over the figures."

With a groan, she shook her head. "I'm tired, Lydia. What do you want to say?"

I sat forward, hiding my trembling hands beneath the table. "Last night, Eric offered me a month's trial managing the restaurant floor section. I trust you're in agreement about that?"

"Of course."

"And Pat still wants to sell his third of the business?"

Her lips tightened, pain flitting across her face before being determinedly smoothed away. "Very much so."

"Okay."

"Lydia, tell me you're saying what I think you're saying."

"I'd like to do the month's trial with a view to purchasing Pat's share of the business at the end of that time, if we're all in agreement that we can work together long-term."

Nell's smile was beatific. "You do?"

"Yes. I know this probably seems sudden, but the idea has been growing in the back of my mind for the last few days. Which still sounds sudden."

She said nothing.

"Anyway, I want to do something I like for a change, sell products I believe in, and I think the Dive Bar could be that opportunity for me." I didn't know what to do with myself. Jump around the room or hide in a corner. Both were viable options. "I realize it's a lot of money, a big commitment, but this feels right to me. I think I'd regret it if I didn't give it a try."

"But you definitely have the money?"

"I will in a couple of days, yes."

Curiosity lit her eyes. "A couple of days?"

"Between you and me?"

"Of course." No hesitation. One of my favorite qualities about Nell was her plainspokenness.

"I have a legal settlement coming through from Delaneys."

"Okay," said Nell. "It is a bit sudden, but you saw the figures. You've worked here, you've seen how much local people like the place. We're not relying on seasonal trade to the same degree as others. This is going to be awesome."

"I hope so." I tried to bite back a smile; it didn't quite work.

"I know so." Nell's gaze dropped to her lap, fingers fidgeting. "In the interest of full disclosure . . . I have some news to tell you. No one else knows about this just yet as I only found out this morning. So I'd appreciate you keeping it to yourself for now."

"Of course."

"I'm pregnant."

My mouth hung open, my eyes feeling bigger than the moon.

"That was pretty much my reaction too." She gave me a grim smile. "It's Eric's. So, yeah. Not exactly planned. Not even remotely."

"Congratulations?" I asked quietly.

Her smile improved. "Thank you. I always wanted kids. I thought they'd be with Pat, but things change, right?"

"Right. And I think you'll make a great mom. No one will dare mess with your kid."

"I do know how to throw knives," she said. "The benefit to knowing this early is we can plan how to handle things business-wise. I don't expect to take too much time off and Boyd can run the kitchen almost as well as me. We'll get another cook trained up along with an assistant. That way I can be back after the baby on reduced hours. It also lets Boyd go to more sci-fi conventions. So it'll work out for everyone."

"Okay."

"Please don't let this scare you off. I swear it won't impact in any big or bad ways on the rest of the business."

I pondered it for a minute. "The fact is, each of us will go through periods when we need to pull back a little, focus on other things. That's life."

"Yeah."

"How are you feeling?" I asked.

"Terrified. Excited. More terrified."

"Me too. And I'm not even having a baby."

Nell picked up her juice again, picking at the label. "I'm really glad you're staying. I lost a lot of my friends in the divorce, so it's good to make some new ones. I know they say not to go into business with friends. But honestly, if you're going to work that closely with people, trust them with your money and your name, I'd rather have friends. The thing is, they need to be friends that you can talk to. Complete honesty."

"I agree." I straightened my shoulders, putting on my brave face.

"If you need somewhere to store your things, there's plenty of empty space upstairs. Also, my apartment has a spare room," she said. "I'm not saying we should be permanent roommates. But you're more than welcome to come stay with me for a few months, until you get something else sorted out. *If* it winds up being needed."

"If?"

"Vaughan's never been like this about a girl before. All over everything to do with you, making sure things are cool and you'll be treated right. I know you've had a fight or two, but he never even stuck around for those before." Her smile was way too hopeful. "Usually women were just temporary, easy. This thing with you . . . it's nice."

Oh shit. "Nell, I really like your brother. I'm sure that's beyond obvious. But hasn't he told you about this Henning Peters guy and the great opportunity with the record companies and everything?"

"I think he felt weird about the fight and then I was sick. Honestly, we haven't spoken that much," she said. "He's going to work with Henning Peters?"

"Yes."

"Wow. That's huge."

"Yes, it is. I'm a distraction, Nell," I admitted, staring at my hands. Except only cowards did thing like that. I raised my face again. "That's the reality of your brother and me."

She just looked at me.

"You're right about this place, your parents' house. Past issues bother him, make it hard to be here. I can only say that because I'm not telling you anything you didn't already know." Unlike the sale of the house. That was his news to share. Oops about the Henning Peters thing.

"I'm sorry," Nell said.

"It is what it is. We're friends." I swallowed hard, doing my best to keep my cool. "Thank you for offering to let me stay, to store my things here."

"Of course."

We both tried to smile. I think hers was better than mine.

Screw men and their devil penises. I had a future to plan.

There were bound to be problems with me coming into the business. For instance, Eric treating the place like his woo palace. Though Rosie had confided the other day, he'd cut a lot of that out since Nell's meltdown at him. He'd barely even bothered hitting on me. Still, I'd be watching. Also, how Eric took the news of his upcoming fatherhood could be vital. If he and Nell were able to continue to maintain a functioning relationship for the business's sake.

But I had a month to settle in, to listen and learn. To see if I could make a go of this. I wanted to be a part of the Dive Bar, to stay in Coeur d'Alene. I had a lot to contribute and, for whatever reason, being here felt right. If it didn't work out, however, I could always make a Plan B.

Chris had derailed me. Hurt my heart and shaken my pride. He'd also, however, shown me the error of my ways. The stupidity of me blindly scrambling, trying to make up for my crap childhood by replacing it with a bigger shinier house and family. Those things as I knew them were just props.

It might sound all Oprah, but my happiness needed to come from me. I knew that now.

I could build my own home, make a future for myself. Not rely on someone else to come along and magically make me feel like I had worth, as if I belonged. I could be strong on my own.

As a by-product of their bastardry, Chris and company had made me grow up and taught me some important life lessons. With my payout from the Delaneys for never suing for emotional or other damages, and refraining from ever telling my story to the press (their fear of Brett Chen being of significant worth), I'd be implementing what I'd learned.

Ironic, really. I might even thank my ex-fiancé one of these days.

Doubt it, though.

Nell needed the office. I left the bookwork and helped Rosie and Masa finish up for the night. Loading the industrial dishwashers, cleaning the tables, mopping the floor, those sorts of things. Mostly any job allowing me to keep a keen eye on the back hallway. Who knew, the mother-to-be might well need emotional backup. It was a tense, high-drama situation. Given my own recent brush with forgotten prophylactics, I felt for her big-time.

Nell asked Eric to join her in the back office. Not a big deal. No one paid any attention. Yet. The owners (with the exception of Pat) had occasional closed-door meetings. Like his brother earlier, he never reappeared. Given he'd doubtless just received news of his impending fatherhood, I'd have used the back exit too.

Vaughan went in next. Two minutes later, he came storming back out, red of face and furious. "Where is he?"

"Who?" asked Rosie.

"Eric." He spat out the name as if it were poison. "Where is he? I'm going to fucking kill him."

"Dunno." Rosie scuttled away. Fair enough.

"He's gone." I stopped pretending to be deeply engrossed in refilling the condiments. Vaughan's evil eye turned my way. Shit. The man was beyond enraged, top lip curled and shoulders heaving. You'd have thought I'd knocked up his sister, the way he was glaring daggers. "He left a little while back."

"Coward."

Not good. With all of the violence from the four-dude epic battle in his sitting room earlier this week, you'd have figured he'd have had his fill of punch-ups for a while. Guess not, though.

"I'm pretty much finished here," I said. "Why don't we go?"

After a moment he jerked his chin. "Yeah. Grab your shit. Let's go."

Oh-kay. I went and grabbed my bag from the now curiously vacant office. Maybe it was international Use the Back Door Day. No puns intended. Or perhaps Nell had also decided she needed to escape unseen.

I'd check on her later. Boyd had keys, he could lock up the bar.

Vaughan threw open the door and stomped out onto the sidewalk. I followed more slowly, giving him some space. Hopefully, there'd be no sign of the baby daddy tonight. If Eric had any survival skills at all, he'd be off somewhere lying low.

All of a sudden, Vaughan about-faced and stomped back, coming to an abrupt stop in front of me.

"Do you know?" he demanded.

"Know what?"

"About her being knocked up by Eric."

"Yes."

He huffed out a breath. "And you still want to stay here, buy into that bar?"

"Nell told you about that too? Okay." I didn't take a step back, just kind of leaned away from him, trying to put a little distance between us. Not that I was afraid of him, but nor was I keen on anyone getting up in my face. "Yes, I do. I've enjoyed working there and I think I have a lot to offer them."

"No. Come on." He about-faced again and started pacing back and forth outside Inkaho, Pat's tattoo parlor. Light shined around the edges of the large framed illustrations hanging in the front window, hiding the bulk of the interior from view. I guess if you were getting your ass inked, having people walking past and seeing in would not be desirable.

"Lydia!" he shouted.

I jumped in surprise, starting to get a wee bit pissed off myself.

He squinted at me like I was beyond recognition. Like I was just some shit on his shoe.

"First you get engaged to a guy you barely know," he said. "Get sucked into that poisonous fucking family. Now you're jumping straight into this? You've only worked there a couple of days."

"I have given this some thought. I've seen how they work, I've looked at their figures," I said, standing as tall as possible. "And there's going to be a month-long trial period to give all of us a chance to assess whether it will work or not. I'm not just jumping into anything."

"Christ." His laughter was so not funny. "What the hell is wrong with you? Do you never learn?"

Huh. Nice to know what he really thought of me.

"Well?"

I just shrugged. "Well, what?"

"Are you going to answer my question?"

"No." I crossed my arms, watching his anger grow and grow. He stared at me, face a mask of fury and frustration. Sucked to be him. "I don't owe you any answers, Vaughan. Not about my business decisions. Not about my life. And especially not while you're behaving like an asshole and insulting me."

He swallowed hard, turning away. "Well, I am not staying here, not for this kid, and not for you."

"Who the hell asked you to?" I shouted, voice echoing up and down the empty street. "I mean, seriously."

He stopped.

"You seem to think this is all some grand conspiracy to trap you in town. It's not."

He scoffed.

"Go and make merry with Conn and Henning Peters in L.A. These people don't need you here," I said, trying to keep my voice calm. "For what . . . ten years? For ten years they've all managed just fine on their own. So shit happened. Shit always happens. The world turns round and people screw up, they make mistakes. Your presence here wouldn't have changed a damn thing."

In silence, he glared at me.

"They don't need you, and neither do I." I stood tall, something inside of me breaking, tears welling in my eyes. "I'm sorry you lost your parents and your sister isn't living up to your expectations of exactly what she should or shouldn't be doing. Thing is, we're all only human and people do die."

His nostrils flared in fury.

"Deal with your shit, Vaughan. Mourn your parents. Get over your guilt. Give you and your sister a break. Do whatever the hell you need to, to be all right." Too many emotions were running wild. I wrapped my arms around me, trying to hold myself together. "But understand, you're not god. Your family and friends here will manage without you if going back to the coast is what you have to do to feel right with yourself."

"It is," he gritted out, hands clenched into fists. Such an angry-man pose. "Of course it is. There's the biggest fucking opportunity of my life back there. Not here."

"Great. Go." I nodded stiffly. "But don't get pissed at me because what I want—this town—these people, are what you're giving away."

Nothing.

And seriously, fuck this. Fuck all of it. "I think we've talked enough tonight. Would you mind driving me home, please, or would you prefer I caught a cab?"

For a minute he stared at me, then he stalked toward his parked car. I stood, staring after him. Fucking males with their fucking issues. Fuck them all. I tried to slow my breathing, to calm my shit.

It didn't really work.

Down the street, he unlocked his car and climbed in, slamming the door shut. Give me strength. The thought of getting into a small enclosed space with him did not appeal. One of us might wind up dead. Maybe I should just walk home. Not home. It would never be home. It was a nice quiet night now that Mr Shoutypants had shut his trap. Of course, I hadn't exactly been a decorous young lady myself.

Gah. Whatever. Stars were shining. The moon was glowing. All that beautiful shit.

Vaughan revved the engine, headlights cutting through the night. Then he just sat there, waiting for me, I guess. My feet stayed put. This was a change. I'd always been so keen to get close to him.

But now, well . . . what to do?

That's when the chair came crashing through the tattoo parlor's front window out onto the sidewalk. Glass shattered, flying everywhere. I fell sideways onto my hip, landing hard on the cement, arms covering my head. The sudden barrage of noise was stunning. The chair skidded past me, metal legs striking sparks against the concrete. It came to a stop against the pole for a street sign, declaring the speed limit.

Then, nothing. Absolute silence.

Cautiously, I raised my head. Two people stood staring at me in shock from inside Inkaho. Fair enough, really. The scene was surreal. Light glinted off the myriad of broken glass. It looked like diamonds or stars or something. Something pretty but bloodletting. No way could I put my hands down, push myself up onto my feet. Guess I might stay put for a moment. Consider the situation.

"Lydia! Shit," Nell yelled from inside the tattoo shop, then ran toward the door, rattling the lock. "Pat, open it."

Instead, the man climbed directly out over the ruined remains of the shop window. *Crunch, crunch, crunch,* came from beneath his boots.

"Are you hurt?" he asked.

"I, ah . . ." I looked around, waiting for my brain to catch up.

"Is she okay?" yelled Nell, watching out the broken shop window.

"Not sure," said Pat.

Footsteps came running toward me. That was Vaughan. His Converse didn't make as much noise as Pat's boots. Why this mattered, I have no idea. I might have been ever so slightly in shock. Despite all the glass, Vaughan didn't hesitate to kneel at my side.

"Babe?" He lifted my face to the light, inspecting me for damage. "Let me see. You all right?"

"Yeah. I think so."

"You sure?"

"I'm really not sure of anything anymore."

A grunt. The man got to his feet, then eased his hands into my armpits and stood me up too. No trace of anger remained. His concerned gaze continued sweeping over me, looking for any hint of maiming. "Does anything hurt?"

"What a weird fucking night," I whispered.

"Hey, tune me in." He gently cupped my face, mouth set in a straight serious line. "Are you sure you're okay? Does anything hurt?"

"I don't think so." I shook my head slowly, feeling out my body from the inside. I wiggled my fingers and toes, moved my head this way and that. All major limbs were still attached. No pool of blood surrounded me. Okay, good. "Just a little where I landed on my hip."

Next came Boyd, Rosie, and Masa, running out of the Dive Bar.

"What happened?" asked Rosie, voice all high and excited.

"Pat got some bad news," said Nell, voice wobbling slightly.

It didn't take a degree in rocket surgery to figure out what the news had been. Nell had told Pat about the baby. Pat had lost it and thrown the chair. Despite their separation. Despite their divorce. Shoulders bowed, Pat seemed lost, wounded. Nell looked about the same. It still didn't give him license to start throwing furniture through shop windows, however.

The amount of yelling, drama, and violence in the last seven days had been insane. In total contrast to my family's own studied indifference. As if caring too much was an error, an embarrassment. Fact is, by the time things disintegrated to this degree, my parents would have long since moved on. I'd been given the same option and yet here I stood.

Staying was the right decision. It was.

Meanwhile, Masa swore while Boyd stood back, scowling.

"Christ, Lydia," said Pat, eyes anguished. He rubbed at his face with both hands. "If I'd hurt you . . . shit."

A police siren wailed in the distance.

"It's okay," I announced to one and all. Despite all evidence to the contrary. "Everything's fine."

"What a mess," said Nell, a tear trailing down her cheek.

I could only agree.

CHAPTER TWENTY-ONE

Baths were a girl's best friend. Screw jewelry, chocolate, and those other things. A big old tub full of warm water had them all beat. Advil wasn't bad either. Despite the monumental bruise covering my side, my hip hardly hurt.

I lay my head back against the rim of the tub, staring off into space. Trying to think constructively about my life, but not really succeeding.

Nell and Vaughan had talked to the police while the rest of us cleaned up the mess. It took a while for Joe to arrive with supplies to board up the window. Joe had stayed with Pat while we drove Nell back to her apartment. All in all, another crazy long night in Coeur d'Alene with the Hewson family and friends.

The voice of doubt had been running through my head. Of course it had. These people were batshit. I was insane to even consider staying here and throwing my lot in with the Dive Bar. Only, when I walked Nell up to her apartment, she'd thrown her arms around me, holding on tight.

I liked that.

As harsh as it sounds, if Vaughan was leaving, sooner rather than later might be for the best. Emotional upheaval and mass confusion where he was concerned had gotten old. He made my vagina happy. Deliriously so. But the rest of me felt tired. Or maybe it was just my head and my heart, the thinking and feeling bits. I'd already faced one major rejection this year, care of my ex-fiancé. Two was getting a bit ridiculous.

At first, I didn't register the quiet knocking. Only when it continued, accompanied with Vaughan opening the bathroom door a little to peek into the room, I sat up in a rush, hugging my knees to my chest, covering up all of the essentials. Like he hadn't already seen everything. A cascade of water splashed over the edge onto the floor. Oops.

"Just checking you hadn't fallen asleep," he said.

"No, I'm fine."

"Mind if I come in?"

I opened my mouth to make excuses. But no go. The door opened wide and he stepped in, some thick candles in one hand and two bottles of beer in the other. He set the whole lot on the bench beside the basin, pulling a book of matches out of his jean's pocket. Small flames blossomed in no time. A finger flicked off the light, plunging the room into romance mode.

No. So much no.

"Vaughan." I couldn't manage a smile. I just didn't have one in me.

With a flick of his wrist a bottle cap fell to the floor. "Here."

"Thanks." Icy glass chilled the palm of my hand. "Um. I'm not really in the mood for sexual healing . . ."

Another bottle cap fell and he knelt by the tub, resting an arm on the rim. After taking a healthy swig, he just looked at me, not saying anything. To have him all up close and personal didn't feature on my list of goals right now. I needed space to figure shit out. Not only to plan, but to understand, what the future would look like here without him.

"Lydia—"

"You know, I don't really want to talk either. Sorry."

"Okay." His eyes were so sad.

The urge to take it all back was huge. But I didn't. I couldn't. Survival skills had to kick in eventually. Protect my idiot heart from getting more wrapped up in him. I was also still rather pissed at him for earlier.

"Thought you should know," he said. "Made a decision. I'm going to head out Monday morning."

"Oh." This was it, the date had been set. My mind emptied, just blanking. It took a moment to find words. "Okay. Right. I'll get organized tomorrow. Get my things out of the way. Nell said I could crash with her for a while. Store my things at the bar."

"I'll help you move."

"Thanks."

We just stared at each other.

He looked away first, glancing at the door. Obviously unhappy. My fingers itched to stoke away the furrows in his brow. To give him comfort and take the same. I'd been lucky with the Chris thing. The way it had come apart, I'd been almost ecstatic. To have avoided falling into his evil marital clasp was wonderful. There'd been anger and embarrassment too. Lots of emotions clouding the scene. But a hell of a lot less heartache than there should have been. Then there likely would be with Vaughan.

"I'll give you your privacy," he said, still not moving.

"We could not have sex."

His brows rose.

"And not talk," I proposed. "Just drink our beers and hang out together. If you want?"

He blinked. "Sure. We could do that."

"Okay."

"Do you mind if I get in?" He nodded to the tub.

"Both of us naked in a tub?" Most dubious.

"Right." He winced. "Might make it a little hard on the no-sex thing."

"Hard. Haha."

A smile. He rose and started toeing off his shoes, pulling off his socks. Basically, not following the recently reached agreement. "I have the answer."

"You do?"

"Yeah. Pull the plug, let some of the water out." With no further warning, he climbed into the tub still dressed in jeans and tee. Not quite normal.

"Vaughan!" I yanked out the plug before we flooded the damn house. "What are you doing?"

"Hanging out with you. Not having sex." The man stood, waiting for the water level to decrease. After a minute, he crouched down behind me, long legs pressing against my back. "Babe, scoot forward a little."

"Shit." I did as told. "But your clothes?"

"They're due for a wash."

I snorted. "I see. Great way to save water."

"Environmental warrior. That's me. This is a bit of a tight squeeze. Hang on." His arm went around my middle for as long as it took to pull me back and up. An easy enough thing to do in the water. Legs stretched out beneath me and I sat on a rough lap. Wet denim made for about as comfortable a seat as you'd imagine. At least I wasn't wearing it. Could you imagine the chafing?

I reinserted the bath plug before we lost all of the water. "Yeah, this doesn't feel sexual at all. Me sitting naked on your lap, bathing by candlelight."

"God, you've got a dirty mind."

I gave him a look over my shoulder. Hopefully it conveyed my complete lack of trust.

"I respect your wishes, Lydia. Nothing's going to happen." Eyes wide and innocent, he drank his beer.

"Mm-hmm."

"Shh. You didn't want to talk."

Asshole.

Spine straight, I sat there, sipping my drink. True to his word, nothing was said, no move was made. Gradually, I began to relax. I blame the shadows cast by the candles. Those flickering flames lulled me. Eventually, I rested my back against his wet-shirted front, got comfortable.

"I'm sorry I yelled at you earlier," he whispered.

"Again."

"Yeah." A heavy sigh. "Again."

"One day, maybe, you might want to talk to someone about all of this. Your parents passing . . ."

Silence. Lots and lots of silence. I prepared myself for the boom. More yelling and swearing, et cetera. He'd made it perfectly plain that he didn't wish to discuss these sorts of things. Yet there I went meddling, diving right back in where my nose did not belong. What an idiot good intentions made of you. Because the thought of him carrying this pain around for the rest of his life hurt. It hurt bad.

So yeah, I waited.

Instead of rage, however, he kissed the side of my face. It was with closed lips. Chaste. Tears welled in my eyes, my breath hitching. Stupid heart.

"Talk to me," I said.

"About what?"

"I don't know. Tell me a story."

"All right." He cleared his throat, his chest rising and falling in perfect rhythm against my back. Pity, being with him always felt so right. My life would be far safer, more straightforward, if I'd been able to retain some semblance of indifference. What had happened to all the cold hard lessons care of my parents? It seemed like ever since I'd seen the home porn of Chris and Paul going at it, something inside of me had come loose. It definitely wasn't desire. Closer to crazy, if anything.

"Once upon a time," he began, voice low and measured. "There was a princess. A beautiful, occasionally annoying princess."

"What was her name?"

"Ah, Notlydia."

I frowned. "Her name is Notlydia?"

"You wanted a story, I'm giving you one. Shut up."

"Whatever."

An even heavier sigh from the man. "Anyhoo, Notlydia was all set up to marry this prince. We'll call him Prince Bag of Dicks."

"Works for me."

"But on the day of her wedding, when she was wearing this sweet dress that served her tits up like they were a fucking platter—"

"Is this an R-rated story?"

"Please," he said, sliding an arm around my bare waist. And I let him. "*R* is for rubbish. If you don't get to see any penetration then you're wasting your time. This is XXX."

I laughed.

"So on the day of her wedding to Prince Bag of Dicks, Notlydia kisses him and he turns into a big slimy two-headed toad with terrible breath and even worse foot odor."

"Whoa." I rested my head back against his shoulder. "Poor Notlydia."

"Hell of a plot twist, right?"

"Never saw that one coming."

"Mm." He rested his cheek against the top of my head.

"What happens next?"

"Well, she's completely freaked out, of course."

"Of course."

"And she takes off into the woods. She's running through bushes, jumping fences, climbing trees, you name it. Nothing's going to stop her from getting the hell away from that toad, Prince Bag of Dicks." He took a sip of beer. "Unfortunately, she loses her fancy dress along the way. She's just down to some skimpy underwear and a corset and with all that jogging through the forest, it's barely holding her in. One decent breath and there's going to be nipple out there for all the world to see. Did I happen to mention she'd been voted Best Rack in the kingdom four years running? Anyway, eventually she finds this small cottage. Now, what you don't know about Notlydia is that she has a shady past."

I tried to look up at him. But with the angle, all I got was stubble and cheekbone. "That doesn't sound like Notlydia."

"Be quiet." A hand covered my mouth. "Notlydia's a dirty, dirty girl. Got a bad side like you wouldn't believe. A little breaking and entering is nothing to her. So into the house she goes. But she's all muddy from running through the woods, see? She can't let people see her like this—she's a princess, for fuck's sake."

The hand remained over my mouth. Which was fine, I had nothing to add to his pornographic fairy tale.

"Notlydia gets in the shower and starts soaping herself. There's lots of bubbles and steam, and she's a modern woman so there's a bit of self-love. She even finds time to wash her hair, shave under her pits. Things like that. But then the owner of the cottage wakes up and hears the water running. He stomps into the bathroom saying, someone's using up my hot water. Notlydia cries out, 'Not me, not me.'"

He craned his neck, meeting my gaze. "See, babe, what did I tell you? That Notlydia is a filthy little liar."

I looked up to heaven. No help was forthcoming.

"Someone's using up all my soap, says the owner. 'Not me, not me,' cries Notlydia." He put his lips next to my ear. "She should be ashamed of herself, shouldn't she? If ever a busty princess deserved a spanking."

I bit at the palm of his hand, teeth catching at the fleshy mound beneath his thumb.

"Ow." He laughed, pulling his hand free. "Then the owner said, someone's been fingering herself in my shower."

"Stop!" I put my hands over my ears, trying desperately to hold in my laughter. "This is the worst story ever. The Brothers Grimm are rolling over in their graves."

"Notlydia throws back the shower curtain and says, 'Oh yeah, big boy, that was me. Come and get it.' And they have wild sex all over the cottage." Vaughan's body jerked beneath mine as he laughed his ass off. "The end."

"No way. Notlydia is virtuous and pure. She'd never pull that sort of shit."

"Nah." He chuckled. "It all happened exactly as I said. Dirtiest princess in all the land."

"Like hell. The owner of that cottage was a pervert and a deviant. Why, he would have picked the lock on a chastity belt. She never stood a chance." Difficult to maintain my pious stance, given I'd started laughing so hard tears were pouring down my cheeks. The funny bastard. "I want to know more about this cottage owner. What's his name?"

"I don't know. Let me think . . ." He rested his chin back on top of my head. "He definitely isn't Prince Charming."

"He could be!"

Silence.

"If he wanted to. Or not. Whatever," I added weakly. Crap. "Let's go back to not talking."

I was a moron.

We'd been all relaxed and laughing. Me and my idiot mouth. Way to go, Lydia. Just shout out any old impossible daydream to the dude who's made it clear there was no future "we." If someone could just direct me to the nearest brick wall, I'd knock a little sense into myself.

On the other hand, it was two stupid words. Surely he could have ignored the last hundred years of Disney perpetuating slick-haired young royals gallivanting around the countryside saving hot babes in distress. For the sake of getting along. God knows, Chris never had any problems ignoring or placating me. I'd seen his thoughtless gorgeous smile aimed my way a hundred times. No, a thousand. If only I'd recognized it for what it was.

Ugh. Just the thought of it made me want to punch the douche all over again.

Maybe I needed a bit more than a week to get over that catastrophe. The money would help. Substantially. I'd never imagined that compromising my morals and taking hush money from such foul woe-begotten assholes would feel so good. Maybe I should sell out more often.

"This, ah, this Prince Charming of yours," he said haltingly.

"Yes?"

Vaughan shifted beneath me, pushing out a heavy breath. "I mean, it doesn't make sense, does it? Why would he be in a cottage instead of a castle?"

"Well . . . his parents, the king and queen of the neighboring kingdom, died in a terrible accident." I stayed perfectly still, waiting to see how he'd react.

"I see."

"And it hurt him so bad he just, he didn't want to be a prince anymore."

Nothing from him.

"Bad things happen in fairy tales sometimes."

A grunt.

"It's not fair, but it happens," I said, feeling my way with more caution than skill. "The prince loved his parents and the castle had too many memories."

"Hmm."

"So he ran away into the woods too."

"Doesn't sound like much of a prince if he can't handle his shit," he said.

"Princes are just men too, human beings. I don't think a crown or a penis gives you magical invulnerability to loss and pain." I stared at the wall, thinking the problem through. "Life is hard. Terrible things happen. We all have feelings. We're all just flesh and blood, trying to do our best."

"Running away from problems isn't doing your best." His voice echoed around the small room, the same as around in my head.

What with holding the Coeur d'Alene title for runaway bride of the year, I had no answer. None at all. So much for my half-assed wisdom.

Hands rubbed the tops of my arms as if I needed soothing or something. As if he wanted out, which involved me shutting up and getting the hell off of him.

"Big day," Vaughan rumbled, drawing me back to the here and now. "Better get you to bed. How's your hip feeling?"

"Fine. It's just bruised." I moved my big butt, crouching at the front of the tub, returning to the "oh god, cover everything so he doesn't see your masses of white flab" position. Pure protective instinct and annoying as hell. There was nothing wrong with my body. I was a strong modern woman, yada yada. Old habits were a bitch to break.

A mighty wave rolled back and forth, sloshing more water onto the floor. He stepped out, dripping all the way. Soon enough the bath mat resembled a sodden puddle. Wet shirt and jeans went splat on the floor.

Man, I loved his skin. All of the art inked into him. The way his body moved, brisk and efficient, limbs moving, muscles flexing. He did nothing unique or peculiar. No acrobatics or aerial feats were involved. Just Vaughan doing his thing, moving through the world, living his life. I couldn't have torn my eyes away.

He wiped off his upper body, then wrapped the towel around his waist. "You need a hand?"

I smiled. "No. Thanks."

He nodded and then headed for the door. My Prince Charming, going, going, gone. It's a pity sex has consequences you can't always anticipate. Changes in emotion, in how you perceive people. Too bad you couldn't buy love.

CHAPTER TWENTY-TWO

Sunday, we worked the dinner shift at the Dive Bar.

Due to an event downtown, it wasn't particularly busy. Boyd, with the aid of Kurt the kitchen kid, was in charge. It seemed he liked to do an all-day brunch on the seventh day. Eggs Benedict, ricotta pancakes with banana and butterscotch sauce, potato and corn cakes with spinach, bacon, and relish, and other amazing things. We arrived just in time to catch the end of it as they changed over to the dinner menu, which mainly included pizzas and pastas. Getting to taste test the remains of brunch on breaks was the best. Issues regarding the size of my ass and hips were problems for another day.

No sign of Eric or Nell. Joe and Vaughan worked the bar.

I'd called Nell earlier and left a message on her cell. After the events of last night, I'd probably want to be left the hell alone too. The rest of the day passed swiftly, and was relatively painless. Despite the countdown to Vaughan's departure tick-tocking in my head.

He slept with me. We didn't discuss it, he just climbed in beside me, boxer briefs on. They remained intact. Things were so weird now. The gratitude I felt when he lay by my side burned.

Love was a bitter pill.

Sleeping in helped with my various aches and pains before we moved my stuff, which didn't take long. We each took our cars to deliver one load to the second-floor storeroom above the restaurant and we were done. Most of my kitchen and household-type items had been donated to a local charity just before the wedding. I thought I'd no longer need them, what with all of those gifts from the Delaneys' fancy friends arriving every day.

"Cover me." A hand suddenly gripped my arm. A male voice coming from directly behind me. "Good job. What's your name?"

"Is this a robbery or something?" I asked, not sure whether to be perplexed or afraid.

The mystery man laughed. "Fuck no. Got more money than I can spend in this lifetime. What's your name?"

"Lydia."

"Okay, Lydia. You're doing great."

"Thanks." I chanced a glance over my shoulder.

"Don't look at me!"

"Sorry, sorry." Despite it being nearly nine at night, the dude wore sunglasses. His face was mostly obscured by a trucker's hat. Strands of long blond hair had escaped the cap, however, hanging down past his shoulder. Bright green T-shirt. Other than that, I had nothing. If I had to describe him to the police, there wouldn't be much to go on, dammit. "I won't do it again."

"I should hope not. Sheesh, Lydia," he said, tone exasperated. "I need you to work with me here. Just act normal. Walk toward the bar like nothing weird is going on at all, all right?"

"All right."

"Let's go."

With slow measured steps we moved toward the bar. It took me a while to catch Vaughan's eye. I tried to communicate several things to him with my look. First, I was not happy. Second, who- ever stood behind me was the definite cause of this unhappiness.

His eyes widened, then his gaze jumped to the person steering me toward the big blond bartender.

"You trying to be in disguise or what?" Vaughan asked, voice oddly calm. Instead of reaching for a shotgun or something, he continued pouring a beer.

"Yes," said the maniac, stepping out from behind me. "Genius, isn't it?'

Vaughan leisurely checked him out then shook his head. "You're a fucking idiot. Get your hand off Lydia, you're freaking her out."

"I'll have you know, Lydia and I are the best of friends. She thinks my costume is awesome," the maniac falsely declared. "Don't you, Lydia?"

"I'm allowed to look at you now?" I asked.

"Knock yourself out," the man said, turning to Vaughan, his voice ecstatic. "This is my favorite part, when they get all excited about me."

"Mm-hmm."

The maniac gave me a broad grin.

Whoever he was, he certainly wasn't afraid of loud colors or stating his musical preferences. He wore a fluorescent green T-shirt with a large picture of Malcolm Ericson from Stage Dive on the front, and a matching fluorescent pink hat. "Mal for President" had been embroidered on the hat. Guess he really loved the drummer from Stage Dive. A lot.

"Wow." I gave Vaughan side-eyes.

He burst out laughing. "She doesn't recognize you."

"Duh. She's not supposed to recognize me, I'm in disguise." The maniac pouted and took a seat at the bar. "And give me that beer."

"Bullshit." Vaughan kept right on laughing, setting the beer on the bar as ordered. "You wanted her to know who you were, you fucking show pony."

The man declined to answer, instead drinking the beer.

"Babe," said Vaughan, smiling. "This is Mal Ericson."

Mal raising a hand in salute.

"From Stage Dive?" I asked, just to be sure.

"Yep," said Mal. "So . . . babe, huh? Don't recall you having a babe before, V-man. How interesting."

"Not interesting." Vaughan started pouring another beer. "None of your business."

"I'd like to buy, babe, a beer." He patted the bar stool beside him. "Sit, Lydia. Let us become friends. Tell your Uncle Mal everything."

"Don't tell him anything," countered Vaughan, brows drawn down. "Biggest fucking meddler I ever met. Always got to be sticking his nose into everyone else's business. And she's working."

"I'd love a drink," I told Mal, taking the proffered seat. "Dinner's basically over, Masa's just clearing the last couple of tables now. A soda and lime, please, bartender."

"You go, babe." Mal started clicking his fingers. "He's not the boss of you."

"Who the hell let him in here?" grumped a female voice.

For the second time tonight, I got accosted from behind. This time, however, it was welcome. Nell gave me quick hug before leaning against the bar. "Mal."

"Nell." The drummer removed his sunglasses, throwing them aside along with his hat. Golden blond hair flowed over his shoulders. Of course, with him revealed in all his glory, there could be no question about his identity. Stage Dive was only one of the biggest bands in the world.

I stared, starstruck.

"Nell, Nell, Nell. Still secretly longing for me, I see." Mal sighed. "You poor pathetic sap."

"Aw. I think it's wonderful that you're so removed from reality, Malcolm. Don't let anybody tell you differently."

He chuckled. "Lydia, did she tell you how when we were kids, she always used to chase after me when we played catch and kiss? Every single time. Not that I minded having an older girl hot on my trail. But shit, running after me every single day. It got a little old."

"I wasn't trying to kiss you, you idiot." Nell turned to me. "One time on the bus, the little asswipe tried to set my ponytail on fire. I kept chasing him to try and punch him, but he was too fast."

"Yeah, sure, Nelly. You keep telling yourself that," stirred Mal.

I looked back and forth between the two, trying not to laugh. Poor Nell's lips were puckered, a heavy scowl in place.

Vaughan slapped down a beer mat, placing my soda and lime on top. Staying out of the twenty-oddyear-old battle. Wise.

"Thank you," I said.

A tip of the chin.

"I was sorry to hear about your mother," said Nell in a softer voice. "She was a wonderful woman."

Mal nodded. "Thanks. I was sorry to hear about you and Pat."

"Yeah." Nell shrugged. "Shit happens, right?"

"Sadly."

"Where's Anne?" asked Vaughan.

"My beloved wife is nose deep in a romance book and doesn't want to be disturbed." With a grin, Mal took another mouthful of beer. "I got a feeling this one's going to be awesome."

"What?"

"Dude." Mal crooked his finger, motioning Vaughan closer. When he did so, Mal smacked him on the forehead. "Listen and learn, you fool. You've got a babe now. You need to know these things."

Rubbing his red forehead, Vaughan did not appear impressed. Or any more knowledgeable. Yet.

"When women read romance books, one of two things generally happen." Mal ran a hand through his lovely locks. "They either want to discuss the book in great depth. And probably, life and your relationship. Now sometimes that's okay. You reach a higher level of understanding with each other and shit. But sometimes it sucks, pure and simple. You wind up getting bitched at for days because of something the dude in the book did that makes you look bad. But if it's an awesome book, however, a hot one? Well then . . . kinky fuckery like you wouldn't believe, man. The ideas Pumpkin has gotten out of some of those books. *Gold.* I could never have talked her into trying half of that stuff."

"Huh."

"Trust me, never mock a romance book," said Mal with all the zest of a manic street preacher. "You have no idea the amount of good they can do for you between the sheets and on the streets. If you love your girl? Buy her books."

A moment of stunned silence.

"Thank god we don't have penises," said Nell, patting me on the shoulder.

"Pretty much," I agreed.

Deep in thought, Vaughan scratched at his head. "Romance books, huh? I'll keep that in mind."

"Give me strength," said Nell. "Everything okay?"

Her brother gazed back at her, face lined. I think we all knew she wasn't asking about the business. So far as I was aware, there'd been next to no communication between them since she'd broken the news of her pregnancy the night before. Given his expression when he stormed out of the back office, he hadn't taken it well.

"Yeah. Everything's fine." He reached out, taking hold of her hand. "How about with you?"

Her smile was grim. "Getting there."

"Know you weren't keen on me selling the house. But with the extra money, I can afford to fly back sometimes. Visit more often," he said, voice soft.

"I'd like that." The joy in Nell's voice spoke for itself.

The siblings held hands. I looked away, it was a private moment. His promises to visit had nothing to do with me. I'd just have to suck it up. And it was a good thing he'd be around more for his sister; Nell would need all the support she could get.

Mal, however, kept watching the siblings, eyes thoughtful. Any trace of his particular brand of crazy appeared to have disappeared for the time being.

"The Closed sign's up, door's locked," said Joe, joining us.

Andre followed close behind. "Hello, everyone."

"Hi." I smiled. Behind us, the restaurant had emptied, all of the lights were dimmed. Cool acoustic songs by a variety of bands played over the sound system. I liked how they kept the music going even after closing. "Time for me to get back to work."

"Stay put," ordered Nell. "Masa and Boyd and the new kitchen kid have got it covered. We're having a small surprise going-away party for my brother. Since he's about as good at goodbyes as he is with letting us know he's in town in the first place."

"I was going to call you that day," said Vaughan.

"Yeah, yeah."

The big blond bear went back behind the bar, taking a dusty bottle off the very top shelf. "Eric said never to touch this one. So we'll start with it."

"Excellent. Have to admit, your brother has fine taste in scotch . . ." Andre inclined his head toward Nell, the smallest of smiles in place. "And women."

"Don't." She threw a balled-up paper napkin at him.

"Ah, speaking of," said Andre, gaze switching to Vaughan. "Pat said he'd catch you later. He's taken his motorcycle and headed up into the wilds of Canada for a week or two to get his head together."

Vaughan nodded. But said nothing.

Andre frowned, looking Nell's way.

A muscle jumped in Nell's jaw. "If you've got something to say, Andre, do me a favor and just say it."

Tonight, Andre wore a particularly cool plaid button-down shirt, hair slicked back. He stopped, focus entirely on Nell. His eyes softened, face not unkind. "Baby girl, you fucked up not fixing your marriage. Pat fucked up giving up on you too easy. Hell, Eric fucked up ever going near you, knowing what the situation was between you two. You know all of this. But if you think for a minute that I don't love you and haven't got your back, then you're crazy. I'll babysit and change shitty nappies if I have to and I fully expect to be godfather, understood?"

Nell hurriedly looked away, sucking in her cheeks. Trying to hold back tears, I'd guess. After waiting a second or two, Andre strode over, throwing his arms around her. The way she clung to him couldn't have failed to move anyone. That kind of unwavering love and support was what I wanted. It was why I was staying here. That's what Vaughan was giving up by yet again leaving. And the longing, the naked emotion on his face showed he knew it, how couldn't he?

It was the price he paid to follow his dream.

My dream wasn't as grand as stardom on the stage. I didn't want to be a rock-and-roll icon. I wanted home and community, a job where I could excel and financially build a future for myself. Sure, if a fairy godmother came along and bonked me on the head with her wand, giving me instant glamour and success as a plus-size model, I'd deal. It would be fun, but it wasn't what my heart yearned for.

"I'm not changing shitty nappies, tell you that much," Mal announced.

"Amen." Joe raised his glass of scotch and they toasted to the sentiment.

"Pussies," I said.

"How are all of the Stage Dive babies doing?" asked Vaughan, accepting his own glass of scotch off Joe.

You had to give it to the guy, Malcolm Ericson did an amazing impression of someone slowly choking to death. By the time his head thunked down on top of the bar, I almost clapped.

"That well, huh?"

Mal groaned. "V-man, if I have to look at one more too cute baby video I'm going to, shit, I'm going to lose it. I just can't take it anymore. I mean, congratulations to them. Their boys can swim. But I don't need to see every fucking thing the fruit of their loins does, you know?"

He stopped to drain the last third of his beer, handing the glass back across the bar for a refill. "I told Pumpkin straight out. I said, my sperm is not to be used for these purposes for quite some years, thank you very much."

"How'd she take it?" I asked.

"She laughed at me." Mal frowned. "Sometimes, I wonder if I'm really in charge at all."

"That's the problem with settling down," said Vaughan, arms crossed over his chest. "She's got the pussy. You want it. Might as well just say goodbye to being your own boss."

"That's your view of relationships?" I tipped my head. A fresh angle achieved nothing, however. He remained a puzzle I could never solve. One that sadly made my heart beat double time. "Seriously?"

"This should be good," said Joe, staring into his drink.

Some snickering from Mal.

Oh good. We had everyone's attention. Andre stood beside Nell, an arm wrapped around her waist. Vaughan had assumed the old blank face. Eyes open and guileless, arms hanging loose at his sides. And yeah, no. We didn't need to do this. I didn't need to know.

I smiled, shook my head. "Forget I said that. A toast!"

Everyone held up their glasses apart from Vaughan. I avoided his gaze, getting on with my life—accepting situations I couldn't change, fighting the inevitable wasted valuable time and energy.

"To Vaughan," I announced, holding my soda and lime high. I wasn't afraid to meet his perfect blue eyes. Not now. Time to pull my big girl panties up and move on. "Safe travels and musical glory. I hope all of your dreams come true."

Compliments and similar wishes were spoken. Drinks were drunk.

"You're not going with him?" asked Mal, voice subdued as conversations continued around us.

"No. We've only known each other a week. It's not . . . and I'm hoping to become a bigger part of things in the Dive Bar." My smile felt staged for some reason. Not that I was lying. "I like it here."

He tipped his chin and said no more. The understanding in his eyes, I didn't like it. Shit, I barely knew the man. I could really do without parading my dumbass heart in front of international rock stars.

"Do you spend much time in Coeur d'Alene?" I asked, eager to change the topic of conversation.

Mal smiled. "Yeah, I've got family here. Bought a place on the lake. You should come over sometime. Meet Pumpkin. I think you two would get along and it'd be good for her to know some people in town. We're spending a bit more time here these days."

"Thank you," I said, eyes wide in surprise. "I'd like that."

"In fact, all of you losers should come visit," he announced more loudly. "Stay the night, bring instruments, I'll organize the eats and drinks. Ben's coming out with Lizzy and Gibson tomorrow. I think Davie and Ev were thinking about visiting too. It'll be fun."

"Won't that be a lot of people?" asked Nell.

"Nelly, the house is big. Like, a bajillion bedrooms or something. No way was I taking the chance that someone's screaming baby would wake me in the middle of the night. Visitors go in the other wing, far, far away from me." He waved a hand, indicating one hell of a distance. "Trust me, you'll all fit."

"Christ, your place has wings?" Joe huffed out a breath. "Last time I saw you, you said you were looking at a log cabin on the water. You didn't say anything about it being a castle."

"Hello, I know we haven't hung out much since school. But, um, guys, I'm kind of rich now," said Mal. "It is a log cabin on the water. It's just a very fucking big one."

"This I need to see," said Joe. "Who built it?"

"Fucked if I know. You can climb over the place to your heart's content, Bob the Builder. Check out how it's put together."

"You had to know he'd be back, shoving his money in our faces," said Andre, a sly smile on his face.

"Haha." Mal flipped him the bird. "Oh, hey. Am I still banned from your shop and have you still got your old man's Gretsch kit?"

"It's upstairs in storage, but I could bring it down."

Eyes excited, Mal rubbed his hands together. "Excellent. Is it for sale?"

"Maybe." Andre sipped his scotch. "If I knew it was going to a good home. As for you still being banned, that depends. You going to try and skateboard in my shop again, you fuckface?"

"Harsh, man. I was fifteen! I've matured a lot since then."

"Hmm."

"You'll let me in. We'll talk about your dad's kit later. It'll definitely be going to a loving home." The drummer started beating out a rhythm on his thighs. He seemed to be constantly in movement. I don't think he ever sat still. "But yeah, you should all come out."

"Rad," said Nell. "But I'll do the eats."

"Sold!" Mal slapped his hand on the bar.

Chatter and laughter filled the space, everyone having a good time. Or almost everyone. I nearly didn't notice Vaughan slinking off. Shoulders rounded and head hanging down, he made straight for the men's room. I walked over and hovered outside, waiting for him to come out. Wanting to touch base with him emotionally, I guess.

When he did, he walked straight into me. Guess I was a crap stalker. No subtlety at all. My balance wavered until he grabbed my upper arms, holding me steady.

"Shit. Lydia," he said, little line back between his brows. "You all right?"

"I was going to ask you that."

He set me free, gaze perplexed.

"It's just that the big house on the lake was your dream."

Quietly, he swore, then grabbed my hand and dragged me into the men's bathroom. It'd obviously just been cleaned. The scent of bleach stung my nostrils. Gray tiles and paintwork matched with stainless steel fittings. It was all very neat and tidy. With the exception of a large piece of artwork on the back wall between a couple of urinals and bathroom stalls.

"Ha," I said. "I don't think I've ever been in a men's room. What's that?"

"Go look." Vaughan leaned against the back of the door, watching me.

A massive red anarchy symbol had been painted on the door, with messy white writing declaring, "I am music. Music is my life. Punk rock forever." Over the top of it all was a sheet of acrylic, for protection. I bent, trying to decode the green and blue scribble at the bottom. A date and a name.

"Andre Senior," I said, smiling.

"Got it in one."

"That's a piece of history."

"Yeah. Apparently he painted it on opening night," he said.

"Glad they kept it." I meandered back toward Vaughan, still

leaning against the bathroom door, chilling. "So you're not having a moment about Mal's palace by the lake?"

"No. Those guys worked hard for everything they have. They're damn good at what they do. Yes, I want what they've got. But I don't resent them for having it. They're my friends." He flicked back his golden red hair, not taking his eyes off me for a minute. "I'm having a moment, as you're calling it, because I yet again made you feel like shit. I opened my fat mouth without thinking. Again. I'm sorry."

I squinted in confusion.

"What I said about relationships was fucking stupid."

"Vaughan." I smiled. "Don't worry about it. You didn't upset me. It's not like what we've been doing the last week could exactly be called a relationship."

His brows drew down but he smiled. "No?"

"No."

"What would you call it then?"

Walking toward him, I laughed softly. "You're leaving in the morning. Does it matter?"

"Go on. What would you call it?" he repeated.

I stopped a bit back from him, trying to read his face. Slight smile, relaxed. His feet were a little apart, arms hanging loose at his sides. All of his focus was on me, waiting for my answer. The problem was, none of the labels fit right anymore. Friends with benefits seemed insufficient, icky. No way, however, was I brave enough to publicly aim for any higher.

"I don't know," I admitted.

"I'd call it important."

I took a deep breath, feeling hope yet fortifying myself for the pain. Where he was involved, in the end there always seemed to be pain. Fucking depressing but true. I needed to write poems about the orgasms he'd given me. Refind my joy.

"Thank you," I said.

We just looked at each other.

"You're beautiful, Lydia. Special. Usually things with me are just casual, hook-ups. No more than a night or two." Mouth serious and gaze somber he paused, searching for the right words. "You're not that. And it's not just that we spent a bit more time together. It's you. You make me wish things were different."

All of a sudden my black flats were fascinating. Totally captivating. And it had nothing to do with the weepiness currently happening in my eyes. Honestly, this man. Every single time I shored up my defenses, mentally and emotionally preparing myself to lose him, he tore the fortress down. Bastard.

"Babe?"

I held up a hand, cautioning him not to speak. Like he hadn't said enough.

He shut his mouth, brows high.

Meanwhile, I breathed. Breathing was good, useful. A really great hobby. Next I walked up to him and got to my knees. I just had to get close to him, to give him something more. Love him in some way to show him he was special to me too. Tiles were a bit of a bitch to kneel on. My favorite blue flares did nothing to soften the hardness. He couldn't have made his speech somewhere sensible, say near a bed or somewhere there might be throw cushions. No way.

Men. Such pains in the ass.

"Um, Lydia?"

I ignored him, busy dealing with his belt buckle before tearing into the button and zipper of his jeans. Goddamn underwear. Today, of course, he decides to wear his boxer briefs. With a heavy sigh of irritation, I slipped my hands into the sides of his underwear, easing both them and the jeans down his hips. Smooth warm skin beneath against my fingertips. Lean muscle and the curves of his hipbone. The scent was just that bit more potent here. Soap, sweat, and him. He made my mouth water.

Touch tender, I liberated his dick, rubbing my lips up and down against the underneath. Nothing felt as hot and silken as the skin on a man's cock. It was amazing. Already, he was hardening, growing. Men had magic in their pants, it's true. Only some took the time to figure out how best to use it, sadly. I traced the thick vein running all the way up with the tip of my tongue. Back and forth, back and forth. His breath caught, stomach muscles flexing.

"Shit." He held up his black Dive Bar T-shirt, the other hand caressing the side of my face.

He filled my hand nicely. Not that size was any great indicator of talent. It helped, but it wasn't the be-all to end-all. In one hand I cradled his balls, rolling them with my fingers. The other hand stayed wrapped around the base of his cock as I sucked him off. I sucked at him, long drawing pulls, before torturing him with my tongue. Giving head could be fun. I circled the head of his cock then licked back and forth across it. Sometimes I'd gently prod the tiny slit of his opening with the tip of my tongue, wiggling it inside just a little.

Vaughan gasped and grabbed hold of my ponytail, wrapping it around his fist. Heavy breathing echoed through the men's room.

The trick was total inconsistency. Never let them know what's coming next. I licked and sucked, tortured and teased, carefully grazed him with my teeth. I loved him with my mouth while my hand kept playing with his balls, tugging on them lightly now and then. I hummed, quite proud of myself. He swelled to admirable proportions and the vibration only helped. The rock-hard length of him slid in and out of my mouth as far as I could take it without gagging.

For a while, he managed to resist fucking my mouth. When I massaged the sweet spot between his balls and his anus with the tip of my finger, however, he lost all control. Hips bucking, he thrust his cock between my lips. Only the presence of my hand wrapped around his base stopped him from going too deep.

"Fuck. Babe," he growled, tugging on my hair.

It was hot, the feral sounds he made, the harsh, guttural tone of his voice. All down to me and all of it got to me. My panties were most definitely wet. His thick cock throbbed and I sucked hard, as hard as I could. Salty creamy cum filled my mouth to overflowing. I couldn't swallow fast enough.

He sagged against the door, still holding my hair in his hand. I kneeled at his feet, catching my breath. And cleaning myself up as best I could. Swallowing wasn't normally my thing. However, let's not ponder that.

Cloudy blue eyes stared down at me. The hint of a smile playing with the edge of his lips. He liked me a lot. Maybe he even loved me a little. Who knew? It didn't matter. He still wasn't going to stay.

"Wish things were different," he said, voice subdued.

"Me too."

By the time I woke up the next morning, he was gone.

CHAPTER TWENTY-THREE

FIVE DAYS LATER . . .

We're going to have to kill him."

I see no alternative." I took a sip of water, watching Masa go about his business. He was serving tables while singing "The Man Who Wants You" by Amos Lee at the top of his voice. People in love were the absolute worst. "He's been intolerable ever since he got back with his girlfriend. It's too bad, he's a nice guy."

"Yeah," said Nell. "Replacing him is going to be a pain in the ass. But we can't have people hanging around being all happy and shit."

I sighed. "No, we can't. The man can really sing."

Nell stopped stirring the pot of soup, moving onto a sizzling pan of bacon. "Masa hosted a karaoke club over in Spokane before this job. Said the driving got to be too much."

"Cool."

At the end of the song, the customers broke out into applause. Even I joined in despite my woe. Vaughan's absence sat like a stone in my heart. A piece of me altered that might never feel soft and alive again. Love was so strange. A collection of shared moments linked together to form this sort of chain of emotion between two people. You witness each other's lives, giving and taking as needed. And then, one day, it's gone. You're alone. Loneliness feels a great burden when you're used to sharing. Used to being part of a couple. Though, I don't suppose it's a party for anyone.

Enough whining. I'd adjust.

The next time Vaughan came to town I'd be polite, friendly. Show him everything was cool. I'd learned my lesson, however. Dating was out of the question. Any hook-ups with friends were likewise. Parties between the thighs only complicated things. It just wasn't worth the inevitable misery. If only orgasms and happy times lasted longer. You should be able to bottle them, let a smidgeon of pleasure and joy fly out when required. How nice that would be.

Wide grin in place, Masa floated past us with a load of dirty dishes. "Wonderful night, isn't it, ladies?"

"Bite me," grumbled Nell.

Well aware of our lovelorn state, the waiter just laughed, carrying on his merry way. I got my butt back into gear, checking on my tables. Joe smiled as I passed by the bar. Eric was busy chatting with two women sipping exotic-looking drinks. Life went on.

"If You Ever Want to Be in Love" by James Bay was on and I hummed along, getting into the groove of things. Super-slick music played tonight. It was Eric's turn at choosing, a duty taken seriously by all members of staff once they were allowed onto the rotation. I had yet to be asked to submit a playlist. Maybe I'd just put one together, and force the issue. If everyone could tolerate Boyd's punk then surely they'd be fine with a couple of hours' worth of my pop and rock favorites.

"Can I clear those for you?" I asked a woman, moving in after she nodded to remove the dinner plates.

"Hold up," said a voice behind me. A very familiar one.

A hand reached around, taking the plates from me and setting them back on the table. The arm covered in tattoos was every bit as familiar as the voice.

I turned, heart stuttering at who stood before me. Lots of stubble and rumpled clothes. His hair was a mess, shadows circling his eyes. Didn't matter. He was the most beautiful welcome sight I'd ever seen.

"Vaughan."

"I got all the way to L.A. and I realized something," he said.

"What?" I frowned.

"I don't know who the first guy you ever fucked was."

Some gasped. Another person tittered.

My mouth opened, but I had no words.

He shoved a hand through his hair, weary face lined. "I told you my story. You never got around to telling me yours, however."

"Oh."

"So?"

I blinked. "You want to hear it right here and now?"

"Sure. Why not." He turned, searching for something. His hand grabbed mine and he towed me across the restaurant to an empty table in the corner. A seat was pulled out for me, and I sat.

"I think I'm having a heart attack," I mumbled.

"Hmm?" He sat opposite me, leaning his elbows on the table. "Oh, I don't know your favorite color either. Isn't that weird? It feels weird. I mean, I should know things like that about you, shouldn't I?"

"I don't know."

"Of course I should!" He smiled, reaching out to tuck a strand of hair behind my ear.

"What's happening?"

"Hmm?" His warm hand cupped my cheek, his gaze soft and lovely.

"What is this? Why are you here?" I asked, shuffling forward in my seat. Stupidly enough, on the verge of crying. My eyes were itchy, swollen. My heart felt much the same. Apparently, heart-break itched. I was obviously allergic.

"I just told you."

Much too much emotion poured through me. I couldn't take it. Not again. I pushed away his hand, shaking my head. "You got to L.A. and turned back around because you don't know what my favorite color is?"

"Yes."

"That's insane."

He shrugged, slouching back in his chair. "I needed to know."

"You couldn't just text?" Oops, my voice got a little loud. I'd say we were attracting attention, but given his odd entry, we already had.

"No."

"No?" My hands were trembling, idiot things. I sat on them, got them out of sight. "What do you mean, 'no'?"

"There's more questions."

"How many more?"

"Lots." Perfect sky-blue eyes. I could have happily gotten lost in them and never left. "I can't give you an exact number."

I pressed a hand to my chest. *Thump, thump, thump.* Heart rate accelerated. Body shaking Sweat covered my back. This was not good. I picked up a menu and started fanning my face.

"Babe?"

"I don't understand any of this," I said, mostly to myself, but he was here too. Whatever.

Slowly, he pushed back his chair. He rose and came over to my side, crouching at my feet. A big warm hand covered my bare knee. I'd decided to wear a black pencil skirt on account of the hot weather. Thank god. Skin to skin with him made everything right. I calmed at his touch. My heart rate eased back to normal, my head no longer felt like it was about to explode. I wished that didn't happen. Vaughan having any kind of physical effect on me did not bode well. I had no say over my emotions. It wasn't too much to ask for my body to keep this crap under control, however. Surely not.

He took the menu out of my hand, placing it back on the table. I gave him my best bewildered stare. Seriously, it was a "what the fuck" masterpiece.

"I came back," he said softly.

"For how long?" I asked, blinking back the tears. Stupid glands.

"As long as it takes."

Yeah. Okay. Enough. I leaned down, getting in his face. My mouth was a mean line. "As long as what takes? Can you please give me a straight fucking answer before I kill you?"

His answering grin was like the sun coming out. Absolutely magnificent.

Then he lunged, grabbing hold of my face and kissing me stupid. I was, however, already a fool so I grabbed him right back. I clung to him, hands fisted in his shirt. Tongues, teeth, we were all over each other. Any children subjected to the spectacle would have required counseling, I'm certain. Apologies would have to be made later.

For now, I had him. And he felt like the whole damn world.

Once the kiss was done, he drew back, lips damp and eyes smiling. "I came back."

"You came back," I agreed, smiling despite all of the questions and the lingering doubt and pain in my heart.

"I'm crazy about you, Lydia. We wished it were different, me being in L.A. and you being here," he said, eyes full of emotion. "So I'm making it different."

I could only stare. It meant too much. I wanted him too badly.

"I'll stay." He cocked his head, stealing another quick kiss. "I canceled the house sale. Financially, I've got some issues. But

Andre said I could start working with him tomorrow. Between that and the Dive Bar, I'll get it sorted out. Haven't worked out everything yet."

"But your dream!"

"Funny thing about that dream," he said. "It now includes being with you."

My heart lurched again. It couldn't be healthy. Any minute now, I'd probably hit the floor dead. "It does?"

"Yes."

"And your band, working with Henning Peters? What about all that?" I demanded. "You said it was a big deal. The best opportunity you'd ever had."

"Lydia, I've been chasing music all my life. But you're the best opportunity I've ever had," he said, tone deadly serious. "I'm sorry it took me leaving to figure that out."

"You broke my heart."

"Babe." Regret filled his eyes. "I'm an idiot."

"Yeah." I sniffed.

"Can you ever forgive me?"

I pretended to ponder it for a moment. The man had done me damage.

"I'm so fucking sorry I caused you pain. I'll do my best to make sure it never happens again," he said. "Can you please forgive me?"

" 'spose so." It's extremely difficult to appear proud and dignified while your nose is leaking. But I did my best.

"Thank you." He stroked my cheek.

"What will you do about your music? You can't just stop."

"No. I'll always want to play. It's a big part of me. I want to record my songs, perform them live. But I don't necessarily need a band for that. I've been rethinking things," he said. "Fact is, you come first for me. I've decided to go solo so I can be based here, organize my music so it fits in with us. But if I have to leave for work, go on tour, I'll come back. Okay?"

"Okay." Despite all of my deep breathing and blinking, tears started falling down my face. "All right."

"You'll move your stuff back into my house?"

"I don't know," I said, nerves buzzing. "You don't think we should date? Maybe take things slow and do this properly?"

He scrunched up his nose. "Problem with that is, my dream also involves having lots of sex with you. I mean, a serious amount."

"I see."

"It's not just about the sex, though. The dream is quite detailed."

"Oh?"

"Yeah." He reached out, wiping the tears from my face with a frown. "Stop that. I don't like it. Didn't come back to make you cry."

"They're happy tears. Leave them alone. The dream, Vaughan," I prodded, slapping lightly at his hand.

He smiled. "It involves us going to sleep together and waking up together."

"Okay."

"And doing coupley shit, you know."

"Coupley shit?" My brows went high. "What is this coupley shit?"

One of his shoulders hitched. "Hanging out, watching TV, being together. Mostly naked, but occasionally not."

"Sounds like a good dream."

"No," he corrected. "It's great one."

I smiled back at him. I couldn't not. "Yes, it is. You're sure, though?"

"I'm sure."

"No. I need you to have thought this through. I don't want you to wind up resenting me. It would hurt if you changed your mind,

decided the musical prospects on the coast were more important."
I grabbed his hand and held on tight. Quietly terrified of what we
were doing. "It would hurt me really badly."

Lines surrounded his eyes, his gaze intensifying. "Babe. This
chance with you . . . you're it for me. You're my number one and
you're staying there. I need you to believe that. This isn't a passing
idea. I didn't hit L.A. and suddenly feel a bit bummed 'cause you
weren't there. I'm not saying I knew you were it for me the minute
I saw you in the bath. To be honest, I was kind of pissed off about
the whole thing. But not much later, things changed. A half an
hour, maybe. Definitely by the time you punched that asshole."

I laughed through the tears. "Ha. You sure it wasn't the breasts?"

"The breasts were definitely a part of it. But I wanted . . . no, I
needed to know everything about you. I needed you to stay," he
said, voice so sincere it hurt. "I just didn't want to change. Not my
plans, not my life."

"What happened?"

Clearing his throat, he rose, lifting me likewise to my feet. Strong
arms wrapped around my waist, pulling me in close. And god, it
felt so good. It felt like my dream. My body relaxed against his, my
arms winding around his neck.

"Vaughan?"

"I know that asshole made you doubt yourself. Made you doubt
feeling like this about anyone." He rested his forehead against mine.
"But you're in me. Have been since the first day I met you. I fought
it for a while, but that's over."

"You're in me too."

"Good." The tip of his nose rubbed against mine. "That's good,
Lydia. 'Cause that's where I'm going to stay."

I buried my face against his chest. Damn tears.

"I mean that literally too," he whispered against my ear. "You
get that right?"

I hiccupped, laughing. "I get that. I want that."

A happy humming noise came from his chest. His hold on me intensified, keeping me safe, keeping us tight.

"I love you, you know," I said, putting it all out there. Taking the leap, trusting in him and us. "I didn't want to, but I do."

"Thank fuck for that," he murmured.

"What the hell?" asked Nell, appearing at our side. Along with basically everyone. Joe, Eric, Masa, even Boyd. Apparently this had turned into a staff meeting.

I subtly wiped my nose on Vaughan's shirt because love was meant to hurt and occasionally be icky. Happily, it was also meant to shine.

"I'm moving back to town, calling off the sale of the house."

I don't know if I'd ever seen Nell so happy. She hid it pretty quickly, however. "And you're manhandling my waitress, why?"

"Because we're going to get married someday and make babies," said Vaughan, relaxed as anything. "Not necessarily in that order. It's up to her."

"Holy shit." My face returned to his shirt. God help my heart. The way it was galloping, I don't think it would ever recover from this night.

"Damn," said Joe's deep voice. "You don't do things by halves, do you?"

"When you know, you know."

"Congratulations, man."

"Thanks."

"To you too, Lydia."

I wiped off my face, smiling like a lovestruck fool. So what. All good. No, all fucking fantastic. "Thanks, Joe."

Others echoed the sentiment. There were smiles all around. Except for on one face.

"Big decision," said Eric, arms crossed. "You going to stick with it or you going to change your mind and leave her high and dry like you did with me being in the band? It's just that, Lydia seems nice. And friends and family, people that are supposed to matter, don't always seem to be important to you."

Silence. And not the happy kind.

"You were out of the band because you didn't take it seriously," said Vaughan. "No other reason. I wasn't turning my back on you as a friend. You stopped taking my calls, remember?"

Eric harrumphed.

"But you're right. I've been slack with keeping in touch with people, looking after the people I love. That's going to change."

"That so?"

"Yes," said Vaughan, neither man backing down. Oh, the heady scent of testosterone was thick in the air. They'd probably start banging antlers any time now. I held Vaughan's hand, standing at his side.

"Nell," he said. "I was wondering if you'd visit Mom and Dad's graves with me sometime soon. Haven't been back since the funeral, but I think it's time."

"We could tell them about Lydia and the baby," said his sister, tears bright in her eyes.

"Yeah, we could."

"What a gathering," said a new voice. Andre joined our circle, huddled in among all of the restaurant tables. Quite a few of them occupied.

"Can we get some service, please?" called out a customer. Fair enough.

"In a minute," said Eric, holding up a hand for patience.

"I think you're going to make a hell of a guitar teacher. Glad to have you on board." Andre reached across to shake Vaughan's hand.

"Thanks for giving me a chance."

"You're serious about this then?" asked Eric. Judgment oozed from the man's pores. Along with some expensive aftershave, no doubt. "Staying here, being with Lydia."

"Yeah," said Vaughan. "I am. You still got a problem with me, don't want me working here. Fine. I quit. I'm not interested in making trouble in the Dive Bar."

A tongue worked behind Eric's cheek, his gaze inscrutable. Then he climbed onto a chair and clapped his hands, calling up everyone's attention, staff and customers alike.

Oh shit. What now?

"Got an announcement to make," he said, looking down at us all from on high. "Two valued members of the Dive Bar family, Lydia and Vaughan, just decided to get married. I'd like to offer them my congratulations."

Applause erupted.

So did I. "What? We didn't do that. We didn't get engaged."

"We sort of did," said Vaughan, kissing my hand.

"To celebrate," said Eric, smiling at one and all. "Drinks are on the house!"

I, however, was not smiling, what with being on the verge of a full-blown panic attack. "I can't get engaged two weeks after not getting married. Who would do that? No one would do that. It's crazy!"

"Babe." Vaughan grinned, enjoying the moment entirely too much. "Don't worry about it. It's just out there somewhere, waiting until you're ready."

"But we're not really engaged, right?"

"I love you," he said, kissing my lips.

"Crap." I deflated, basically collapsing against him. It was all too much and my heart was on the line. Again. Blood rushed behind my ears while people clapped and whooped. Champagne corks were already popping. And there Vaughan stood, waiting patiently for me to get my shit together.

"If you go away, you'll come back?" I asked.

He met my eyes without a shadow of fear or doubt. "I'll come back."

"Okay. All right."

This wasn't Chris asshole Delaney. This was Vaughan. My Vaughan. He didn't say shit he didn't mean. He loved me. But what's more, I loved him.

"I'll be waiting," I said.

"Babe." His smile, the blue of his eyes . . . everything about the man. Everything.

Unable to hold back, I launched myself at him.

Customers were treated to quite a show, Masa started singing again (something by the Stones this time), me and Vaughan were rolling around on the floor. Things were crazy in the Dive Bar.

Thing is, sometimes crazy works.

Stay tuned for
TWIST

Book #2 in the Dive Bar Series

Visit Kylie Scott at
www.kylie-scott.com
for updates!

Book one

Lick

Waking up in Vegas was never meant to be like this . . .

Evelyn Thomas's plans for celebrating her twenty-first birthday in Las Vegas were big. *Huge.* But she sure as hell never meant to wake up on the bathroom floor with a hangover to rival the black plague, a very attractive, half-naked tattooed man next to her, and a diamond on her finger large enough to scare King Kong. Now if she could just remember how it all happened . . .

One thing is for certain, being married to rock 'n' roll's favourite son is sure to be a wild ride.

Book two in the Stage Dive series

Play

Mal Ericson, drummer for the world famous rock band Stage Dive, needs to clean up his image fast – at least for a little while. Having a good girl on his arm should do the job just fine. Mal doesn't plan on this temporary fix becoming permanent, but he didn't count on finding the one right girl.

Anne Rollins never thought she would ever meet the rock god who she'd plastered on her bedroom walls as a teenager – especially not under these circumstances. Anne has money problems. Big ones. But being paid to play the pretend girlfriend to a wild, life-of-the-party drummer couldn't end well. No matter how hot he is. Or could it?

Book three in the Stage Dive series

Lead

Can rock 'n' roll's most notorious bad boy be tamed by love?

As the lead singer of Stage Dive, Jimmy is used to getting whatever he wants, whenever he wants it – now he's caught up in a life of hard partying and fast women. When a PR disaster serves as a wake-up call and lands him in rehab, he finds himself with Lena, a new assistant hired to keep him out of trouble.

Lena's not willing to take any crap from her sexy boss and is determined to keep their relationship completely professional, despite their sizzling chemistry. But when Jimmy pushes her too far, he just might lose the best thing that's ever happened to him. Can he convince his stubborn assistant to risk it all and let her heart take the lead?

Book four in the Stage Dive series

Deep

Positive. With two little lines on a pregnancy test, everything in Lizzy Rollins' ordinary life is about to change forever. And all because of one big mistake in Vegas with Ben Nicholson, the irresistibly sexy bass player for Stage Dive. So what if Ben's the only man she's ever met who can make her feel completely safe, cherished, and out of control with desire at the same time? Lizzy knows the gorgeous rock star isn't looking for anything more permanent than a good time, no matter how much she wishes differently.

Ben knows Lizzy is off limits. Completely and utterly. She's his best friend's little sister now, and no matter how hot the chemistry is between them, no matter how sweet and sexy she is, he's not going to go there. But when Ben is forced to keep the one girl he's always had a weakness for out of trouble in Sin City, he quickly learns that what happens in Vegas, doesn't always stay there. Now he and Lizzie are connected in the deepest way possible . . . but will it lead to a connection of the heart?